Sally's Got A Taser

Terry Hornby

Published by Terry Hornby, 2024.

Also by Terry Hornby

For Linda and Pam

Linda, my birth sister and much loved sibling.

Pam, my sister by marriage and a cherised family member

How lucky can one man be?

And, as always, to my darling Glenda, my wife, my best friend and the leader of my cheer squad.

Chapter 1

Across from the darkened house, a tired man watched the young woman fumble with the front door. His car seat sagged with fatigue, conceding the fight to gravity and neglect. The windscreen reflected patches of dead insects and smears, streetlights highlighting his poor housekeeping.

The young woman finally negotiated entry into the house. Shutting the door behind her, the street returned to its sleepy quiet.

The big man sat silently for a further five minutes, his watch gleaming as he pushed the light button. At 1.10 am on this starlight Monday night, he opened the car door and emerged on the next stage of his task. Moving quietly, he crossed the road and entered the grounds of the little cottage. No light shone from his chosen window, no noise came as he stood listening, black leather shoes compressing a small flower garden.

Inside the house, Sally sat in the darkened lounge room, her eyes adjusting to the gloom of the night. She looked at the bookshelves with their unreadable titles, and the entertainment console supporting a large TV screen. She listened to the house's stillness, unaware that another stood nearby. The big man with his dark coat, wrinkled shirt and stained tie. He listened. She listened.

Listening is a skill. Patience is a virtue. The big man had long ago lost regard for his sense of virtue, but he had made patience a tool. With hands quietly by his side, he listened, experience holding him still. Dark jacket and grey slacks dissolved his outline into the shadow of the house. The shoulder holster had pushed a permanent bulge into the material of his coat. He heard a noise from within the house, a creak of leather, the sound of someone standing up.

Sally moved from the lounge room into the main bedroom. The late hour conspired with the flat bedspread to remind her of fatigue. She was tired, longing for sleep, but some duties remained. Her eyes moved around the room, looking for something out of place, something to inform her task, to further her quest. The queen-sized bed was well-made, the floor clean of debris. No sloppy housekeeper lived here; photograph frames glinted in the weak light filtering between the heavy blinds over a large window. When opened they would reveal the backyard, morning sun would strike any sleeper and make a comfortable lie-on very difficult.

She crossed to the wardrobe and slid open the mirrored door, a reflected self causing her to start briefly. The image of a young woman dressed in jeans, a dark button-up long-sleeved blouse and black sneakers flashed across her vision. A flood of chemicals rushed into her brain before reason clamped down on the fear and apprehension. She bottled her emotions, again resolving not to start at shadows, especially not shadows of herself.

She was armed, she had her Taser. But a woman alone at night inherits the hardwired fear of society; the night holds the attacker, the rapist, the molester. The man.

Outside the big man moved, slowly opening the unlatched window. More flowers died beneath his leather shoes before he swung himself to sit on the windowsill, one leg silently moving into the house. Gradually he transferred his weight onto this foot and, ever so carefully, eased into the house. Garden soil fell onto the carpet. Again, he stood, listening.

The woman looked at the exposed shelves in the wardrobe. Enough light filtered in for her to make out the neatly piled clean clothes and, on the centre shelf, a wooden jewellery box. Reaching out she lifted the lid which caused the front of the box to lean forward. It was a false front, lowering it on the hidden hinges exposed three shallow wooden drawers, each with an ornately carved centre recess. She placed one slim fingertip into the recess of the top shelf and slid the slender drawer out, a fragrant aroma of sandalwood wafting from the box. Accompanying the movement of the shelf was a very gentle sliding sound, this she expected. She did not expect, however, to hear a metallic noise from another part of the house.

She froze, terror of dark places again flushing her system with adrenaline. Terror of the noise in the night, the imagined breath on the back of her neck, the footfall, the clutching arm, the hand across her mouth. She needed to be strong, she thought. But I'm not tough, I'm not strong. And I'm all alone.

With an effort she controlled her fears, but realized her nerves were making the evening more and more distressing.

She stood and listened, looking back into the lounge room through the open doorway. She could not see with any clarity, the darkness of the doorway was only slightly less gloomy than the surrounding walls. She looked for movement, for a darker shadow to cross the doorway. She stood, listened and quietly screamed panic into an overtaxed mind.

The big man slowly moved his left arm away from the table lamp, his watch striking the metal shade had sounded like a gunshot to stretched senses. Again, he stood quite still, forgetting his eyes and their inability to see in the dark. But his ears were straining, hearing was the sense that still functioned perfectly, it did not need the bright glare of light. He listened, fearing to hear a sound yet needing to know where the woman was positioned. Was she even now waiting to strike at him, the interloper, the barbarian invader of her evening? He stood and listened.

The gentle noises of the night crept into their ears, the darkness edged against their exposed necks, the house swallowed them in blackness. Outside an animal cried, and a dog howled in the distance. Further afield, each heard the random sound of traffic noises, faint reminders of the bustle of the day. The sound of their own blood beat heavy into their ears, their breathing seemed forced, rasping and asthmatic.

The silence blended with the darkness to produce the dry-mouthed fear known to creatures threatened by night. Time passed slowly as the woman and the big man stood quietly, each listening and yet fearing to hear.

The woman's brain finally asserted its dominance, turning her back to the open shelf. By now her eyes were seeing well into the dark, she saw black shapes of jewellery nestled on the shelf, and off to one side, secluded from the rest by space and function, she saw a small rectangle of blackness. Reaching out she touched the object with a fingernail, a small click, the tap of nail on plastic. Not metal, but plastic. Her fingers closed around the dark shape, and she gently pulled it from the drawer. The slight change in weight caused the drawer to rock briefly, sending a louder click of wood against wood throughout the house. Again, the night noises died away, she froze in apprehension. Where did that noise go? To whose ears? She held her breath and waited.

Nothing.

The big man heard the noise. His head turned to the doorway into the bedroom, his eyes searched the dark rectangle for some clue, for his quarry. He moved gently towards the doorway, adjusted eyes now able to see the waiting traps of furniture. He eased one hand into his holster and began to pull his pistol free. It stuck, his thumb found the strap clipping the gun in place, a small press stud preventing the weapon from falling accidentally. Working his thumb under the strap he paused next to the doorway, back pressed against the wall. Slowing his breathing, extending his senses as far as he could, he pressed his thumb gently but with increasing force against the strap.

It came free with a very definite, very loud noise. Click.

Both people had made a small noise. Now they stood only a few metres apart, separated by a wall and the night. To each the sound of their breathing seemed to rush into the dark, screaming their presence. The woman turned to place her back against the cupboard door, ready to face whatever leapt at her from the pit of her nightmares. The big man eased his pistol out, willing his ears to grow and capture every sound. His eyes flicked from the doorway to other parts of the room, never pausing. He knew that darkness played tricks with vision; staring at one place made the shadows move and imagination became the dictating factor, not reality. He changed his vision, hoping to sense any attack or invasion in time to evade. His legs throbbed with adrenaline overload, his breathing came in bursts. They stood, each a little crazed with the dark.

The woman was the first to move. Clenching the small dark rectangle into one fist she took a step forward and stopped. Then another step, then another. Slowly she edged to the open doorway. Finally, they were so close they could have touched, save for the wall separating their beating hearts.

Quelling her imagination, she summoned her will to thrust down jangled nerves. She stepped into the doorway.

The man placed the barrel of his gun against her neck and said, "Stand very still."

Chapter 2

Alarms flashed into her brain, her body rigid, mind cascading with questions. Who was he? What danger does he bring? Flee! Fight!

She remained still, slowly her emotions came under control even though breathing remained a series of pants. "Who are you?" she asked, "What are you doing here?"

The big man looked at the woman standing before him. He could feel the waves of fear drenching her mind and body. He was worried, standing in the dark with this unknown stranger, this potential threat. Holding the gun against her neck he put a hand against the wall, fumbling up and down, searching.

"I could ask you the same questions, Miss. And I intend to. Stay where you are." Light blossomed as he pressed the overhead light switch. She blinked in the sudden blaze, grateful for the harsh light. She felt safer, surely no vile crime could be accomplished in this stark glare.

"What now?" she said, not daring to move from her uncomfortable mid-stride. The cold barrel of the gun chilled her body. Her right leg began to twitch with the tension of keeping her balance, but she dared not move and call forth a violent response.

"Sit down, please," said the big man.

She took a step towards one of the leather chairs, turned and sat down gratefully. She was exhausted, the ebb and flow of emotions had depleted energy and drained vitality. Her left hand still held the rectangle of plastic she had taken from the jewellery case. As she sat, she placed this hand next to the gap between the chair and cushion. Relaxing as much as she could she carefully opened her hand to allow the object to fall into the crack.

The big man still held his gun on the young woman. He did not know her, did not know her abilities and until he was sure he intended to keep her secure. "Now," he said, "perhaps you can tell me who you are?" He looked at her studying the face for clues, for motivation, for anything.

He saw a young woman, late twenties, long dark hair and dressed in clothes that would blend in with the night. A shoulder bag sat near her feet. Her eyes and the set of her mouth conveyed intelligence, her brow unlined with worry, eyes devoid of the lifeless lustre common to those who had lost their way.

"My name is Sally. Sally Grant." Silence, no reaction from the big man. She caught his eyes and held the gaze. Keeping her voice even she continued "And this is my home." She looked him full in the face, watching for a reaction. Nothing showed on the big man, his gaze never faltered.

"Are you a rapist?" she asked.

His eyes widened at the question. For a moment he felt empathy for the young woman, admired her courage. Finding an armed stranger in your house at night would send most people almost catatonic. Not this girl. "This is your house, is it Mrs. Grant?" he asked.

She sat back, feeling slightly surer of her ground. She had no reason for feeling safer, but it seemed unlikely that a man bent on evil intent would turn the house lights on and engage in casual conversation. Her hand pulled unconsciously on the strap of her shoulder bag, tugging it closer to her body. It was an age-old gesture, one used by women all the time, bringing the valuable closer.

The man barked, "Leave it alone!" His gun snapped up, his posture changed to aggression. The room tensed, the woman froze in her seat.

Both were again still, caught in the unreality of the moment. She watched a bead of perspiration form on his forehead and run down his face. She could feel her face gone to stone, fear roared behind her eyes.

"Kick it over here!" instructed the man, gesturing with his pistol. His voice was harsh, tense with the need to do something, yell, scream, vent the adrenaline. He felt his shirt sticking to his back, nerves causing him to sweat.

Her whole body rigid, the woman pushed the bag with her left foot, sliding it across the floor. She kept her eyes fixed on the gun, the black hole at the end filled her vision, it drank her life.

She felt the strap fall to her lap and let it slide to the floor. The uncontrolled movement made the big man jerk. "Sit still!" he commanded.

He stepped forward and placed the muzzle of the gun against her cheek. The cold metal had a sense of threat far greater than any she had ever known.

With his foot, he kicked the bag further from the woman, well out of her reach. She could feel the man's heavy breathing, rapid heartbeats matching her own trip hammer. Felt the quiver of his hand down the barrel of the gun and onto her face.

He stepped back and both of them exhaled, tension draining away, shoulders slumping with nervous fatigue.

Silence lay between them. He took some deep breaths as if recovering from a race.

"You say this is your house, Mrs. Grant?" he asked again.

"Miss. Yes, it is," she replied. She carefully kept her body still, not wanting to provoke another reaction. Her voice was small, diminished by the surreal events of the night. "What...," she swallowed, "what are you going to do to me?"

The big man blinked. Her answer was confusing, it made no sense. The gun never wavered, "Why would you be wandering around your own house in the middle of the night with the lights out?"

The question surprised the woman. She had expected violence or even simple threats. Not calm, innocuous questions. As her breathing slowed, she looked again at the man before her. He stood with the hateful gun still pointing, jacket unbuttoned and creased, tie askew, hair a little unruly. She put his age somewhere in the late forties, face tracked by care and worry.

Leaning back, she carefully placed her hands in her lap, the small plastic object safely tucked into the chair. "Look, if you're here to rob me you'll be out of luck. I've little cash. Take the TV, take everything but just go!" She waved around the room, indicating all the contents, but her eyes stayed on his face. The man with the gun.

The two people were still, a small, frozen tableau. He scanned the room, saw the books, saw the TV, went back to the woman. She waited for his reaction, her breathing a little shallow, waiting for the next act in her private drama. Was surprised when it came.

Opening his jacket, he put the pistol back in the holster, wiping the palms of his hands on his trousers. Standing up straight he ran a hand through a mop of hair. Everything changed, he was no longer a vicious threat, no longer her imminent doom. "Look, Miss Grant, we may have got off on the wrong foot."

She looked at this stranger, gone was the heaving terror of the unknown assailant. He gave her back a small smile, a little embarrassed cough.

"I'm a police detective."

Chapter 3

"What the hell ..." began Sally, her voice rising.

The big man placed his hands out to placate the woman, to stem her tide of anger "I saw you entering the house, you looked suspicious. I thought you might be a burglar."

"You thought!" she said, voice rising in pitch. "You thought! You thought you should sneak into my house and hold me at gunpoint! What sort of a brain do you have?" Sally rose out of the chair, eyes flashing. "Show me your badge! How do I know you're a detective?"

The pair stood facing each other, a brief pause after the woman's tirade. She was now the aggressor, he wilted back, shrinking a little into himself.

"Take it easy, Miss Grant...," he began, again holding his hands out placatingly.

"Don't you 'Miss Grant' me, you... you..." She sputtered to a halt. Taking a slower breath, she calmed herself. "Just show me some ID," she finished, voice weary with battle fatigue.

The big man opened his jacket, causing the woman to flinch again, he slowly extracted a small leather folder. Flipping it open he showed her his badge. She bent forward and peered closely, examining the ID card and photograph. "Well, Detective Howard," Sally began, "perhaps you will be good enough to get the hell out of my home." She straightened up and looked around the room, spotting the opened window. "Well, well," she went on, "breaking and entering as well as threatening behaviour. You're quite the man, aren't you? For goodness' sake, what were you thinking? You scared the daylights out of me."

The big man replaced the folder and stood abjectly in front of the woman, his posture admitted defeat. "I'm so sorry, Miss Grant, we've been chasing a burglar in this neighbourhood for two weeks now. When I saw you, something didn't seem right, so I followed you in here."

Sally hesitated, "What do you mean, 'something didn't look right'?"

The big man shrugged his shoulders and took a step away from the woman. He stopped by a low coffee table and looked at the large picture book on display. The front cover showed a diver on SCUBA giving the thumbs up; the book title sparkled in shades of blue "Great Dives of the USA."

He looked back at the woman, "Do you dive much?" he asked.

Folding her arms, Sally walked around the room, shut the window and then turned back to face the detective. "Not anymore. Tell me, what did you mean by 'something didn't look right'?" The couch formed a barrier between the two, the woman slightly safer on the other side of the room from this strange man.

The big man raised his head, looked at Sally and nodded towards the kitchen. "Do you reckon we could have a cup of tea? I'm dead beat, been on my feet all day."

They stood looking at each other. Sally was surprised, flashed a panicked glance at the kitchen. He was a detective, she was sure of it. Still, who asks for a cup of tea at half past one in the morning? "I don't know, it's late. Look, why don't you just go. Just get out. I won't report you or anything. Just leave." She waited, willing him to move towards the door.

Again, the silence held, they stood motionless.

He moved, "Yeah, you're right. Again, I'm sorry for scaring you." He took a step towards the front door, stopped, "It's just …"

The moment hung.

"OH, GOD!" SALLY EXCLAIMED, "All right, I'll make you a cup of coffee!" She moved to the kitchen, grabbed the electric jug, filled it with water then fussed a few moments before turning it on. "Anything to get you out of here."

He moved to one of the stools at the kitchen bench and sat down, "I prefer tea. Look, it's just there," he pointed at a small wooden tray holding a variety of teas. "Wouldn't have a chamomile, would you?"

Behind the bench, Sally stared at the man in astonishment. "You've got a nerve. You break into my house..." She looked around for something to drink from.

"No, I didn't," interrupted the man.

Sally stopped opening cupboards looking for cups and turned back, "I beg your pardon?"

"I didn't break in. The window was unlatched." He gave her a gentle look and regretted his interruption as she leaned over the bench and confronted him with a baleful glare.

"Listen to me, buster,"

"Isaac," he said.

"What?"

"Isaac. My name's Isaac. Isaac Howard."

Sally took a deep breath, trying to quell the surge of indignation and then gave up. "I couldn't care less what your name is, Mr. Detective bloody Isaac Howard! You are sitting in my home drinking my tea and interrupting everything I say! Now just shut up and tell me what was so unusual that you had to break into my house!"

He thought about mentioning the difference between breaking and entering, looked at her furious face and changed his mind. Swallowing slowly, he carefully spoke, "I saw you walk back and forth in front of the house a few times, you kept looking at your hand like you were looking for an address. I was parked across the road, it just looked unusual, that's all. And ..." He stopped, his voice fading.

Sally shifted her weight and leaned against the bench, "And what?" She crossed her arms, tapping one finger against her arm.

"Um, and you haven't given me any tea yet so I'm not actually sitting here drinking it." He hunched his shoulders, wondering why he would say something so stupid.

"You take the cake, Isaac, you really do," replied Sally, her voice low. "What a cheek." The fire seemed to have gone out of her, perhaps it was just exhaustion. She finally opened the cupboard containing some mugs, pulled one out and placed it in front of the detective. "Make your own tea."

Sally moved out of the kitchen to sit back in the leather chair she had vacated earlier. Stretching her legs out she tried to stay calm, tried to relax.

The big man moved into the kitchen, took the teapot from the bench and placed a spoonful of tea into the pot. Pouring the boiling water over the leaves he inhaled the gentle aroma. "Ah, good stuff," he said.

"So," he went on, "were you?"

Sally's chair faced away from the kitchen, its position focused on the television in the corner. Without turning her head, she responded, "Was I what?" She thrust her hands deep into her pockets and waggled her feet to disperse some of her tension.

The big man picked up the teapot and mug and moved towards the couch. Sitting down he placed the mug on a small coaster showing 'I LUV NY' and poured out a cup of the aromatic brew. As he poured, he said, "Were you looking for this address?"

He sat back and sipped his tea, swivelling to watch the woman. Sally's mouth hung open, her brain stuttered, "I can't believe I'm hearing this. What do you want, proof that I live here?"

"Could you do that?" he asked.

"Put the tea down and get out," Sally said tersely. "Get out or I'm calling the police."

He looked mildly surprised but put the mug back on the coffee table, "Where's the phone?" he asked.

Their eyes locked, she flared and stood up, grabbing her shoulder bag as she did so. "I have my mobile right here."

Before she could unlatch the bag, the big man leapt to his feet and pulled out his pistol. They stood frozen again, she half rose from her chair, face caught like an animal in a car's headlights. He with his gun pointed at her head, crouched in a shooting stance.

"Do not put your hand into that bag," he said, slowly and with menace.

Sally swallowed, her throat suddenly dry. "I...' She stopped, then started again, "I don't know what's going on here anymore." She sat back in the chair.

The big man stood up, gun steady on the woman's head. He moved closer until the barrel dominated her vision, filling her world. "Where is the phone?" he said.

Sally looked up, fear again flushing her body with unwanted chemicals. "My mobile...it's in my bag...please, please don't hurt me..." Tears ran down her cheeks, mascara formed streaks of misery and anguish. "Please..." she spoke softly, all power gone.

Satisfied that the woman could not reach her bag for any hidden weapon, the detective sat back on the couch. Keeping the gun pointed at her face he asked, "This is your house. Correct?"

A tear-stained nod. Hands twisting in her lap. Feet close together, body aching.

"Then show me where your phone is," he demanded, voice calm, rational, reasonable.

Sally waved her hands at her bag, but he interrupted, "Not your mobile. The landline. Where do you keep your phone?"

A mumble. Head down, hair falling over the tear-streaked face.

"What's that?" he said, "I couldn't hear you."

Sally lifted her face to look into the eyes of this strange, threatening man. He had not touched her, had made no move to lay a hand on her body yet she felt violated. Used up and wrung out.

A small voice, "It's not my house."

Chapter 4

Howard sank back into the couch, feeling exhausted. He had pushed and prodded and found what he needed to know. Not her house! Of course, it wasn't her house! They both sat, bodies limp, brains at their limit.

"What happens now?" asked Sally. She leaned forward, arm reaching for her bag. All she could think of was the need for a tissue.

The big man pushed himself erect and walked past her chair, "Leave the bag alone, Sally. I need to look inside." So saying, he bent down and picked up the leather bag, opened the flap and moved back to the couch. Rummaging inside he felt a small travel pack of tissues, he pulled them out and tossed them to Sally. "Just sit still for a while, please," he said. The bag was full of bric-a-brac, used tissues, keys, and an old express delivery envelope. But no discernable weapons except for a long stick. He pulled it out.

"What's this?" Isaac asked.

Sally spoke in a small voice, "It's my Taser."

Isaac turned the object over in his hands, it didn't look like the police issue tasers, they were big and bulky. This was slender and long, with a small battery pack at one end that could be held in the hand and then a small rod with a slightly gnarled shape. It looked vaguely familiar, but he couldn't place it. "This thing's a Taser?" he asked. "Looks a bit weird. Does it work?"

"I don't know," said Sally. "I got it off eBay. From the Harry Potter online store. On special, they were closing down."

"Harry Potter?" asked Isaac.

"Yeah," she said. "It's supposed to look like a magic wand."

Isaac looked at the girl, looked at the Taser and wondered why human beings were so bizarre. A Taser built to look like a magic wand. Oh, Lord, he thought, preserve me from idiotic marketing schemes. "Well," he said, "good luck with that."

Sally opened the tissue packet and fought down a surge of gratitude towards Howard. He had seen her need and reached out! He had given her tissues! Shaking her head, she thrust the thought away, blew her nose and wiped her eyes. A small bundle of tissues built up on her lap.

Quietly, she put a clean tissue into the palm of her hand and gently slid it down into the crack between the cushions. Her fingers found the plastic rectangle and pulled it into the tissue; pulling it up, she mimed wiping her nose. Finally, she turned to look at Howard, hands together in her lap, secrets hidden.

He was looking at her, his gaze steady. A small shock went through her body.

"Everything all right?' he asked.

"Yes." A small voice. "Am I under arrest?" she asked. "I've never done anything like this before." She looked so fragile and small, dwarfed by the big leather chair.

He smiled and held up her wallet, releasing one finger he allowed it to fall open to show her photo ID. "Rubbish, Miss Sally Grant."

Sally stared at her traitor photograph. Emblazoned across the top of the card was her name, "S. Grant." The next line calmly stated, "Private Investigator."

"You're a private investigator?" he asked. "Really?"

"I've got my Cert III." A small fire blossomed in Sally. "What qualifications do you have to be a detective?" Her chin was up, her eyes confronting this ... this man.

Howard moved closer to Sally, shifting to the arm of the couch, his worn face opened with a smile. "Been doing a bit of breaking and entering yourself, haven't you Sally?"

She folded her arms, shrugged and looked at her feet. "Dunno," she replied.

"Come on, Sally, you're done, girl." He sat watching her face, searching for clues. "I've got you breaking into the front door, sneaking through the darkened house. Found you in the bedroom." He stopped and glanced towards the open doorway leading to the bedroom. "What were you after, Sally? What's in this house to interest a PI?"

Sally pushed her legs out to full stretch, tucking her folded arms under her shoulders she again shrugged, "Dunno." She kept her eyes on the tips of her shoes, using all the tricks she learned at school when confronted by authority. Admit nothing, deny all. Have no eye contact.

The big man stood in some frustration. He swung back toward the kitchen, "You didn't know where the cups were, no idea how to make a cup of tea." Reaching the kitchen entrance, he turned and focused on the small girl, "You're not real good at this."

"Not my fault," she murmured. No change to the stance, no eye contact, just those few words.

He took a step forward, "Not your fault!" Voice rising, "Not your bloody fault!" at a shout. "That has to be the stupidest excuse I have ever heard. Well, whose fault was it, Sally? Who forced you in here with a gun to your head? Who twisted your arm behind your back?" Howard stood in a rage, eyes bulging, drops of spittle flying from his lips. "Of course, it was your fault, you stupid, stupid woman!"

Sally had shrunk back into the chair, retreating from the violence of the detective's intensity. She looked up at him with fear, astonished at his vehemence.

Howard strode quickly forward and grabbed a heavy floor lamp, dragging it over to Sally's chair. She winced as if attacked, curling away from this madman who seemed intent on mayhem. Plucking a pair of handcuffs from the back of his belt he latched one cuff onto the lamp. While she watched in shock and astonishment, he grasped the hand holding the tissue-shrouded prize and clicked the other end of the handcuffs into place.

"Stay still," he said. Under the harsh glare of the overhead light, he loomed as a surreal presence. To Sally it seemed she had entered another world, one encompassed only by the four walls of this room. A real sense of dislocation infused her fatigued brain and limbs. For Howard, the night still stretched ahead, another in a long line of late, late nights. More discoveries needed to be made, more revelations exposed.

Standing, he looked down at his captive. Feeling she had been secured sufficiently, he stepped back and turned around. He looked at all parts of the room, searching for something amiss. Ignoring the young woman he moved to the front door, disappearing down a hallway.

Sally realized with a start that she was alone, the room seemed larger, not so awful. Her tormentor had gone! Standing, she slid the handcuff to the top of the lamp, looking for release. The fixture for the bulb blossomed into a stylish bulge, big enough to trap the cuff onto the pole. An examination of the base showed a heavy, carved circle of metal. With only a brief hesitation she hefted the lamp with her free hand while clutching her prize tightly into her left hand.

Howard re-entered the room, retracing her original steps into the house. He was confronted by the woman on her feet, struggling to hold the heavy lamp in one hand. They both froze, eyes locked together as if each had discovered the other in some intimate, private moment. He moved a hand inside his jacket, enough for the woman to understand his threat, "Sit down, Miss Grant," he said softly.

Sally sat.

Keeping her in his peripheral vision, he moved to the open doorway into the bedroom. He paused, looking into the darkness, flicking his gaze back and forth to his captive. His jacket hung in untidy folds over his shoulders, merely a piece of cloth to serve a purpose, not an item of fashion. Not the stamp of the successful man. From within its confines, he extracted the hateful gun and, holding it loosely in one hand, stepped into the bedroom and flicked on the light.

He surveyed the neat room, the clean lines of the bed. Eyes roved around the pictures and finally rested on the open wardrobe door. He saw the jewel box lying open, the front panel folded down, the slender drawer exposed and raw. Naked and violated.

Sally watched him staring into the room, saw him see the results of her handiwork. She was surprised when he stiffened for a moment, felt a thrill of fear as his gaze swung towards her like a gun barrel.

Without a word he turned and stepped out of the room back towards her, gun by his side, one arm giving him support against the doorway frame. The detective had a different look in his eyes now, Sally saw the distaste, saw what could be hatred. She felt real fear, not the fear that went with her earlier discovery, but the fear born from confronting the enraged beast before her.

She shivered, hand clutching the plastic prize, the other hand thrust forward to protect her defenceless form against attack. Legs curled back into the chair, head sunk downwards.

"What is it?" she whispered, "What's wrong?"

Howard stopped before the chair. Anger and restraint warred to keep him still, "What did you take?" he asked, voice low and still.

"I didn't take anything," Sally replied, small, vulnerable, fragile. "I don't know..." Her left hand curled around the tissue with its hidden trophy, this hand was still attached to the lampstand. There had been no opportunity to transfer it elsewhere, so she continued to clutch it within its protective screen. Every girl holds a tissue in her hand.

Howard quelled the urge to hit, knew he would never have struck the woman, he was not a coward, had never beaten a woman, never would. But the urge was there, he controlled it, sent it back into the abyss. Violence would not solve this problem, it never really solved any issue.

Instead, he used words. Words communicate, words prise open secrets.

"Sally," he said softly, "Sally, I know you have something, I know you took something out of that jewellery box." He waited, watched the small form. Sally kept her head down, face shielded by hair, legs now pulled up under her body on the chair. Only the hand clamped to the light pole extended from her body. All the rest of her was curled and foetal.

She shook her head, hair waving, face down, and uttered a soft mewling noise. A hurt animal, trapped and scared.

If words would not work, then Howard must resort to older skills. Observations, deduction, surmise. He looked around the room again, scanning objects, weighing evidence, dismissing the irrelevant. He had searched her bag; she had not been able to go anywhere else in the room before he caught her leaving the bedroom. If she had taken something, and he was sure she had, then she must have it on her person.

Where?

His eyes travelled across her body, not seeing a small and vulnerable woman but a human being with something hidden.

Where?

The handcuffs clinked with a small movement, drawing his eye.

"Open your hand," he instructed.

Sally stopped moving, all became still. She was again a little girl standing before her father, caught in the act. She knew the falsity of the emotion, recognised that it was a remembered passion of her youth. Knew its siren cry and intellectually rejected its claim.

But emotionally, it moved her.

She opened her left hand, exposing the tissue. A small sob. Why couldn't I be made of stronger stuff, she asked herself.

The detective reached forward and gently removed the white, shredded paper with its central core of hard plastic. He unwrapped the tissue, exposing the rectangle of plastic, plucked it from her hand.

"What's this?" he asked.

"Dunno." Head down.

Howard crouched before the young woman, holding out the tissue. Sally saw it between strands of hair; saw the gentleness in the man. Accepting the offering, she used her free hand to wipe tear-soaked eyes. The detective reached into his tired coat and extracted a small set of keys. He used them to unlock the handcuffs, freeing her from the stigma of helplessness.

"Sally," he said, voice soft and gentle, "do you know what this is?" He crouched again so she could catch his eyes without having to look up and acknowledge obeisance.

Another tissue disappeared as she blew her nose. Raising her head a little, she looked at his opened hand, seeing the plastic clearly for the first time, knowing what it was.

"Yes," she answered.

They remained together in silence, he crouched before the woman. She leaned back into the chair.

"It's a LifeChip," she said, head resting on the comfortable leather. "It's the download of a human personality."

She looked him in the eye, a challenge.

"If it's been used, then it contains a person's life. You have in your hand, Isaac, another human being. Someone has stolen a life and kept it in a little wooden box."

She saw the big man swallow and look at the chip, seeing it with different eyes.

"Worse than slavery, Isaac, worse than kidnapping."

The night was far away, they sat in their cocoon of light, separate from the world.

"Someone has stolen a human being," Sally finished.

Chapter 5

"That's a bit strong, isn't it?" asked Isaac.

Sally stretched, looked longingly at the kitchen and said, "Do you think we could make another cup? Coffee this time. I've had a big night."

Isaac stood, making a small groaning noise as he did so. "I'm getting too old for this caper. Come on, let's see what we can find." They moved back towards the workbench, downlights washing the scrubbed bench top in a blaze of clarity.

Sitting on a tall stool Sally asked, "So, what do you know about LifeChips, Isaac?"

The detective filled the jug with water, returned it to its original site and pressed the switch. He raised his voice a little to rise over the soft gurgling sound as the water boiled. "LifeChips. Pretty common to your generation, I should think. Not so with people of my vintage. A lot of us, but not a majority, I would think. Technology discovered too late."

He opened a cupboard, peered inside and pulled out a glass coffee pot with a plunger.

"Real coffee!" exclaimed Sally, sitting up with delight, "Well done, Mr. Detective." She looked at him with a bemused expression as she watched him rummage through the kitchen extracting coffee grounds, a grinder, milk and sugar. "What about you, Isaac?"

"What about me what?"

"Do you have a Life Chip?"

He stopped fussing, hands on the bench, left hand still around the small electric grinder. After a moment he shrugged, "Yes, I've got one. So's my wife. Our parents were forward thinkers. Unfortunates missed out. Funerals are a bit rare for me now."

He plugged the grinder into a power point, measured coffee into the compartment and closed the lid. "You?" he asked.

Sally opened her mouth to answer. Isaac grinned at her and depressed the switch. A loud noise erupted into the house, drowning out any response from Sally. She gave him an exasperated look, opened and closed her mouth again before sitting back and waiting for him to finish the grind.

"Sorry, what was that?" asked Isaac, pulling the cord out of the wall and opening the lid to the small machine.

Rolling her eyes, Sally said, "Boys and their toys." Leaning onto the bench she continued "Yes, I've got one. Just here." She tapped her chest, fingers hitting the hard sternum. Where's yours?"

"Same place. I read that some surgeons are putting them in the brain cavity now, for more protection. Techniques weren't that advanced in my day. A bit of chest bone was the best we could do." He poured the ground coffee into the plunger pot, added the boiling water and replaced the lid.

The atmosphere had again changed between them, their relationship seemed gentler, more at ease. Sally looked at this man who had threatened, cajoled and terrified her. But he had never actually caused her harm, most of the grief and angst she had suffered came from her sense of guilt and culpability. He had just forced her to confront it. He seemed to be capable of real tenderness, a poor man beaten by a harsh world who still could find some space for restraint.

"Penny for your thoughts?" he asked. From under the bench, he produced two more mugs and set them down ready to receive the aromatic brew.

"I was just thinking that it's a pity the coffee didn't taste as good as it smells," she responded.

Isaac poured out the coffee and each cradled their mug for a moment before sipping. Both emitted a satisfied "Aaah" sound, Sally giggled and Isaac smiled.

"So," he said, "can you tell me anything?"

"About what?" Another sip, shoulders relaxing, Sally's mind wandered away briefly.

"About why you're in this house," said Isaac. He had the unnerving ability to become completely still when asking a question. It threw people off track, like the background music in a movie ceasing moments before a climax.

Sally, caught off guard, stammered, "Umm, no, I don't know why...look....um," She shut up, cross with herself for acting like a schoolgirl. Taking a deep breath, she went on "Honestly, Isaac, you change gears so fast." Another sip of coffee, "Look, I'm a private detective on a case. I can't go blabbing, especially not to the police. That's why people hire private detectives, they usually don't want the police involved." She looked up at his face, a bit more able to read its crags and fissures. "Sorry."

"Would you prefer to be arrested?" He still hadn't moved, voice very calm, no threat. A simple question.

For a moment Sally's mind did not comprehend the question. Why should she be arrested, aren't we just a pair of friends sitting over a cup of coffee? Then her brain caught up and she ran over the evening, she concluded that breaking and entering, plus a little light burglary, probably did add up to the wrong side of the law.

Again, she looked at Isaac, trying to judge how serious he was about the threat. Suddenly his face was that of a stranger, unreadable. Where had that kind man gone? Who was this anonymous, faceless lawman in front of her?

Another crumple. "No, of course not. But I can't tell you much." More coffee, more silence.

"Who hired you?" he asked.

She breathed out slowly, "I was contracted by mail. Yesterday an express envelope was delivered to my office. It gave me instructions. And a cash card." A much-needed influx of funds.

Isaac studied the downcast head. He still did not know how much to trust this strange woman. Was she playing him? Keeping his voice flat, he asked again, "Express envelopes have return addresses. Who sent it?"

A sniff. "It's in my bag."

He remembered seeing an old express delivery envelope. Telling the woman to stay where she was, he moved back into the main room, picked up the bag and returned to the kitchen. Resuming his position behind the counter, he placed the bag on the bench and opened the large cover flap. Again, he surveyed the disorganization of Sally's life. Down one side, beneath a pair of sunglasses, a coin purse and a tissue, was the colourful corner of the envelope. He extracted it carefully and flattened it out on the counter after moving the bag back onto the floor near his shoes. He still did not want to take any chances with Sally reaching inside and pulling out a surprise. Or her Taser, even a patently ridiculous one.

The return address sullenly stared back. "Not a lot of use, I would think," he commented. "Mr Smith of 123 Main Street, Sydney" Looking up at Sally he said "What do you think, Miss Grant? Know anyone called Smith living in Sydney?"

The young woman raised her head, "I didn't check, all right? The cash card was good, I went online and put it into my account. I got paid." She was getting tired of this emotional roller coaster. "You just do what you have to, okay?"

"Did you know what you were looking for when you broke in?" he asked.

"Yeah, the instructions gave me all the details, told me it was a LifeChip. I had to get the chip and verify the identity with the chip reader in my bag."

Again, he retrieved the bag, waded through the tissues and found the small case containing the chip reader. Flipping up the small screen he inserted the LifeChip and pressed the power button. The small LCD panel came on.

Isaac stood very still as he looked at the display. The name bore into his skull, questioning, condemning. His face reflected the soft glow of the screen, the screen gently stating the identity of the person whose life, whose history, whose entire existence, was stored on the chip:

Name: Mary Hodges.

Date of Birth: 1/1/2017

Date of Implant: 1/1/2017

Sally could not read the letters, but she could see the impact they were having on Isaac. His face had drained of colour, his mouth slightly open. "Uh, are you all right?" No response. "Isaac?" She fell back onto detail, ignoring his reaction. "Anyway, after the verification – which I haven't seen yet, by the way – I was to forward the chip to another address."

"Another address?" Isaac took the envelope and held it to the light, looking for any extra information. Without looking he reached down, pulled open the second drawer and withdrew a pair of scissors. He used them to cut the envelope so it could open out and sit flat. He placed it back on the bench and hunched over the exposed interior, carefully studying the surface.

Sally sat very still, panic again flooding through her tired body. Staying a little bit slumped, she searched the bench, looking for anything she could use as a weapon. She was scared, scared of this man who seemed to know far too much about this house. He hadn't even looked at the drawer to find the scissors, he knew they were there.

"I need another tissue," she said in a small, weak voice.

He looked up, almost surprised to see her there, "What?"

"I need another tissue," she said. "I've used all the ones you gave me. There're some loose ones in my bag." She sat still, trying to look as harmless as possible. "Can I have one, please?"

Isaac's brain spun its wheels for a moment before comprehension set in. "Oh, yes. Sure. Just a minute" He bent down, opened the flap and looked inside the bag. Spotting a tissue, he reached in and pulled it free.

"Here you are...," he began, straightening back up to the bench.

Sally hit him flush on the side of his head as it cleared the bench top. The electric jug was still half full of water and it struck with a solid, meaty blow. She immediately let go of the jug and swung herself atop the bench. Looking down she saw Isaac crumpled on the floor, one hand to his face where the jug had split his cheek. She jumped down beside him.

Still groggy, Isaac felt his jacket being pulled open. The pain in the side of his face was intense and he was only slowly beginning to regain coherent thought. Opening his eyes, he looked up to see Sally crouched over him, the barrel of his own pistol approaching his right nostril.

Sally jammed the weapon in tight, anger forcing her teeth clenched as she snarled, "Who the hell are you? How do you know so much about this house?"

"I..." started Isaac before Sally pushed the barrel in harder, "OWW!" he finished.

"The truth, dammit! You didn't even look for those scissors; you knew where the grinder and coffee were kept! The grinder! Nobody just walks into a strange house and knows that stuff!" She panted, eyes ablaze, manic intensity making her arm quiver.

Isaac could feel the cut on his cheek bleeding, but it was a small irritation compared to the pain of cold metal softly tearing his nasal tissues. The gun trembled, he feared for his life if this mad woman lost all her control.

"I ...," he began, then stopped as more pressure was forced along the gun and into his pain-wracked nose.

"It's my house," he finished.

A NIGHT SCENE, ANOTHER place, different people, the same world. The empty street trickled through a small warehouse region; wet asphalt glistened from a water spill, a lone overhead light looked at its own reflection, trying to ignore the pair of arguing females.

The taller of the two women opened the car door and slid into the driver's seat. Parked in this dark street the meeting was unlikely to be observed; the hour was late and all the good folk were abed.

These were not good folk.

"Shut your face, bitch," she snarled up at her still-standing interlocutor. Her car growled to life, the throb of the engine counterpointing its driver's passion. The other woman leaned on the roof of the vehicle, one arm thrusting out and allowing her face to slowly lower to the open car window. She continued down and squatted, expensive jeans and tailored cowboy boots hugging a lissom body, a smile raising scarlet lips into a mocking smirk.

"I mean it," spat the driver. "Tell your vile employer to never...," she paused for effect, almost a struggle for self-control, "... ever presume on our arrangement again." She fixed her glare at the woman outside the car; it was not rage that drove her to these words, it was the impertinence of it all. No one dictated to her, no man and certainly no woman.

"You do not call me," she said. "Ever." She let the silence send its message, its own level of threat. Then she continued, "I will call you. When I choose." The car pulled out into the street and accelerated with a jerk and a roar.

Alone on the pavement, the bejeaned woman shifted her weight to squat on a booted heel, a more comfortable pose and far more in keeping with her external cowboy appearance.

"Like I give a shit," she said, softly, just a whisper. She rose, stretched, looked up and down the street before pushing manicured hands into pockets and strolling away.

A soft susurration accompanied her, an MP player chortling out some late-night jazz.

She skipped a step or two before turning the corner into a small alley. The street blinked and went back to sleep.

But not for long, a new engine roared into life and a motorbike erupted from the alley, all chrome and noise. Astride the throbbing engine sat the young woman, now encased in a black full-face helmet and leather jacket. She throttled back and came to a halt at the street entrance, boots resting on the wet road surface, hands on hips, bike balanced between her thighs. She saw the deserted street, the wonderful road stretching off before her wheels, the night was all hers, hers alone.

She raised the visor, carefully placed her hands back on the handlebars, stretched her fingers once and then accelerated with a quick twist of her right wrist. Her steel-capped boots dragged for a few meters on the road sending cascades of sparks from the metal toes to accompany the near deafening roar of the bike.

She grinned at the sheer visceral pleasure of the event. She was alive; young, fearless and beautiful.

The bike accelerated into the city.

Chapter 6

S ally pulled the trigger.

Nothing happened. Getting herself under control, she withdrew the weapon and sat back on the kitchen floor. Sally fell back, hitting the floor with a soft thump, gun held in one hand, eyes wide, mouth open. Mind gone away in disgust.

"Safety's still on," he said.

Isaac felt his abused nose, holding a hand onto the damaged tissue, trying to will healing through the warmth of his palm. A throb began, beating gently but insistently from his nostril, through his damaged cheek and into his brain. Each beat of his heart caused a corresponding throb of pain. He knew from experience that it would not stop, rather, it would escalate, very gently, very painfully. It would dominate his tomorrow.

With a groan, he sank back into the promise of future pain. So much hurt in his life, so many nights spent with the insistent beat of his own blood inside his head.

"That hurt," he said.

She looked at him. Sitting there, holding his damaged nose, blood gently dripping from his cheek, he seemed like damaged goods. Heaving the heavy pistol up, she again pointed it at this strange man, this chameleon.

"Shut up," she commanded.

They sat looking at each other, she with the gun, he holding his injured body.

"Bit of a mess, aren't we?" he asked, with a soft chuckle. "Lord, you hit me hard. What time is it?" he glanced at a wrist, "Two a.m. What a top night!"

He leaned back, placing both arms behind him for support. Blood trickled from his cheek but streamed from his nose. Sally looked at this shaggy, bloody, obstinate and frustrating man. The gun became too heavy, she let it tug her hand down until it rested on her outstretched leg. "Are you really a copper?" she asked.

"Yeah," he replied, "I really, truly am. And this really, truly is my house. And we are in a bloody mess." Pause, silence, looking at each other. "Why did you break into my house, Sally?" he asked.

"Told you," she replied, tiredness coating her words. "Got the job in the mail. Got paid. Got a simple task. Ticks in all the boxes."

She felt it was time to throw him a curve, he had been the one doing all the pitching so far. "So, Isaac, tell me. Who'd you kill? This person on the chip?" she asked.

Frost entered the room, flowing from the big man leaking blood. She felt the emotional temperature drop as surely as if it were a blizzard. His teeth clenched, lips curled over bared fangs. She felt his anger.

"What the bloody hell would you know?" he snarled.

Sally slowly rose to her feet, tugging the huge cannon with her. "I know I've got the gun, Isaac. I know you are a painful man. I know that you... that you... Damn, I don't know! You've got the LifeChip of someone in your closet! In your jewellery box."

A thought hit her, "What are you doing with a jewellery box? You're a man. Women have jewellery boxes. What...? Oh, God, more mysteries."

She looked at the name still displayed on the LCD screen, Mary Hodges, it said. She noted the unusual birthday, the first day of the year, and bet she didn't get separate presents at Christmas.

"So, who's Mary Hodges, then," she asked.

"My wife," he said.

SALLY LOOKED AT HIM, yet another face he showed. "You are one sick animal, Isaac."

The kitchen light sent shadows under benches, between the gaps. The detective's face had long shadows each time he looked down. "True enough," he said.

The floor tiles were large squares of alternating patterns, black and white. Sally felt she was looking down at a giant chessboard. With Isaac a fallen piece, messing up the neat array of order. The rest of the kitchen was clean lines and straight edges. Except for their bench top, it was littered with the debris of their supper. Just like this moment, she thought, a neat place squandered by a blotch of mess, a splash of blood.

"You killed your wife. Killed her and then opened her up to extract the LifeChip. What did you use, Isaac, a tin opener? Maybe a knife?" She felt disgusted by the refuse before her, this pathetic crumple of a man. "Kept her for a trophy. You sick, sad, sorry man."

The young woman examined the pistol and, finding the safety, she flicked it off.

From his seated surrender, Isaac heard the sound, knew its importance. With his face turned up to the kitchen light he was the subject of a mercy painting, a bloodstained, pitiful man pinned against the harsh glare of justice and contempt.

"I loved Mary." He stopped, sank his head a little, "Two years ago she stepped out of the house, stepped out of my life. Went shopping. To the Mall. Never saw her alive again. My Mary went away, she...," a choking sound, "she ...," tears rolled down his cheeks. "I lost her that day, couldn't find her, she ... disappeared."

Sally looked down at the helpless man, crying softly below her. His pain seemed real, a part of him had been ripped away. For a brief moment, she wondered what that sort of love must be like. Would anyone cry for her the way this man wept for his lost love?

"What do you mean, Isaac?" she whispered, "What happened?"

Rubbing one sleeve across his eyes the big man drew dignity and control over himself like a cloak. "Mary was listed as missing. Her body was found ...," a pause, "was found in the forest two weeks later. She had been, oh God, abused and," ... another choking sound, "cut." Anger and rage welled within Isaac. "Some... person... thing... cut my Mary up!" He clenched his teeth, rolled his mouth and grasped his loss and grief with an iron hand, forcing them back into the controllable box.

She reached down a hand and gently pulled Isaac to his feet. Again, he crossed an arm across his face, the surge of tears wiped away.

"Isaac...," she began.

He waved her into silence, pulled himself erect, gathering his dignity, cloaking his nakedness, "Don't. Just ... don't." A deep breath. "This is the first time I've seen that chip. The first time I've seen ...," pause, "my Mary."

The big man stood, shoulders slumped, eyes seeing other vistas. Clothes and wounds ignored; life unimportant after the light had gone away.

Sally stared at him, swallowed and made a decision. She committed herself to righting a crime, saw another human in need and reached out to say, "Isaac, here's your stupid gun. We need to find out what's happened here tonight. We've been played. Someone is having fun at our expense. Help me, Isaac."

She reached out a hand, the hand holding the pistol. Isaac looked at it, looked up to her face and raised his arm to take the offered weapon. Without a word, he replaced the killing lump into its holster and flicked back the tired jacket over the weary bulge.

Smiling at the young woman the big man said, "Thanks, Sally. Let's find this mongrel."

She smiled back, "Too right. Bloody painful man."

THE RIDER THROTTLED back and leaned her bike into the turn. Ahead, the entrance to the underground parking lot gaped, a security drop gate kept the impertinent out. Stopping next to a metal box she tugged a glove off with her teeth and used the now free hand to unzip a side pocket in her jacket. She pulled out a small card and inserted it into a slot.

The security gate wriggled and lurched up, this gave her time to replace her glove and prepare to enter the garage. The night ride had been fun, giving cheek to the snotty woman in the car had been even better. But now, this part of the ride, this was the best bit.

As soon as the gate was fully raised, she accelerated down the short ramp and opened her throttle; the bike snarled and roared, the noise magnifying as it echoed back from the side walls of the entrance tunnel, a blossoming bubble of sound encasing bike and rider. After a few turns the tunnel opened into the parking bay proper and she again accelerated, leaning the bike steeply into corners, sometimes running through the now empty parking bays. She had the entire floor to herself, to herself and the bike.

And the noise. The lovely, lovely noise.

THE PHONE RANG. NOT a mobile, the landline, the phone connecting Isaac's home with the wider world. They both looked towards the sound. "Bit late for a call," said Isaac.

Holding a tea towel to his nose he reached under the end of the bench where a small ledge held a telephone, pencils and assorted small pads for notes.

"Hello, Isaac Howard speaking." Sally noticed the neutral telephone voice, the standard identification. She never announced herself on the phone, not the done thing for cool singles.

= Good evening, Isaac. So good to talk to you again.

The voice meant nothing to the detective, conjured no images.

"Who is this?" he asked, sliding down to sit on the floor, back against a cupboard.

= Ah, yes. Very good question, Isaac, very good. Let me see, …mmm, yes… you can call me 'Leonardo'. Bit of a clue there, old chap.

"What?"

= Do try to keep up, Isaac. Perhaps you would be so kind as to put me on speaker. Just want to say a quick hello to Sally.

Isaac looked at the handset in bewilderment. Sally was watching him, a slightly quizzical expression, intrigued to see who would be calling at this time of night. She saw the big man's astonishment, saw him turn to look blankly at her. Then he pushed a small button on the handset and another voice entered the room.

= Jolly good. Well done, Isaac. A very good evening to you Miss Grant, I trust you are well?

She looked a question at Isaac, he shrugged. "Uh, yes…fine, thank you…"

= Lovely. Forgive the lateness of this call, terribly inconsiderate of me, I'm afraid. Nonetheless, needs must when the devil drives and all that. Now, to the point of all this unpleasantness…

Before he could continue, Isaac blurted, "Listen, you creep, I don't care who you are or what you want." He stopped, drew breath and went on in a fiercely restrained voice, "But when I find you, and I will, we will be having a little chat…"

= Oh, very good, Isaac, very good indeed. Love your work. Now then, aren't you at all curious as to how I knew Miss Sally Grant was going to be in your home tonight? And what she would find. Do go on, I am, as they say, all agog.

Sally and Isaac looked at each other, each could see their thoughts reflected on the other's face. Confusion, apprehension, rage, and a little fear.

"You say your name's Leonardo?" asked Isaac.

= Actually no, Isaac, I did not say my name was Leonardo. Bit more listening from you please, more of the sleuth, less of the flatfoot. I did, however, say you could *call* me Leonardo. Subtle distinction, old boy. Next question, fire away, bated breath at this end. Perhaps one from the lady?

Sally realized her mouth was open, "Uh…"

= Come along, Miss Grant. Opportunity knocks.

With a rush, she asked "Why…how did you know I was here?' She stopped, gulped and then said "No, not that. Answer this. How did you know what I was going to find?" She looked at Isaac, moved to sit beside him on the floor, telephone between the two of them. Isaac was impressed by the question.

= Oh, yes. Very good. Do take note, Isaac. How did I know what you would find? In the jewellery box, top drawer, right-hand side? Well, I must confess I am playing little mind games with you. Especially you, Isaac. Now, listen carefully because here comes another one. I knew, because … roll of drums, please… because I put it there! Do go on, this is such fun.

Isaac started, realising another person had broken into his house. Sally spoke first "Why?" she asked.

= The clock on the wall tells me it is approaching 3 in the morning. So late. Or early, I daresay it depends upon one's perspective. Must dash, things to do and so on. Isaac, I'm finishing up a small task here and then I'll fade away. If you would like to stop by for a chat, I suggest you pop on over now. I'm at a charming little bistro on Eagle Street labouring under the quite garish name of "Mama Luigi's Late Nite Lasagne". Night is spelled 'Nite', regrettable, I'm sure.

"You'll stay until we get there?" asked Isaac, still grappling with the various twists and turns of his evening.

= Good heavens, no, dear boy. I will stay until my current little chore is complete and then I shall, as they say in the classics, make like the wind and blow. I have taken the liberty of contacting the local constabulary and informing them of the break-in at your current premises. You may wish to stay and chat with them, in which case you shall miss me. Terribly sad.

Sally nudged Isaac and said, "Let's go" in a whisper. They both climbed to their feet, Isaac still cradling the phone.

= Aren't these modern telephones amazing? Pick up the faintest of sounds. Congrats, Miss Grant, on your leadership. Still waters there, Isaac. Best hurry, though. Naughty me, I told the thin blue line of your latest acquisition, viz a viz, the LifeChip. Correct me if I'm wrong, Isaac, but I do believe possession of one with a personality imprinted is still against the law?"

The detective looked around the room, saw the chaos, and realized there was no time to restore order. Placing his thumb over the mouthpiece, he said to Sally, "We have to go. Now. Come on." He moved towards the door, carrying the telephone handset with him. Speaking into the phone handset he said, "Yes, it's illegal. But we can sort all of this out easily. Just stay where you are, no harm will come to you, I promise. We'll be there soon."

= How rational you sound, Isaac. Wonderful stuff. I'll sign off now and you, of course, must dash. Look, now this is just between you and me, but I may have let slip some information to your colleagues. Now what was it? Oh, yes. Look, do forgive me Isaac, but I left a bit of incriminating evidence in your house. Sort of drops you in it, I'm afraid. Sad to say, Miss Grant, you don't get off scot-free either. If you have a moment, pop your head into the main bathroom. Toodle-pip.

The line went dead.

Isaac dropped the phone, turned away from the front door and ran down a small corridor to the bathroom, Sally behind him. He stopped outside the door, pulled out his weapon and gently opened the door. Making sure he did not enter the room, he reached in and turned on the light.

Sally craned her head over his shoulder, looking into a neat and well-kept bathroom. White tiles on the floor and running partially up each wall. A small shower nook, handbasin and bath completed the décor.

The tiles were streaked with blood, red glistening starkly against the purity of the white. In the bath lay the body of a woman. The drain hole in the centre of the floor had blood trails leading to it, drag marks showed where the body had travelled across the floor and placed in the bath.

Although fully clothed, the woman's chest had been split apart, bone pulled to one side, chest cavity glistening wetly in the harsh light.

On the edge of the bath, balanced neatly on one end, was a LifeChip.

Sally heard the sirens.

Chapter 7

The elevator containing the young woman rose, she had left her leathers and helmet on the bike; they were perfectly safe in the building, and if they were stolen, she would buy some new ones. She liked new things and money was no problem, her boss could afford it.

She winked at her reflection in the mirrors, liking what she saw. The ride still tingled through her veins, the buzz combining with the music from her earphones to give her a little slice of heaven. She danced, body swaying, head sweeping back and forth, long hair washing over shoulders and face. She liked the classics, she especially liked hearing what was pumping out of the earphones now - AC/DC and "Dirty Deeds Done Dirt Cheap."

When the doors opened, she was still dancing, eyes closed, stomping booted heels into the floor in time with Bon Scott's raw vocals, joining him for the chorus.

"DIRTY DEEDS" ... stomp the feet for a few beats ... "DONE DIRT CHEAP!!"

She opened her eyes to see the white-coated figure of the doctor standing at the now open elevator doors. She stopped singing and straightened, brushing hair back off her face. She wasn't embarrassed but the moment had passed.

"Heya, Doc!" she chirped. "How you doin'?"

"Don't you think it's time you grew up, dear?" asked the doctor. "How old are you now, Evie? Twenty something?"

Thrusting out a hip, Evie chewed her gum and gazed at her boss, "Reach 30 and die," she said. She moved past her boss into the corridor and turned into a private office. "Got anything for a girl to drink, doc?"

The doctor followed Evie into the room, "Please don't call me 'doc'. I know you're compensating for our difference in status but I find the word demeaning."

Evie opened a wall cupboard and surveyed the selection of bottles now displayed, "Yeah, sure, doc," she absently replied. She was reaching for a bottle of vodka when pain erupted across the back of her head. She staggered forward, hands catching the shelf briefly before blackness closed over her mind. It was only for an instant, her arms slowed her fall, the carpeted floor making a spinning pattern before her eyes.

She stayed on hands and knees, blinking back tears, trying to fathom what had happened. A heavy glass ashtray landed on the floor beside her left hand, she could see a bit of skin and hair stuck on its unforgiving surface.

"You can leave anytime you like, Evie," said a voice somewhere overhead. "If you stay here then do as you are told. Don't call me 'doc.'"

The young girl breathed deeply a few times and before slowly getting to her feet. She felt the back of her head; a spot of dampness on her fingers, the beginning of shock and pain sweeping from her damaged head. Her eyes looked at the blood on her fingertips before moving to the figure now seated at a desk, "Damn ...," she whispered.

"Pardon, dear. What was that?"

"Nothing," said Evie, "nothing..., Doctor."

Their eyes clicked for a few moments before the doctor continued "Now, tell me all. Did you see the stuck-up bitch?"

Evie slumped into a seat across from the doctor, "Yeah, she came all right; said the same thing about you. Gave me a mouthful of abuse."

A knock at the door interrupted their meeting, the doctor stood up, her white lab coat blossoming open to reveal an expensive dress from a label Evie recognised. She hated herself for the momentary pang of envy, Evie liked to think she was above such trivial lusts.

"A bit late for callers?" she queried, the young woman turned her head to the door, following the doctor's progress across the carpet. Evie saw the fleeting glimpse of confusion in the other woman's eyes, this caller was unexpected. Two women alone at night and a knock at the door, Evie stood up and prepared for the worst. She'd had the worst before and didn't intend on it happening again without extracting an appropriate amount of pain. Bloody men.

The doctor opened the door and a young man entered the room, Evie saw the doctor's shoulders relax into a more casual pose. Her boss knew this character. Evie glanced at her watch, well after two in the morning.

Who came calling at this hour? And how had he gotten in the building?

"Joshua...," said the doctor, then stopped herself from saying any more.

The young man smiled at the doctor with an expression full of pleasure before seeing Evie, his face froze for a moment before it adopted a neutral, guarded look. A small smile of expectation came to his lips, that smile people have when they want to be polite but not start a conversation. He was an average looking young man, Evie noted, not the midnight lover type and certainly not dangerous. It was a wonder he could see at all with those milky eyes, she thought, must be a patient.

"Just pop into the next office," instructed the doctor, "this won't take long. We'll continue our conversation in a moment." Evie held the doctor's eyes for a moment, noticed the body language which assumed obedience for the instruction to be carried out.

Evie stood up. In doing so, she noticed a mobile phone in the young man's hand.

"Whatever," the young girl muttered. She crossed to a door in the side wall and entered a smaller office.

As the door shut on the duo, she heard the young man say "You get great mobile reception here, even in the stairwells..."

The doctor lives well, she thought, keeps the big room next door with big chairs and lots of space and can still afford another office like this one, just for the humdrum details of administrivia. She sat at the desk and clicked her fingers on the surface for a few moments, boredom came easily to her, boredom and impatience. An expensive laptop sat on the desk, lid down but the power light showing it was still active.

"Well, well," she said, opening the top of the computer, "Got any secrets, doc?" she whispered.

THE DETECTIVE IN ISAAC scanned the room, his civilian brain urged flight. After a few moments, they both agreed. "Come on," he said, "Let's go. We're done here."

Sally followed him back to the front door, watched silently, numbly, as he peered outside. Turning back to the woman he instructed, "Out the door and across the road. Quick".

He pulled open the door, gestured Sally out and together they moved to his parked car. As he crossed the street, he deactivated the car lock, a small beep and a flash of the side lights indicated the doors were unlocked. "Round you go," he commanded and Sally moved to the passenger door, opened it and got in. Isaac fitted into the driver's seat with a fluidity born of much practice. He started the car, indicated before pulling out into the street. Keeping to a steady acceleration he soon reached cruising speed.

As he drove, his gaze kept flicking to the rearview mirror.

He saw the flashing lights of a police car far behind, when he saw it pull over in front of his house, he activated the indicator and made a gentle left turn. His hands gripping the steering wheel were taut with restraint and panic, a war his body would pay for with a headache as the darkness swallowed the car.

Sally looked ahead, shocked, still seeing the dead woman, the entrails draped over the bath, clothing askew and the silent mockery of the LifeChip. She heard Isaac say something, "Sorry," she said, "what was that?"

"I said," he repeated, "Where's your car?" The dark road was dotted on each side with small cottages, low trees at intervals stretched down beside each footpath. The street was nice, thought Isaac, calm and peaceful. An unknown land for him.

She looked at his profile, suddenly a colleague, no longer an assailant, "I don't have a car."

"What? How'd you get her?" he asked.

"Bus."

"You're putting me on." Isaac did not even know where the bus stop was in his neighbourhood. "What sort of private detective uses a bus? What do you do for a hot pursuit, catch the 490 and then leap to a 102?" He chuckled.

"Yuk it up, big guy," she replied. "Thing is, I'm broke. I'm beyond broke. I'd have to save up to be broke." She looked out the window, seeing a world she had read about, seen on TV, but never experienced. "That cash card let me eat, pay a few bills. Catch a bus." She swung back to face him, "And I got to meet you, can't tell you what a thrill that's been."

He drove in silence for a while, body on automatic, mind roaming free. Her words were spoken in softness, no venom or malice behind them, yet they echoed in his mind. "Where are we going now, Isaac?" she asked.

"Eagle Street," he replied, "I know where Mama Luigi's is." Flicking a glance in the rearview he continued, "So you took this job to break into my house and get Mary's LifeChip. Didn't strike you as odd, a person keeping a LifeChip in the cupboard?"

She slid further into the seat, head resting on the window. The quiet conversation was lulling her to sleep, "I'm new at this PI stuff, Isaac; got bored with being a shopgirl, did a TAFE course and here I am." She closed her eyes but kept talking "Are Mary's cells still viable? Can you bring her back?"

"Maybe." The traffic was thickening as they approached the city centre, "When she was declared legally dead, I asked for her cells to be kept. Kept hoping I might find the LifeChip." Lights reflected off the windows, traffic nudged and flowed around them. "I checked with LifeCorp last month, they said the cells were still viable. If the ...," he swallowed, "...the data on the chip is still good then all should work."

She looked across at him again, "Yeah, the chip. That's the thing." Silence. "You need to get that chip validated, Isaac. It might not even be Mary, those readers can be fooled." No response from the big man. She tried to reach out again, "Isaac ..."

He flashed a taut face at her, "I know!" Back to the traffic, "I know already. I know the chips lose data when they're out of the body, I know they store and transport them in a protected environment. I know that if it is my .... my Mary... then she might ...be ... damaged..." His voice faded, choking off the last words, "I know..."

Sally wanted to heal the poor, wretched man. Wanted to make it all better, wanted to be somewhere else. She shut her eyes tight, held her breath, and did not move. Perhaps when she opened her eyes it would all have gone away. All a bad dream.

She opened her eyes. Isaac was still wrapped in his isolation. Deciding on distraction she asked him, "Do you know this character on the phone? Leonardo? Sounds like you have a history."

"I don't know," Isaac grunted. "All I can think of is that he was the one who did the original killings. We had no clues then, didn't even know if the killer was male or female. We only guessed it was one person, not a gang."

"How many murders?" she asked.

"Four"

"Four!" Sally sat up. "When was this? I don't remember hearing of four murders in the papers, what aren't you telling me, Isaac?"

He seemed to slump further into the seat, shoulder pressed against the door, head almost touching the window, the words came out slow, voice gravelly, a litany of observed grief. "The killings finished two years ago, Mary was the last one. Before that, we found three other bodies, all gutted like that one in the bath tonight. All with their LifeChip missing." The night held them both still, traffic had eased, the big man turned the car off the main roads and entered the labyrinth of city side streets. The sound of the indicator was a clock ticking away some dark life.

"I found the first one, a schoolgirl." He paused as the memory blossomed. "We thought we had some sort of rapist or sex killer, poor little kid. I was in the city, looking for a particularly nasty stand-over merchant who had used up all his favours."

"What do you mean, 'favours'?" she asked.

"You can't treat everyone the same. The law says we all have the same rights and the same responsibilities, but a good copper has to make trades. This character, Pig Saunders, was a racist, a bully, probably a killer but we never found any proof. I didn't like him, not many did. But he was used by various members of the citizenry when they needed some unpleasantness done. We'd had a complaint from a newspaper vendor that Pig had beaten him up, probably didn't pay his bookie, but it was one complaint too many for Pig."

Isaac drove through the deserted streets, dawn came early in these latitudes; for now, the car was alone in this between time of the day. "He'd given us some useful information from time to time, helped us take the odd bigger thug off the streets. This gave him some credit with us; so long as he didn't get too carried away, we could ignore him. Then he went too far, became very violent. The newspaper vendor was Asian and Pig lost control, almost killed him. I was in the back streets heading to a little club I knew he used, came down an alley and saw a leg sticking out behind a dumpster."

THE YOUNG MAN NODDED acquiescence to the doctor's request but did not sit in the chair before the desk, the chair recently tenanted by Evie. Instead, he moved to a small couch against the wall, a couch that formed a smaller meeting area within the large office. Before it was a low coffee table, another lounge chair sat to one side making an intimate spot for private yet personal conversations. This was an area for secrets to be shared, not business to be conducted.

He spoke from the couch, running a hand through his hair, "Sorry to bolt off like that, doctor, I'm just in the middle of a little project and had to check in with one of my employees."

"You have employees, Joshua?"

He smiled deprecatingly, "Sort of, they just don't know it yet. Anyway, I'd like to continue our conversation from earlier."

"Certainly, I'm all yours."

"I didn't know you had a visitor," he said, nodding towards the adjoining office, the one in which Evie now sat. The doctor wasn't thrown by the question, a lot of her life involved misdirection, guarded interviews and armchair psychology. She also understood that her answers would be scrutinised by this young man, this quiet young man now sitting on her couch in the small hours of the night.

This young man who mildly terrified her.

"My turn," she smiled. "She's one of my employees. I can send her away if you wish." Behind the doctor was a large glass window, in the morning it would reveal a bird's eye view of the city, blue sky and buildings. A breathtaking panorama. She rarely looked at it, just liked knowing she owned it.

But tonight, she felt the outside darkness, she felt the size of the night, sensed it as the childhood bogeyman peering over her shoulder. She didn't want to turn around and see that darkness, some small part of it seemed to have entered the office with Joshua.

"Wouldn't know her birthday, would you?" the young man asked, still with his gentle smile. He sat back deeper into the couch, the soft leather creaking, a gentle fragrance of the oiled surface wafting into his nostrils. He scanned the room, not really looking, he'd seen it before but still enjoyed the opulence of it all. He enjoyed playing the searching game, looking at each item in the room and working out why the doctor had chosen it and the reason for its placement. The doctor was a trickster, he knew, playing her games.

He did like a good game.

"No idea, Joshua. We could ask her if you like." She paused, "Why this sudden interest in birthdays? You wanted to know mine last week; I thought you might be planning a birthday surprise."

He ignored her question, "Lovely night out there."

A fright caused her to catch breath, why had he referred to the night, had he sensed her anxiety? She swallowed and reached out to shift the heavy glass ashtray a millimetre along the surface of her desk, "Is it?" she said, twirling the ashtray on the spot, "I haven't been out tonight."

"I have," he said. "Lovely dark. Clear sky, lots of stars."

Chapter 8

The big car pulled into the curb, Isaac stopped the engine, turned and looked at Sally, "She was fifteen, still in school uniform. I still see her, lying on her back, head to one side, eyes open, face so young, so... surprised. Her chest had been cut open with some big blade, we thought a machete or cleaver. Ribs pulled apart." Sally stared, Isaac took a breath before continuing the story, "The killer left a note saying, 'This is number one and we're having so much fun'. We knew we were in for a bad time." He stopped. "Don't like this job sometimes."

Sally gazed in helplessness at the detective. What possible words could she say to make his pain less? Her mind gibbered in helplessness, the utter pointlessness of any words stood in stark contrast to this very real, almost tangible horror. Another world had reached out and touched her, a world where mad things existed, where incomprehensible cruelty lived and slavered.

She reached out a hand and touched the poor man's coat, squeezed the arm.

"Numbers two and three both had notes, taunting us. One said, 'Catch me, please!' Might have been a cry for help, but probably just the killer being sadistic." Number three said, 'Random killing is so boring!' Then came Mary, her note said, 'Now I have a plan!' We had no idea what it meant."

"That's Mama Luigi's," he said, indicating a shop front about three car lengths away from where they were parked. Light blazed through the large glass windows, no one was visible behind the shop counter. Isaac opened the car door, Sally noticed the interior light didn't come on. She realized Isaac must open his door at night a lot, open it and prowl the darkness, keeping her and the rest of the world safe.

She opened her door, but before she could exit the vehicle, she heard Isaac say to her, "Stop. No. Damn." She turned to face him, each sat with their doors half open, she had one leg out of the car already. "You should stay here," he said.

Exiting the car, she said, "Yep." Her legs shook with nervousness, she wanted to stay in the car but ... but he needed help.

Isaac stood and shut his door, activating the locks. He leaned on the car roof, both hands clasped as his outstretched arms took his weight. He fiddled with the car keys, looked at the young woman. "Sally, you saw the body in my house. There'll be a car full of uniforms here soon, we've all got trackers in our vehicles. When they arrive, I'll be in there," he pointed to the shop. "I'm not looking forward to finding what's inside but there's a chance he might still be there. He sounded pretty full of himself, probably wants a chance to gloat. If we wait for the sirens, we'll miss a chance."

"But it's my chance, Sally, my job. Not yours. I get paid to stick my head into dark places. Please stay here."

She looked at the big man, he looked back. "Nope," she replied. 'What was she doing?' Her brain demanded, 'get back in that car, you are not cut out for this sort of work!'

"You're a grown-up, make your own decisions," he said. "Painful bloody woman." He pulled out his weapon, crossed to the footpath and started walking towards the shop front, gun held loosely at his side. Sally was surprised he wasn't insisting she stay behind, she realized she would have preferred to sit tight and wait for every policeman in the world to show up and stand between her and whatever waited in that shop. Her moment of bravado had come and gone, but she had told Isaac she would not stay, by implication she had said she would back him up.

He hadn't argued, hadn't given her instructions, hadn't treated her like some helpless female. He had taken her at her word, had accepted what she said. This scared Sally, she wasn't used to people dealing with her this way.

Suck it up, girl, she told herself. Get after the big guy. She moved on shaking legs towards the shop.

Isaac was waiting at the front door. He looked at her, nodded and pushed into the shop. He went in first, Sally came after, both went to different sides of the doorway, Isaac crossed quickly to the counter and looked over.

There was no one in the front part of the shop. Behind the counter was another doorway, presumably leading into the kitchen area, a large servery window opened beside the doorway. The food preparation space could clearly be seen in the next room but again no other person was visible. The lights were on, shining down stark and bright, pools of black shadow lay under counters and shelves. Stainless steel bench tops reflected the brightness, the air conditioner hummed to itself, sending wafts of cool air through vents into the front part of the shop. Sally felt its cool breeze from time to time against her cheek.

A glass display case took up half the counter area, inside its controlled environment sat an array of lasagnas, cabana sausages, and other strange and vaguely repellent food offerings. None of it made Sally hungry, her appetite sat watching the unfolding drama, not wanting to intrude.

Isaac surveyed the room, he sensed Sally off to his right, heard her quick breathing. Tough girl, he thought. Tougher than she thinks, he believed. On top of the display case were small boxes of snack foods, chocolate bars, and impulse items. He listened, sending his hearing out to explore. After a few moments of silence, he stepped forward, pressed against the counter and leaned forward. He was trying to see what surprises might be in the kitchen.

The bench top stopped short of one wall where a flap allowed entrance to the business area of the shop. Isaac crossed in front of Sally and moved to this entrance. Holding his pistol in the ready position, he stepped into the space behind the counter, body pressed against the back wall next to the servery window. Again, he waited.

Sally watched the big man move, his actions sure and practised. She was unsure what to do, deciding to stand still and not get in the way. Remembering her Taser, she opened her shoulder bag and pulled out the device. She had never used it but felt better with it in her hand. Better than standing here shaking like a leaf, she thought.

Again, they waited. Isaac listened. A lot of Isaac's job seemed to be waiting and listening, she realized. I could learn a thing or two from the big guy.

He peered over the corner of the window. Nothing moved inside, at least nothing he could see. Ducking under the window he slid along the wall until he was next to the doorway into the kitchen. He looked back at Sally, saw her standing in the centre of the room, hair tousled, eyes black with a lack of sleep and an excess of tears. In her hand was her ridiculous Taser, he hoped it was a useful weapon. She looked so young, like a kid about to cast a spell with her pretend magic wand. Just a child in some dress-up game. Her eyes followed his every move.

She was scared, he could feel her nerves as she stood exposed in the harsh fluorescent glare - a moth pinned under a lamp. Disliking the analogy, he gave her a grin, nodded to indicate he was about to enter the kitchen. He realised she was sacred, even terrified, but also understood that she was brave, brave enough to go into the dak places. Quite a girl, he thought, and moved into the room.

Sally saw the nod, gulped and tried to remember the last cop movie she had seen. As Isaac disappeared around the corner she burst out of her stasis, ran around the counter and darted past the servery window. Flashing a look inside she sped past, saw Isaac's shoulder for a moment crouching, scanning the room for threats. By the time she had reached the open doorway, he had moved off deeper into the room.

A small wall jutted into the kitchen, screening the back section of the room. A row of pegs held aprons and jackets, a rubbish bin was tucked under a small sink. From his crouch in the centre of the kitchen, Isaac could see around the wall to the beginnings of a back door. A whiteboard took up wall space near the door, originally it had held a roster, but the bulk of the names had been erased. In a cleared patch of the board was a note written in blue pen:

Couldn't Wait

Must dash –

Left something in the fridge.

Leo

Isaac shuddered.

Sally moved into the room, seeing the detective standing in a non-aggressive pose, she hoped all was well. Then she saw the slump to his shoulders, noticed the gun hanging limply from his right hand. She took three steps to stand beside him, saw where his eyes were fixed and read the message on the whiteboard.

Isaac recovered a little when Sally moved beside him. He was the professional, dammit, he was the one who should be setting the pace. But he was feeling worn out and used. As Sally tried to comprehend the implications of the message, he looked over her shoulder to the large door leading into the cold room. A wide band of stainless steel wrapped itself around the front of the door as a broad handle. Pulling this bar would release the door from its closed position, an overhead track showed how it could slide aside easily.

Clutching the gun tightly, he walked to the door, looked back at Sally to ensure she was out of direct sight of whoever, or whatever, was in the cold room and grasped the handle. He took a breath and heaved the door outwards and along the slide. As it began to move, he swung into the cold room, crouched and scanned the room, weapon tracking with his eyes.

Two bodies lay on the floor, both female, both slit open exposing the naked privacy of internal organs. One was dressed in a cream outfit with the words 'Mama Luigi' embroidered on the sleeve. The other was a nurse, still in her sea blue uniform from City Central Hospital. Isaac shook as if struck by a blow; the women were dead, both in poses reminiscent of his dead wife. He stepped out of the cold room, fell backwards onto his rump and leaned back against the wall, his gun hand relaxed allowing the heavy weapon to pull his arm to the floor. He sat with legs outstretched, hands on the floor beside his drained and shattered body. Sally saw the bodies, crept out and curled against his side, huddling for warmth and a need to share the grief. She sobbed against his shoulder, he felt his own tears run down cheeks long used to suffering. She wasn't tough.

EVIE TRIED ANOTHER password but the laptop resolutely refused to acknowledge her efforts. "What if Miss-High-and-bloody-Mighty-call-me-doctor has put a limit on the number of trials for the password?" she muttered.

She was running out of options, she considered typing in the doctor's name, her phone number and any other piece of random data that might be a password. All had failed. She glared at the screen and chewed a nail, what was the infuriating woman's password? A thought struck her, she typed in "Joshua".

The screen cleared to a welcome message, the wallpaper showed a photograph of a wrecked motorcycle. What sort of weirdo background is that, wondered Evie.

And why was this Joshua character so important to the doc?

IN THE ADJOINING OFFICE the doctor was reseating herself in the large chair behind the desk, "Would you like to sit down, Joshua?" She was glad of Evie's presence next door, an ally if needed. "Do you have a response to my message?"

Joshua sat in the recently vacated chair, he ran his fingers through his hair before rolling his shoulders to relieve tired muscles. He sank into the soft leather and said, "Jimmy reckons he's solved the last bug, I got this message from my middle man, he deals with Jimmy and then contacts me. He says Jimmy is ready for a demonstration but wants payment before he hands over the tech – he wants two clones. He'll use them to demonstrate his cleverness before selling the bits off to the black market. You gotta love a free market economy." He looked at his fingertips, idly examining the state of his nails. "What do you want me to tell him?"

The doctor hesitated, "Just a minute, this is big." She thought quietly for a few moments, if Jimmy had indeed solved the interface issue, they were on the brink of making a fortune. Current technology allowed for the upload of data from a LifeChip and into a blank mind, but the mind had to be in a clone of the deceased person. But this new tech promised other options. Illegal, nasty options. Joshua let his gaze wander around the room, mind pleasantly in neutral. Finally the doctor spoke again, "Do you believe him?"

The young man smiled, "What do I care?" he replied. "You pay me to run messages to criminals, not to evaluate their responses." He looked at his watch, "I'm on a deadline here, ma'am. What do you want me to tell him?"

The doctor came to a decision, "Tell him he has a deal. I'll give him the clones, he can use them for the demonstration."

"And he'll give you money," said Joshua.

She smiled, "Oh, yes, Joshua, he will indeed. Lots of lovely, lovely money. Now, run along."

She handed Joshua a set of keys, "Downstairs in the carpark is a Medical Transport Vehicle, I've two clones in the back. Sedated, of course, they're on gurneys in the back."

Joshua's eyebrows rose a little, she enjoyed the sensation of his surprise. "I like to be prepared," she finished. "Is there anything else you need?"

"Whoa, hold on there, boss lady," said Joshua. "I've still got to arrange a meeting with Jimmy, a face to face. And I certainly don't want to be driving around the city with a couple of black-market clones. Keep them here, I'll call when I need them but I want someone else to drive the vehicle. Any suggestions for a driver?"

The doctor thought of the young woman next door, "You ring me and I'll have Evie bring the clones to you. Is that acceptable?" She again pondered the delicate dance she took when negotiating with Joshua, a strange young man, she thought. Strange, fortunate, and damaged in so many ways.

He nodded, stood up and left the office. The doctor felt the entire room exhale as the door closed behind him.

And now for Evie, she decided. She stood up and crossed to the door between the two offices, before turning the handle she placed her ear against the wood, listening for any sounds. I wonder what she's been up to in there, she thought.

She swung the door open in a smooth and quick motion, a childish part of her wanted to catch the younger woman out at something. Possibly with her hand in a drawer, or a face covered with jam – where did I get that image from, she queried herself. – and then the look of astonishment on the culprit followed by a decisive "aha!" from herself. All this flashed through her mind as she opened the door, a whole range of childhood incidents where she had been caught by her mother at some piece of mischief flooding her mind before her rational self asserted dominance and sent her inner child back to the playroom.

But she kept the 'aha!' ready, just in case.

EVIE WAS NOT AT THE desk, nor in the office chair. Moving further into the room the older woman looked for her younger companion, finally spotting a booted foot protruding from in front of the desk, on the other side to the chair and the doctor's laptop.

The doctor was an organised woman, capable, meticulous and careful in all her planning. But she chided herself for leaving her laptop on the desk, alone and exposed. She crossed to the booted foot and gazed upon the sleeping form of Evie, stretched out on the floor, a pile of office literature and her jacket forming a pillow for her pretty young head.

Had Evie accessed the laptop? The doctor tapped the sleeping woman's foot to stir her into wakefulness and then moved to sit at the desk. She raised the lid of the laptop – and questioned whether she had left it open or shut – and waited for the welcome screen to show up.

The motorcycle picture fluttered to life on the screen, followed by a request for a password. Evie struggled to her feet and slumped into the visitor's chair, yawning and scratching. Tousled hair completed her image, catching the doctor's eye she winked and softly broke wind. Then she smiled.

"Such a pretty thing you are, Evie, a joy to watch emerge into wakefulness. I'm sure your young men must love it."

"What's not to love?" asked Evie. She ran fingers through her hair and waited for the doctor to ask the question.

"Did you try to gain access to my laptop, Evie?" The doctor was very still, the question soft and gentle, the threat unstated.

THE BIG MAN HEARD THE sirens, the running feet, the clatter of boots in the kitchen. Heard the shocked gasps, felt the stagger as each visitor to the new abattoir entered and saw the desecration of two human beings.

A voice emerged from the pulse of people, "That you, Isaac?"

He looked up and saw another man standing in the doorway, a black man. Although not in uniform the badge pinned to his belt identified him as a policeman, "I need your gun, Isaac" he said.

The big man tried to will his brain to clear; he needed to function normally, to think clearly. Of course, he had to surrender his gun, he had fled his own house, a crime scene, only to be discovered here at another. He knew this detective, had seen him at the station. He raised his hand holding the pistol, ready to surrender the weapon.

"Freeze!"

His brain looked through eyes lost in confusion. He saw the black detective in a shooting stance, a weapon pointed at Isacc's head. Two other uniformed officers were in the room and had spun at the command, one also had his heavy calibre pistol held in the approved two-handed grip. A big bore barrel soaked up Isaac's head, filled his world. The other policeman stood in the centre of the room, stunned into frozen apprehension. His eyes widened at the scene; guns, noise, smoke and mayhem were about to fill the despoiled kitchen.

Isaac held his right arm motionless, saw his pistol held by the grip and realized his mistake. Sally sat rigid beside him; he could feel small shivers through her hand grasping his left arm.

"Easy, guys, easy," he said, "I'm going to open my hand now, let you see I don't have my finger near the trigger. Be cool, now." He waited a few beats, holding the rest of his body tense and still, ensuring no other limb so much as twitched. Slowly he lifted his thumb away from the gun, then gently eased his trigger finger up and straight. He repeated the motion with other fingers until he held the pistol with his middle finger pressing it into his palm. He rolled his hand slightly to take most of the weight onto his hand. There they all stayed, Isaac watched the patrolmen, waited for someone to move. The gun was heavy, pulling his arm down. He saw the uniform with the gun flick a glance towards the black detective.

"Get his weapon," he heard the black man say.

The nervous patrolman holstered his gun, secured it with a clip and swallowed. Extending his hands he moved slowly across the floor, eyes fixed on Isaac's gun. The other uniform moved to a covering position and drew his gun, pointing it at the seated man. Step by step the uniform moved in, arms outstretched. "Sit still, man," he murmured, over and over again. "Sit still...still..."

Finally, he placed a hand over Isaac's weapon and the big man allowed himself to relinquish his sidearm. He kept his hand elevated for a few more moments, waiting for the uniform to step back. Slowly he lowered his arm, sinking back against the wall. A long sigh escaped through his dry mouth.

"Top night," he murmured.

Chapter 9

The tension eased out of the room, Sally and Isaac rose to their feet and assumed the search position against the wall. A uniform patted each down, extracting ID from Sally's bag and Isaac's coat. The black detective holstered his weapon and examined the documents.

"There's a bulletin out for you Isaac," he said. "Don't know anything about Miss Grant, though. Let's get out of here, we can wait outside for forensics, have a chat about what happened here."

There were a couple of small tables with cheap plastic chairs in the front part of the shop, old magazines lay scattered across their surfaces. Something to read while waiting, all the magazines were several months old, torn and tatty. Isaac, Sally and the black detective sat down, Sally took a chair and leaned her head against the side wall, it felt deliciously comfortable, so restful.

"I'm Harris," said the black man, his aboriginal status strongly writ across a face saddened by the detritus of life. His nose was broad and flat, skin a mesmerizing depth of night but his eyes looked into Sally's with a look she had already seen in the gaze of Isaac. Men who had seen too much. "Want to tell me what's going on, Detective Howard?"

Before Isaac could answer a cell phone rang. Each of them patted pockets, Sally watched them from within her fatigue and then jolted upright. That was her ringtone! She grabbed her big bag and delved into the chaos, finally coming up with her phone. It continued to chirp brightly.

"Hello," she said.

= Evening, Sal. Pop us on speaker, would you?

Sally looked in shock at Isaac, moving the phone away from her ear, she pushed the speaker button.

= Hey, gang. How's every little thing?

"Leonardo?" asked Isaac.

= Got it in one, Zac, old boy. Say, Isaac, are you Jewish? You know, the name thing and all. Not a bigot or anything, old man, just idle curiosity.

Isaac looked at the phone, his brain stumbling. Harris spoke, "Who is this?"

= A new voice! How nice. Would you be another terribly brilliant detective man, then? Friend of yours, Isaac?

Harris glowered at the phone and leaned towards it aggressively. Sally placed it on the table, not wanting to touch anything with links to their tormentor. "This is Detective Sergeant Harris, identify yourself, please."

= Wait one.

In the pause that followed Harris raised his eyebrows in interrogation to Isaac who gave him a non-committal shrug in return.

= Yes, got you, Detective Sergeant Harris. Don't you just love the internet? Well, well, a black man, one of our indigenes. Whatever is the city coming to, leaving the defence of its citizenry to blacks and Jews? ... Just kidding, Isaac and I are old friends, aren't we, Zaccy-poo?

Finally, Isaac spoke, "What do you want, Leonardo?"

= Just checking in. Couldn't wait for you, I'm afraid, had to make a call. As a concerned citizen, I felt obliged to inform the local fuzz of a disturbance at Mama Luigi's. Say, Isaac, pop, quiz: 'Who would have thought the old man had so much blood in him?'

The line went dead.

Isaac and Harris looked at each other, then Isaac burst to his feet. Running back through the kitchen he flung open the door into the service alley. Lying against the side wall was the body of a man, his throat cut, the blood had run in torrents from his savaged neck across the alley. The man's river of life flowed past a dumpster to finally disgorge itself into a wastewater grill in the centre of the alley. A stray cat sat lapping at the congealed stream.

It was obvious the man had been dead for some time; Isaac noted his chest was intact; the only wound was the red and screaming mouth of his grinning neck.

Harris called to the uniforms, told them to search the alley and called for further backup. While they stood in the alley, a forensic team arrived and asked them to leave the area. Returning to their table, Harris again asked for information.

Isaac talked, he told Harris about his evening, about finding Sally in his home. And he told of his wife's LifeChip. As he spoke Sally's eyes slowly closed, her breathing deepened, and gentle snores came from the young woman. The human mind can only handle so much, and she had reached her limit.

Other detectives arrived, paused to listen before going back and examining the carnage. At some point, three cups of something hot were placed on the table. The men sipped and murmured, Sally snored on. The bodies were wheeled out to waiting vehicles, passing the now silent trio. The Medical Examiner followed the last corpse, that of the dead man. He pulled up a chair and joined the table. Reaching across he picked up Sally's cup and drained most of it in a few swallows.

"Cold and tasteless. My favourite." He put the cup back on the table and looked at the big detective. "Evening, Isaac. Bit familiar this, isn't it?"

"Hello, Frank," said Isaac "Yeah. Thought we'd seen the last of these two years ago." There was an uncomfortable silence as the men remembered the identity of the last body.

"You in charge here, Bill?" the medical man asked, directing the question to Harris.

Harris looked in his empty cup, a final check for something worthwhile. "Yeah. We got a call that a murder had been committed, report said there were gunshots and screams."

"Doubt that, no gunshot wounds on any of them. Screams? Don't know, but wouldn't think so. Think you've been fed a few lies, Bill. Anyway, I'll give you a full report in the morning." He looked out the window and saw the first glimpses of the new dawn. "Maybe lunchtime." He looked at Isaac "So, what are you doing here, Big Fella? And who's the girl?"

Harris replied for them, "Fed the same line as me, Frank. Girl's a consultant," Isaac looked at the black man but was able to hide his surprise at the half-truth. "Got anything to tell us before you do a full autopsy?"

The Medical Examiner stood up, "Nope, two dead females, one dead male. That's it. One had her LifeChip stolen, just like in the bad old days." He moved to the door.

Isaac called out, "Wait a minute, Frank, what do you mean 'one LifeChip'? I know the man wasn't cut up but both women were. How do you know only one chip was taken?"

Turning at the door the ME opened his bag and took out a document wallet, a secure bag for collecting critical evidence. "Because the other one is here. I found it in the body cavity of one of the victims. Looks like the killer extracted the chip and then dropped it back into the body. Bit gruesome. Gotta go." And he left.

Harris said, "What the hell is going on, Isaac?"

Before a reply could be made Sally's phone rang again.

THE YOUNG WOMAN LOOKED at her interrogator. She scared Evie, scared her at a deep, deep level. She was a little girl again, found out by her mother in the act of stealing from her purse. She was in school, being berated by a teacher for sloppy work and a poor attitude.

But none of these people ever hurt her, none had ever threatened her with death. Or worse.

And neither had the doctor, this distinguished, well-dressed, educated and articulate woman who hired Evie to do little tasks. Strange tasks, unpleasant and exciting tasks. Well paid tasks.

No, the doctor had never actually threatened her with anything. She just did it. Like hitting her with the ashtray next door. No warning, no anger or emotion, just the violent and painful act. And Evie knew that the smiling woman across the desk from her would still be smiling as she carried out whatever act she deemed necessary. Joshua was not the only shadow employee she had seen, the doctor knew several very bad people and it was one of these who had brought Evie into the older woman's orbit of influence. She had done a simple task, a trial, a little test to see if she was worth using again.

"Do you remember the first job you did for me, Evie?"

The young woman started, unnerved by the parallel course her thoughts had taken alongside the doctor's question. She shrugged noncommittally, trying to keep the necessary cool she had acquired on the streets, "Maybe," she replied, forcing herself to let her gaze wander around the room with as much casualness as she could muster.

"The young man was the son of a man who had done me some harm," said the doctor. "Nothing significant, I can't recall what it was but his wedding day presented me with the opportunity to do the family a little disservice. When you flounced down the aside dressed in that quite revealing little number I was sitting in the back row, very interested to see how you would carry out my instructions. I must say, you did look like you were enjoying yourself."

Evie smirked at the memory, "Too right, I was," she said. "Got the chance to play up and get paid for it. God," she snorted, "the look on his face when I kissed his bride! Fair broke me up."

The doctor was also reliving the event, "Yes, the wedding was looking rocky already and your little performance pushed it a bit more over the edge. Kissing the father of the bride on the way out was pure gold, especially when it was obvious he knew you."

"He knew me alright," said Evie, "I let him pick me up the previous night in a bar, had a bit of a fondle in the carpark before he went home. What a hoot!"

The doctor tapped the lid of the closed laptop with one long, manicured nail, "And now, Evie, dear, please answer my question. Did you try to access my laptop?"

The smile died on Evie's lips, she thought she was sharing a bit of camaraderie with her employer, a bit of bonding down memory lane. But there was no bonding with the doctor, just obedience. Obedience and fear. She swallowed and decided honesty might get her through the next few minutes. "Yeah. Well. I tried to but couldn't get past your password." Perhaps not complete honesty, but hopefully close enough to skirt the danger area. Evie hadn't looked at the data, just loaded all the recently used documents onto her memory stick for reviewing later. Probably nothing worth knowing about them anyway but old habits die hard. What was her employer going to do now?

The doctor opened the laptop and noted the initial screen, the one asking for a password. "How many times did you try, Evie?" she asked with a deceptively idle nature.

"Just two. I figured if I locked myself out of the machine because of too many incorrect codes you would find out anyway."

"How many tries do you think it would take, dear?"

"Dunno. Usually, it's three, so I stopped when I realised what I was trying to do."

"And what were you trying to do, my young villain?"

Evie gambled it all, "I realised I was trying to access data which may have been quite personal to you. Personal and private. And therefore, dangerous to me. It was stupid, just an old habit; I'm sorry, I didn't see anything, I don't want any trouble." She'd said it all, gone as close to the truth as she dared, her fear was real and she let that show, let the apprehension in her heart be reflected by the nervousness in her actions and speech.

She wasn't acting scared. She was scared.

The doctor gazed at her young companion and considered her options. She looked at the password screen and asked, "Two tries, you said?"

Evie nodded, her face a misery. The doctor typed in a name at random on the password entry screen and hit the enter button; another message appeared, "Too many incorrect entries. The keyboard is now locked."

"Damn!" she whispered. It meant a visit from a technician tomorrow, a glance at her watch told her that the next day was only hours away – not a major inconvenience, then. "You are a very silly girl, Evie. Although you were unsuccessful, I am still very annoyed with you." She mused a moment "Still, no harm done, I suppose." She stood up, "For now, stay here and get some more sleep, you can nap on the couch next door; we'll discuss your actions later. I will have a small task for you in a couple of hours, driving a Medical Transport Vehicle to meet Joshua. And Evie," she said, "Don't look in the back of the vehicle, Joshua would not like that. Understand?"

Evie nodded, feeling momentarily like a rabbit caught in headlights; she pulled herself together and stood up, making a delivery to Joshua would leave her sanity in tatters but hopefully there wouldn't be any other consequences. She moved next door and stretched out on the couch. When she was safe, she would look at whatever was on her memory stick. As she began to doze, she sighed, grateful she had reset the password cue.

Sometimes, her dance was very near the edge.

The doctor watched the young woman leave, walking her to the door and escorting her through the outer office. She stood looking at the door, mulling over the actions of her two employees. Joshua was obviously involved in some private scheme, she would have to ensure that all links to him were erased; that meant a bit of work on her laptop – the motorcycle background would have to go.

And since Evie had seen them together then she would have to go, too. Joshua could do that little chore, bring the body to her private lab for a spot of recycling.

She smiled at the word – recycling. Yes, she thought, I am a bit of a greenie after all.

THE RINGTONE SPEARED into Sally's consciousness. She swam to the surface as from a great depth, opening her eyes to sights she had never seen. It took her several moments to recall how she had ended up sitting in a takeaway food shop with two grim men while dawn spilled through the windows. Her hands grappled with, and found, her mobile of their own volition.

"Hello," she stuttered.

= Wakey wakey, Miss Grant. The games afoot.

Sally pushed the speaker button and again set the phone on the table, she wanted to go and wash her hands after handling the contact with Leonardo.

"Leonardo?" asked Isaac.

= Morning, Isaac. Is young Bill still with us?

"What do you want?" said Harris.

= My, quite the tetchy one, isn't he? So, how's the head, Isaac? Going round and round in circles yet? Not getting anywhere? Have to start calling you 'wingnut' won't we?

Isaac burst out, "We're going to get you, you sick mongrel!"

= Of course you are, dear boy. Goes without saying. Still, two years ago I gave you so many chances and what sort of response was there? Not a sausage. Let's face it, gentlemen, on a good day you have trouble finding your backside with both hands. I mean to say, you hadn't even found all of my people at Mama Luigi's until I gave you a clue. Honestly, some people.

"How did you get my number?" asked Sally.

= When was the last time you looked at your advertisement, child? Just under quite a lovely photograph is your mobile number. Have a nice doze, by the way.

Isaac twisted, searching the room for the speaker. How did he know about Sally's sleep?

= Settle down, Isaac, you'll do yourself a mischief. Lovely morning isn't it, my favourite time of day. Well, I must pop along to my exercise class, just thought I'd give you a bell. Toodle-pip.

"Wait!" begged Isaac "Wait. Why are you doing these things? Let us help you!"

= Aww, Isaac, that's sweet, thinking I'm in need of help. Far from it, old man, I'm a bit unkillable really. No, I just woke up one morning and killed someone. You ever have the urge, Isaac? No, of course not, pillar of the community and all that. Tell you what I'm going to do, though. Give you a sporting chance, drop you another clue. That's ANOTHER clue, Sherlock. Ready? Pencils poised? No repeats here, just saying it the once. Okay, here we go: School days are the best days of our lives – discuss.

The line went dead.

They looked at each other. "What the hell was that all about?" asked Harris.

Sally did not join the conversation; she was in a meeting with people who knew how to do this sort of thing, who knew about crime and criminals. She decided to keep quiet and not reveal her ignorance of this world.

"We can't talk here," said Isaac. "Somehow he's watching, we need to move."

"Yeah, right," said Harris, "We need to get detailed statements from the two of you, anyway. Let's go down to the station, try to sort this out and you could do with some rest, Isaac, you look like something the cat dragged in."

They stood and moved outside, the morning was fresh and clean, all bright and new. She followed Isaac back to his car, Harris went with them. "I'll get a ride back with you, if you don't mind" he said.

Sally looked back at the shop; through that doorway, she thought, was a place not of this world. This morning was for new life, the sweet scents of the trees down the footpath, the brightness of a flight of birds overhead, their cries counter-pointing the rosy hues of dawn.

But through that door was blood, stink, ugliness and death. A dark, dark world.

Chapter 10

Isaac unlocked the car and grimly entered. He knew why Harris was riding with them, it wasn't for a lift, it was to keep an eye on them. Until someone in authority gives us the all-clear, he thought, Sally and I will be 'helping the police with their enquiries'. He was grateful Harris had been present for the phone calls, at least it gave weight to their story.

He pulled away from the curb, "He was watching us."

Sally sat back in the seat, tired to the bone, "How?"

They drove. "I don't know," replied the big man. "It was close to dawn, maybe he was outside with a telescope or something. The light came right through those big front windows, he could have set himself up anywhere to watch. A car, rooftop, lots of places." He glanced across at Harris in the front seat beside him, "What do you think?"

The black man was listening from the back seat, gauging the ebb and flow of conversation. The phone calls could have been fake and could have been made by an accomplice of these two. The simplest explanation is usually the right one and the simplest explanation was that these two had done the killings. He knew of the body in Isaac's house, and they were discovered in the shop, in the same room as two gutted corpses.

"We need to have a good talk. I think three, no four, deaths need investigating. That's all, I think. One step at a time, Isaac, we need to get you guys downtown and try to get to the bottom of this."

Isaac yanked the wheel hard, the car swerved over and stopped at the curb, badly parked with the rear jutting out. A car following behind honked in disgust.

"I think you need to listen to me, Harris," said a tense Isaac. "We had nothing to do with these deaths; you heard that maniac! He's playing with us. For some reason he has decided to torment me, I don't know why but I sure as hell know I don't need your veiled threats!" His hands shook on the steering wheel, a combination of fatigue and shock reducing his tolerance level to nothing.

Harris was grateful he had given the big man's pistol to the uniforms. Looking at the man in the driver's seat, he saw himself in a few years, worn out by the job. Had something given way in the depths of Isaac's mind? Was there a part of him that had collapsed under the weight of grief over his wife and anger at the world? Were there two Isaacs?

"Keep your hands on the wheel, Isaac," he said, quickly removing his pistol from its holster. Placing the gun in his lap he pointed it down and to the front, muzzle pointing towards the rear of the driver's seat, but each knew it could snap up in a moment. "Now calm down, man. You know the routine, we have to get your statements and then someone higher up the food chain gets to make some decisions."

Sally couldn't see the gun from where she was in the front passenger seat, she saw that the two men were arguing but didn't recognise the nearness of violence. "What sort of decisions?" she asked.

Isaac realised that Harris would have a weapon out. He lowered his head to rest on the steering wheel, sleep a distant memory, when had this day started? "He means that someone else will decide our fate," he replied, "Just like this Leonardo character, someone else will be pulling our strings."

"But I don't understand," said Sally, "We told you what happened. What's the problem?"

The two men exchanged a glance, one of fellowship and common understanding. Isaac sighed, "Maybe we lied." He turned to make eye contact with Sally, then smiled a sad, sad smile. "Maybe I lied." Slowly then "Maybe you lied."

"Me!" It made no sense to Sally, "But you were there, Isaac, you know what happened!" She looked at the big man, "Isaac! Tell him! Tell him I didn't do anything!"

Slumped against the driver's side door Isaac rested his head on the cool glass. "I'm a copper, Sally. If I pull back from my personal involvement, I can see how it looks. Harris here knows you were at my house; you left prints all over the place. He knows there was a body there. So, you may be the one who put it there. He found you here again tonight, more bodies. You're a common factor. You could be responsible."

"But you were there, Isaac, you know what happened," she pleaded.

"Yeah," he answered. "And I could be the one who did it all, lured you into it. Or it might be the two of us. Face it, Sally, we're the most logical suspects."

Harris spoke up, "How are we going to play this, man?" His gun twitched, and Isaac's words struck a nervous chord. He could be in a car, all alone, with a pair of mass murderers. He was thinking he wasn't too bright, probably should have had another car follow them.

Isaac raised his head, saw the bead of sweat on the black man's upper lip, and deduced the reason. "Don't worry, Harris. For what it's worth, I didn't do it. Pretty sure Sally's in the clear, too."

"Pretty sure!" she exclaimed.

"Settle down, Sally," said Isaac, "I think you're on the up and up, but there's always a slight chance you're a bad guy."

"Bloody hell, Isaac!" she declared, folding her arms and sitting back in the seat. She glowered at the two detectives.

For some reason, Harris felt embarrassed. He was holding a gun on these two, almost sure both were innocent. But then, being almost sure can get you killed. "Let's go, Isaac," he said.

"Yeah, no worries," said the big man. He engaged the drive and pulled forward, running over the curb and bouncing back onto the road. "City Central, here we come."

They drove for a while, the morning sun deepening the sky away from its gentle blue until it settled down into the pure azure of an Australian summer. The birds fled for shade, people began showing their faces, joggers fleeing down sidewalks, and late nighters looking for a bed. Early risers stepping sprightly, all shiny and clean, fresh and sanctimonious.

On they drove, past the closed shops, avoiding a drunk in the gutter. City Central loomed ahead, Isaac showed his badge to the officer on duty and was allowed into the underground garage. He pulled into an empty space, turned off the engine and looked over at Harris. "Want the keys?" he asked.

"Better have them," came the reply. Isaac handed him the car keys. They exited the vehicle and moved to the elevator. Isaac pushed the button.

"Are we ... am I under arrest?" asked Sally. She still had her bag, it contained the Taser and all her odds and ends.

"Just go with the flow, Sally," said Isaac, "As Harris said, someone else will have to make some decisions about us." The elevator arrived, they entered and rode the few floors upwards in silence. With a gentle ping, it deposited them onto the ground floor. Exiting the small box, they were faced with a large empty room, front doors opening onto the street, a large expanse of shiny floor finally finishing in a tall bench behind which sat a severe looking uniformed officer with sergeant's stripes. He was another large man; big, beefy and bored.

Two small glass cubicles flanked the room, in each of them was a heavily armoured uniformed officer carrying a large and lethal looking weapon. Bad guys might gain access, but they would pay a price. The cubicles would not just be glass, thought Sally, must be some horribly hard but clear stuff able to keep attackers at bay.

The trio approached the desk, Harris in the rear. "Morning, John," said Isaac.

The sergeant towered above them on his raised platform, the height adding to his already imposing presence. His face reflected a life replete with a history of argumentative people, rowdy drunks and aggressive hoodlums. He was the immovable object, the looming presence, the embodiment of rumpled authority.

"What's good about it, Mr. Bloody Detective?" responded the sergeant. "And why are you making my reception area look untidy, Isaac? Who's the bint?"

Harris pushed between Sally and Isaac. Handing the sergeant the big man's pistol. he said "The young lady's name is Sally Grant. She and Detective Isaac Howard are under suspicion of multiple murders and are to be placed in an interview room pending further enquiries." He stepped back leaving the sergeant facing Isaac and Sally.

The height of the bench gave the uniformed sergeant huge stature, he was the personification of unamused police. From his immeasurable peak, he looked down at the two lesser mortals beneath him.

"Bugger me," he muttered.

THERE DIDN'T SEEM TO be any appropriate comment to the sergeant's observation. In truth, Isaac agreed with it. Sally maintained a neutral face, not willing to let her inexperience with police sergeants cause her to make some social slip. She wondered what the correct etiquette was for being placed under arrest. Something must have shown on her face because the sergeant turned his slab-like face towards her, pinning the young woman with a gaze terrifying in its intensity.

"Something on your tiny mind, Miss Grant?" he asked.

He had picked up a pencil and was pointing it at her like a spear. Sally noticed the last two fingers on his hand were fused together, her eyes were dragged by the spectacle.

"Um," she managed before she was able to break her stare and look into the sergeant's eyes. "No," she finished, her voice soft and small.

"Probably noticing your delicate paw, Flannery," said Harris. He pointed at the sergeant's hand, "John's got a few bits and pieces mixed up, haven't you, Flannery?" he asked.

The sergeant grunted. Sally was still mesmerized. "John's on his third life now. Been a bit of a lad, used to be a skydiver until that fateful day. Tell us about it, Flannery," said Harris.

"Bugger off," said the sergeant. Isaac was leaning against the high bench, he looked at Harris and they both grinned.

"Did you ... die?" asked Sally. She had never actually met someone who had used up all of their lives before. "Was it your parachute? Oh, God, it must have been awful, falling and falling."

"Parachute was fine, jump was perfect," said the sergeant. He looked at the two grinning detectives and resigned himself to another retelling of his least favourite story. "I got caught in a crosswind, it blew me away from the drop zone, no big deal. Landed fine."

"Landed in a quiet country road," injected Isaac.

"Yes, I landed on a bloody country road, all bulldust and flies. Just me, standing there pulling in my chute, no problems."

Sally was confused, how did the sergeant's skydiving result in his death?

"And then...," prompted Harris.

Sergeant John Flannery flashed a look of contempt at his two tormenters, "And then some mullet in an old Ford came tearing around the corner and cleaned me up."

Both men exploded in guffaws, "First recorded death of a skydiver in a hit and run with a Ford!" roared Harris.

"Talk about your dangerous sports!" laughed Isaac.

Flannery sighed and gave himself up to the moment, "Bloody detectives," he said, smiling at his friends, "Can't leave a man alone with his dignity."

"That's what mates are for, John," said Isaac.

Sally watched the three men, knowing they shared that peculiar bond of friendship that Australian males seemed to encourage. A reluctance to take the world too seriously. But she was different, she had questions. Into the lapse, as they drew breath she asked, "What about the second death?" She wanted to join the group, be a part of the inner conversation.

Flannery looked at her, this insolent human daring to ask private questions. The other two men had stopped laughing and were in a different mood, Sally knew she had entered uncharted territory, another social faux pas. "Sorry," she said, "None of my business."

The sergeant looked at her a moment longer, shrugged and said, "No big deal. I was in my new body about a week when some bugger shot me." He activated his computer console and began tapping keys, "Better get you two logged in. Want to empty your pockets?" He pushed a tray in front of Isaac and another to Sally. "Everything in," he said.

Isaac had begun placing all his pocket contents into the tray. Sally was caught off-guard by the request. In her mind, she was still discussing the sergeant's deaths. The skydiving story was spelled out in far more detail than the shooting, surely the second death had more behind it. Unthinkingly she put her big shoulder bag into the tray and emptied her few pockets, her eyes filled with moisture. And now I'm going to cry, she chided herself.

Patting his pockets for any missed items Isaac felt a small bulge, instantly his mind recalled the earlier events, finding Sally in his house. And his dead wife's LifeChip. His hand stopped, he stopped, even his breathing stopped.

Sergeant Flannery had been in the game too long to miss the signs. His right hand crept under the counter where it was out of sight. It closed over the grip of the cut-down riot gun he kept there. A quick pull on the fast-release clips and it would drop into his hand, he could have it over the bench top and blasting the detective's face into mash in a heartbeat. His right foot moved over the floor mounted alarm button. The rest of his body caught its breath and waited.

Harris was behind Sally and Isaac, all according to the regulations. He stepped back to give himself room to draw and fire if needed.

Sally continued to dither, not noticing the tense drama unfolding, too enmeshed in her confusion. She kept thinking about how embarrassed her mother was going to be when she found out her daughter had been held by the police for questioning. Her tough as nails, no-nonsense daughter. The one who stood now with quiet tears running down her cheeks.

Isaac was not in the room, he was standing in a church, watching his bride. He was sitting in a movie theatre, holding hands with the woman he loved. He was looking at Mary's face, watching the wind gently tousle her hair.

Some movement brought him back, perhaps he sensed the sergeant's movement, or his subconscious heard Harris' footsteps. He was back in the room, reaching for the LifeChip. "I've got something special here, John." He extracted the object.

Flannery had seen it all, but even so, a LifeChip was a big deal. He sucked in his breath and held out an open palm. Gently Isaac placed the token of his lost wife into the sergeant's meaty hand.

"It's Mary," he said.

Flannery looked at the chip, then raised his eyes to see the broken man before him. He knew the story, all the station did. He knew of the suspicion that had fallen across Isaac in the days following his wife's abduction. But he also knew of the man's reaction when she was found, cut up and mutilated. He had heard the call while in the station, realized that Isaac was calling in his wife's body. He had grabbed the two nearest uniforms and driven a squad car like a madman to the scene. In the wood they had come across the detective, sitting against a tree, gazing at the wreckage that was his wife. She was still dressed in the khaki uniform from her volunteer work at the Sydney Zoo. He must have been there for twenty minutes before Flannery had arrived, looking at his wife's dead eyes, staring at the face of a husband she would never see. Flannery knelt and blocked the body from Isaac's view, he had not moved, had not objected, just sat, looking. Flannery never wanted to see a face the like of which Isaac showed to the world that night. It was a man condemned.

"Bugger me," he whispered.

Gently, the sergeant placed the chip in a secure container and continued to log each person's effects. He entered an itemized list into his computer and printed out a copy. The room had regained its sense of normalcy while he carried out these mundane clerical tasks. Harris made a small joke; Isaac laughed, he seemed to be rejoining the human race. Flannery was grateful for small mercies.

"Sign here," he said. They both did. "Any more weapons? What about you, Isaac, got any funny stuff tucked away?"

"My whole body is a weapon," said Isaac, straight-faced.

"God save me from funny coppers," said Flannery. "What about you, Miss Grant, anything else?"

Feeling very meek and vulnerable, Sally replied "Just my Taser. It's in my bag." Something else seemed required; in this company of aggressive and confident males, she felt the need to make a statement about her capabilities. "It's very powerful," she said, sounding tiny and harmless in her ears.

Flannery picked up the imitation magic wand, examined it a moment before casually tossing it back into the box, "I'm bloody terrified." He pushed a hidden button and a door to their left opened, "Move through that door, first two rooms. Day shift doesn't start until eight, if we're lucky a detective might saunter in around nine after his morning latte."

Harris walked over and held the door while Isaac and Sally moved through. Each of the rooms off the new corridor was labelled with a small sign. The first two said "Interview Room" followed by a small one or two. Isaac entered the first and Sally was guided by Harris into the second.

Inside each room was a small table and three chairs. A small electronic box attached to a wall held recording equipment, in the corner a red light blinked to indicate a live camera.

Isaac crossed and sat in a chair, slouching down. He was alone, as was Sally. He knew he had a few hours of waiting, waiting for the detectives to arrive, waiting while Harris made his report, waiting while the brain's trust in the department worked out what to do with him.

He took off his coat, folded it neatly and put it on the table in front of him. Then he changed his seating position, resting his head on the makeshift pillow. In moments he was asleep.

In the next room, Sally fretted.

Chapter 11

Joshua pushed through the door and entered a dimly lit room, not a bar or tavern, not a dive. At least, not one that fitted the normal understanding of the word. Around the walls of the room were small desks, partitioned from each other by a slim but soundproof divider.

At each desk was a very comfortable chair, many occupied, and it was to one of these chairs that Joshua moved. He put a hand on the shoulder of the man sitting in the chair, the man whose eyes were fixed on the screen before him. Joshua scanned the rest of the room, noting which booths had occupants, aware of the intense scrutiny each person had on their own computer screen. More booths filled the centre of the room, the dim light allowed for the glow of each screen to illuminate the chair's occupant. Although the people were in the room in body, they were really elsewhere.

When the seated man felt the hand on his shoulder he glanced up in irritation, his concentration broken for a moment. When he registered Joshua's identity his gaze changed to acceptance before shifting back to his screen. "What are you playing?" asked Joshua.

"Dota," replied the seated man, "just started a new character. Want to know what I call him? J-Man!" he chuckled, "Got him just for you, my friend."

Joshua watched the man move his character about for a few moments, saw the small avatar running towards a collection of buildings on the screen's horizon. "Can you talk while you do that, Frankie?" he asked.

"No problemo, buddy," said Frankie. He continued to manoeuvre his character but flicked his gaze up to Joshua from time to time, "Grab one of those spare chairs and come down to my level," he said, "That way we can talk and I can still earn a living."

Joshua looked around and saw a stack of spare plastic chairs, he moved across, pulled the top one free from the pile and returned to Frankie's booth where he managed to wedge himself in next to his companion. He watched the other man's screen for a few moments before continuing his conversation, "So that's me, is it?" he indicated the small figure on the screen. Above its head flashed the small label 'J-Man'.

Frankie grinned "You betcha. I made you an Orc warrior, all muscles and teeth. What do you reckon? Any good?" The small figure had reached the town and now moved through streets crowded with other avatars, each bearing a name over its head. Some were generic names – guard, villager – but most glowed with the representation of another human being's imagination, their own choice of name for adventuring.

"I couldn't care less, Frankie. You know this stuff bores me to tears."

"To each his own, my man. Now, what's the news? Is the doc going to go ahead with the deal?"

Frankie felt his shoulder squeezed hard, "Don't call her 'doc', give her the respect of her full title. When you demean her, you demean me." Joshua held the grip for a few more seconds until he saw fear blossom in Frankie's eyes. He liked to see that.

"All right!" gasped Frankie, he kept his eyes fixed on the screen. There he was in control, there he entered any number of combats, none of which hurt him physically – merely a loss of pride. But the man beside him lived in the real world and more than that, he lived in its underbelly. His pain was real and, to Frankie's certain knowledge, that pain was often followed by death. "Let's keep it professional, Joshua. I'm sorry, okay?"

Joshua nodded acceptance of the apology, not caring that the other man was unable to see the gesture, Frankie's avatar was now entering one of the buildings, moving about a large room in what seemed to be a tavern. Other avatars were seated or walking about. "She has agreed to the next stage, I want a face-to-face with Jimmy. I need you to sort out the details, when will you see him next?"

"Right about now," replied Frankie. He pointed at the screen as his "J-Man" figure stopped before one of the other avatars, this one bore the label "Clone1". He opened a small dialogue box and typed in a sentence:

—Clone1, what's the good word?—

"What are you doing?" asked Joshua.

"Having a meeting with my contact" replied Frankie.

"Your contact is in the game?"

"Pretty cool, huh? No chance of being jumped by bad guys or rumbled by the law. I set one of these meetings up each time I have a deal to put together. We share the name of the server and a location and time."

"How do you know it's them?"

"Passwords" replied Frankie, "we use all the spy shit – dead letter drops, secret handshakes, you name it. If it's been in a movie then we copy the routine. So now I'm waiting to see if this dude is my contact."

"What's he have to say?"

"Just wait," said Frankie, "You're gonna love this."

A reply came on the screen:

—I spy with my little eye something beginning with 'C'—

"That's your password?" asked Joshua, "A game of I Spy?"

"Yeah. Who's going to want to play a dopey game like that in Dota? Hang on, he needs my response." He typed in another sentence:

—C, for Copy of a dead man. How about a game of snakes and ladders?—

Joshua watched as the conversation continued, a reply came back after a moment:

—So, what's the deal, man? Is the doctor in?—

Frankie typed:

—All good, usual fee –

From Clone1:

—When do you want to start?—

"What'll I tell him, Joshua?" asked Frankie.

Joshua thought over his response, a few moments passed while Frankie held his fingers over the keyboard, all poised for action. "Tell him..." then a thought struck Joshua, "Do we know if we are talking to a man or a woman?"

"No idea. Is it important?"

A young man two booths away leaned back in his chair and stretched, yawning loudly. Joshua silently watched him and only resumed speaking when the player had again immersed himself in his game. "Not really. I want another meeting meet with Jimmy and have a demonstration of his tech; the doctor has given me two clones."

"Yeah, man. How does she do that?" The moment the question passed his lips Frankie knew he had made a mistake, "No, don't worry, man. I don't want to know."

Joshua leaned in and smiled closely into Frankie's face "I don't mind telling you, pal. Of course, then I'd have to kill you." He stayed there for a few moments while the fear again blossomed in Frankie's eyes. He did like that reaction.

"It's cool, man, you know? Just chill." This was why Frankie liked meetings to be electronic, if things went bad you were a million miles away. Now would be a good time to be a million miles away. Joshua scared Frankie, he had come into the other man's orbit of acquaintances through a girl, a girl who liked to live on the edge. Bloody Evie.

Joshua didn't live on the edge, Frankie decided, he was way over it. Another message appeared on the screen asking for a response about the deal - Frankie opened up the dialog box and soon the time and place of the meeting was agreed. Joshua contributed a few suggestions for his own security but left most of the fine tuning to Frankie.

This took a few minutes, during this time Frankie became lost in the task, the real world around him faded and he lived in the screen. This was why he liked computers and games, he was in control, he could forget the tribulations of his hunger, his aches and pains faded, all the demands of the world went away. They just went away for a little while. As a drug of choice, it had few side effects and no long-lasting detrimental outcomes. All it took from Frankie was his time, his hours, his days, his life.

"You got that little package for me, Frankie?" asked Joshua.

Frankie started, again aware of the presence of Joshua, a looming darkness he could not turn off and from whom he could not walk away. He looked at his strange companion in bewilderment while he replayed the question in his head. Then he remembered, he reached into a jacket pocket and withdrew a memory stick, "Here you go, my man. A few files from my contact at Police Central, as requested; addresses of those women you, er, wanted to know about." He caught himself before his natural curiosity caused him to ask for the link between the women and Joshua. - what was he thinking? he chided himself. "Plus, the code word for tonight's foot patrols."

Joshua accepted the stick and said, "Thank you, Frankie." He placed his palm gently over Frankie's hand as it rested on the mouse, "Now, I want you to remember something for me."

Frankie's mouth dried, he could feel his hand gently trembling under Joshua's palm. There was no pressure, certainly no pain from the gesture. Nonetheless, he trembled, and he knew that Joshua knew he was trembling.

"Sure, man, anything" Frankie's voice had an artificialness to it, wavering on a small falsetto.

"I'm not 'your man.'"

"S-sorry, Joshua."

"And get rid of that stupid character. Do not use any form of my name again in any of your endeavours. Do you understand me?" Joshua's voice was soft and calm, no threat, no menace.

Frankie was terrified, "N-no problem, Joshua. W-won't happen again. Promise."

"Excellent," said Joshua, standing up. His voice brightened, "I like you, Frankie. You're fun to be around, I look forward to our next meeting. Sadly, I must away and check up on the progress some friends of mine are having with a little treasure hunt we're playing. Toodles." He strode off, disappearing out the door of the Internet cafe.

Frankie's chest heaved as he sucked in deep breaths, his body was wrung out with the tension of the meeting, his mind stressed over the desire to fight or flee.

"Next meeting," he murmured, "oh, dear Lord, a next meeting...."

TIME PASSED, ISAAC dozed, Sally continued to fret.

Her room was unremarkable; she looked again at the bare, slightly dirty walls, the single light embedded into the ceiling. From time to time, she stood up, walked to the door and opened it. Outside stood a female uniform who politely asked her to wait inside. It was accompanied by a smile and a steely glare. Sally never knew what might happen if she tried to force herself out of the police station, but she suspected the smiles would stop and the steel would come out. She preferred the velvet glove.

Without her confiscated phone, she had no measure of the passage of time. Sitting in the silent room allowed her time to think over the events since receiving the letter with the job offer. The task of breaking into Isaac's house. The wooden chair slowly assumed a level of comfort she would not have believed, she stretched out her right foot and snaked it around the chair on the opposite side of the table. A few judicious jerks pulled it into just the right position for her to be able to place her outstretched legs up onto its seat. She sank back into the chair and released a deep sigh. Slowly her head dropped onto her chest, and she dozed.

HARRIS AGAIN RECOUNTED the events of the evening to his uniformed superior, Chief Inspector Blackburn. Elizabeth Blackburn.

Elizabeth was a female in an historically male dominated culture. To rise to the rank of Chief Inspector had taken a small amount of luck and a large dose of ability. She was good at being a police officer, ferocious in managing people, intelligent and task oriented. Her dark hair and emotionless stare had stilled the heart of many adversaries, the hair was blacker than nature ever intended, a colour known only to a bottle and a hairdresser. She knew her nickname. Black Betty. She agreed with it.

Harris stumbled over the fourth recount, stopped and looked up at Black Betty, "Give me a break, boss. I haven't missed anything, honest." He stood silently, eyes fixed on the wall over his seated superior's head.

Elizabeth studied the black man, blinked and made a decision. "All right, there is nothing to link Howard to these killings. Except for the fact that the first one was in his house, and he was present when you found the other three. That's hardly a clean bill of health, but there is no other physical evidence." She stood and moved to one corner. Black Betty needed to move while she thought through issues, so she paced. Harris stayed very still, watching a brain work.

"No one's seen them yet?" she asked.

"No," replied Harris, "Isaac would know the drill, but I doubt the girl has enough experience of police procedure to know our little ways." He stopped at a glare from his boss, regretting the flippant reference.

More pacing. "What about this LifeChip? Has it been confirmed it's his wife?" she asked.

"Yes, it's Mary Howard. Forensics have it now. They think it could be viable."

She stopped, "Viable? After two years out of a body. I didn't think that was possible."

He shrugged, "Well, there's viable and there's viable. All the signs are that she could just be uploaded into her clone, after the usual six-month growth period, of course."

"I can sense a 'but' coming on." The Chief Inspector was standing close to Harris, not too close, but close enough for him to want to be elsewhere.

She smiled inwardly as he took a casual step back, retreating before her dominance, yielding her the floor. Another small victory in her continuous struggle to prove herself.

"But," he went on, "there is always an element of risk with a LifeChip which hasn't been removed from a body and placed immediately into one of their specialized storage units. All ambulances and Life Retrieval Teams carry them but I'm pretty sure your garden variety mass murderer doesn't keep one as standard kit."

"So,' she said, "bottom line?"

"Bottom line, if she is uploaded into a clone there's a big chance there'll be a problem. Memory loss, personality disorder, it's the equivalent of our bodies having a stroke. Her brain's been damaged. Maybe."

Harris watched Black Betty pace some more, the room went silent. Back and forth, back and forth, finally she returned to her seat. Interlacing her fingers over a clean desk she looked at Harris, "Get their statements, all the routine stuff and let them go," she decided.

Harris almost asked her if she thought that was wise but caught himself in time. Black Betty had a sharp tongue and one way of hearing it was to randomly suggest she was doing the wrong thing. It was different if you had evidence, then she would listen, would welcome the disagreement. But to ask her to reconsider based on no new information was a good way to be flayed.

"What about his gun?" he asked.

She keyed her computer screen active and began typing, moving on to a new task. She answered him with only part of her concentration; she had finished with this matter and had other work to do.

"He's a copper. Give him what he needs." She stopped typing and looked back at Harris, "Do the interviews. Turn them both loose and hope they find this madman, but be close. This Leonardo character seems to have decided to pick on Howard; use him as bait." Harris was again awed at Black Betty, she was ruthless and implacable.

God preserve me from my boss, he prayed.

Chapter 12

E vie saw Joshua waiting at the curb, he didn't wave at the vehicle or perform any action which may have caused him to be noticed. Arrogant bastard, thought Evie, probably just expects me to see him and pull up.

Which is exactly what I'm going to do, she chuckled to herself – I want to walk very carefully around this one.

Joshua climbed into the front seat of the van and greeted his companion, "Afternoon, Evie. The doctor tells me you're a reliable sort, a girl who can keep her mouth shut. Would this be true?"

Evie looked into the milky eyes and nodded, this wasn't the time for wisecracks.

"Jolly good," he went on. "Off we go, dearie, drive on and I'll direct you as we go." Evie moved the vehicle into traffic, quite happy not to engage in idle conversation but Joshua seemed to want to talk, "Now, have you checked our cargo? All's well, I trust?" he asked.

Evie was confused, "I ... uh ... I haven't looked in the back at all. The doctor told me not to." Was this some sort of test, she wondered?

"Really? How extraordinary." Joshua continued without missing a beat, "Well, I think I can let you in on the little secret; we have two bodies in the back."

The van swerved a little as Evie tugged the wheel in shock, "Bodies! I've been driving two dead bodies all over the city?"

"Scarcely all over the city, dearie, just from the doctor's office to here. Surely that's only a few blocks?"

If he calls me 'dearie' one more time, thought Evie, I will run this tree into a pole, "Why are we driving dead bodies around, Joshua?" she asked.

"Oh, they're not actually dead," replied Joshua, he paused before adding, "dearie." He waited for a reaction but Evie dredged up her last vestiges of self-control, a vaguely remembered skill from her childhood but perhaps one which may save her life in the current conversation.

Joshua was enjoying himself; this young woman was used to men doing her bidding, anything to be rewarded with one of her smiles or perhaps something even more physical. He knew she expected him to fall under her spell and was enjoying pushing her buttons. He doubted whether any other man called her 'dearie' and treated her like a not-too bright child. He could see her clenched hands on the steering wheel and the occasional flare of a nostril. People were such fun to annoy.

"They're clones, Evie. The good doctor is engaged on a little business transaction and we are, as they say in the classics, middlemen." Joshua continued to give directions for their route, directions which Evie could follow easily while carrying out her end of the conversation.

She knew that possessing clones outside of a regeneration facility was highly illegal; she stopped herself before pointing this out to Joshua and risking his bemused retort. Of course, he knew it was illegal! But she wanted to find out more while he was in a chatty mood, information was always a commodity she valued because it could be bartered or sold. A girl's got to make a buck any way she can.

"What's the plan, Joshua? Are we delivering them for organ harvesting?" She tried to sound casual about the deed but she knew she was playing with the big boys now. Organ harvesting was up there with murder, a long way from her usual petty theft and occasional public nuisance behaviour.

"Not quite, my dear," went on Joshua; he was quite willing to discuss the project with his young companion; particularly after the final instructions from the doctor. Poor little tyke wouldn't last the night, he thought, as he looked at her and catalogued the options available for her demise.

"We're taking them to the other interested party in the deal, a young computer whizz-kid who claims he can take data from a LifeChip while it is still in the original host and put it into another clone."

Evie's eyes opened a little larger, "What? What's the point? Why would anyone want to? And if it works - what do you get? Yuk, do you end up with two of you?" It sounded like pointless science; she could not see any benefit from the process except mental instability.

Joshua issued more directions before continuing, "Not your concern, Evie."

But Evie couldn't leave it alone, "But why not just use the original LifeChip? Why bother making a copy – just take the chip out of the original body?"

"Imagine you have a jaded personality and wish to try something a bit different," replied Joshua. "Perhaps something a trifle illegal and dangerous where the loss of the LifeChip was highly possible. I have no interest in such frivolous pastimes. My recreation is solving problems and puzzles - so mind your manners. As regards using the original LifeChip, it's a good idea except the little beggar is firmly embedded in the host's body. Extracting such a piece of technology is possible but tends to make a mess of the body; the big hole in the chest is hard to hide and upsets the host rather terminally. And that is what Jimmy has now devised – a piece of tech which allows us to take the personality from the LifeChip without disturbing it, now shut up, we're here – pull into that garage."

Evie did as she was instructed, the roller door slid shut behind the van, cutting them off from the outside world. She helped Joshua unload the two clones and managed to hide the creeping heebie-jeebies when she saw the forms laid out - even though they were concealed by a merciful white sheet she knew she was very close to strange things; clones without a personality. Zombie movies had taken a whole new twist with the arrival of clone technology.

When the two trolleys were positioned outside another set of doors, she stood wondering what to do next. Joshua spoke into a small grill and a buzzer sounded to unlock the inner doors.

Joshua pushed one of the trolleys through and then turned to Evie, "Come along, dearie, walk with me a while. And bring our friend."

Evie started to push her trolley after him and wondered how she was going to get out of this mess. Down the hall she went, following the back of her strange companion, he was taking her to strange and dangerous places. She shivered.

Up ahead Joshua chuckled.

SALLY HAD SAT FOR SEVERAL hours, dozing on and off. Finally, the door opened and a uniform came in with another detective, one she had not seen before. He sat and asked for her story. Bit by bit she revisited the events of the previous twenty-four hours, taking her back to another life, or so it seemed.

Sally had sat for several hours, dozing on and off. Finally, the door opened and a uniform came in with another detective, one she had not seen before. He sat and asked for her story. Bit by bit she revisited the events of the previous twenty-four hours, taking her back to another life, or so it seemed.

The detective asked for some points to be expanded, why she took the job, how did she know how to break into houses? Grudgingly she gave up bits of herself, explained about her failed relationship, told of how she had sometimes had to break into their own house after her partner had locked her out. She felt again the shame and guilt which she thought she had expelled, she found herself justifying her actions to the detective. Over twisting fingers, she looked up and saw his blank, impassive face and stopped talking, dragging herself back to the events of the night. Her life was hers and hers alone, not for the empty ears of a bureaucrat.

She wondered how she ended up in a police station at night. Because I wanted to change my life, she realised, I wanted it to mean something. I wanted to make someone else's life better, and not just by smiling at a customer. Well, girl, you got your wish, now suck it up.

After teasing out bits of her story he left the room, returning moments later with a printout of her words. She was impressed with the technology, good voice recognition software was expensive. Then again, she thought, an accurate rendition of a criminal's confession probably ranked with the high priorities. Certainly more than dictating a shopping list.

He thanked her and left her alone again. No explanation, she was just alone again, in her own room, one she knew well by now. At the point she had decided to leave, the door opened and Detective Harris beckoned her out.

"Sorry about all that, had to wait for the shift change. We've got your statement and you are free to go. Follow me down to the foyer and we'll get your stuff."

He turned and walked away, Sally jumped a little in surprise, then moved quickly after him. These corridors were familiar territory to him but a strange land to her, she did not want to be left lost and alone in the jungle. With an effort, she restrained herself from reaching out and holding the back of his coat for security.

Harris came to a heavy door with a keypad entry, he tapped a few keys and pushed when he heard a click. He and Sally walked through, she felt a discernible change in the atmosphere as she left the corridors and re-entered the light of the foyer.

Standing at the Sergeant's counter was Isaac, picking up his possessions from a tray and placing them in various pockets. As she walked up, he retrieved his huge pistol and slid it into his shoulder holster. If it wasn't for the gun, she might have hugged Isaac, he was like an old friend.

"All good?" he asked.

She gave him a smile and looked up at the desk sergeant. It wasn't Flannery, this man was smaller, somehow neater. His uniform fitted correctly, he was less rumpled, more concisely efficient as opposed to Flannery's badly dressed rawness. She decided she preferred Flannery to this interloper from the day shift.

The neat sergeant held out a form listing all her possessions and insisted she go through each one. When she picked up the Taser she flicked a glance at him, looking for a reaction.

"Be careful with that, Miss," he said, "It's a dangerous weapon."

She definitely preferred Flannery.

Harris was waiting in the centre of the foyer, Isaac and Sally joined him after signing several forms. "Set to go?" asked Harris.

The three stood together, other uniforms and plain clothes traffic moving past on various errands. Sally felt the strangeness of the situation, around her people were treating this day like any other. But now she knew, now she knew the world outside was different, she knew it held dark things at night, things to come and creep into your nightmares. But the people who jostled her shoulder had no idea, the ones entering looking all young and fresh, they could not possibly comprehend the world she had seen last night.

Then she looked into the eyes of the two men with her, really looked. She saw a vast history of horrors, of night interviews with grieving parents, of blood and fear, of chasing vile things into dark places. A shudder rippled through her small body.

Isaac saw the change in Sally's eyes, saw her gaining the secret knowledge. He smiled at her and nodded.

She moved her shoulder bag into a more comfortable position, looked out through the large front glass doors and tried to work out her next step. A bus home, shower, and sleep seemed to be the best course of action. But she was reluctant to step away and break her links with this strange series of events. She also felt she had unfinished business with Isaac, they had a common antagonist.

Isaac saw her standing, sensed her thoughts. He had appreciated her bravery in the previous night, she was willing to go into dark places, that seemed to deserve something. "Want a ride home?" he asked.

"Thanks, I could do with one."

Harris led the way to the elevators, punched in the key code to unlock the doors and stepped aside for Sally to enter first. As they rode down to the garage, he asked, "Can you give me a ride to Albert? Got to meet my partner."

"Sure," grunted Isaac, his eyes fixed on the glowing numerals above the lift door. His brain had taken the easy option, looking at familiar things, idling in neutral. His gaze wandered around the front of the elevator, falling on the back of the black detective's neck. "Say, Harris," he began, "I've been in Central for a while now, haven't talked to you much at all. What's your story?"

The black man spoke over his shoulder, "Been here about three months, came down from Newcastle. Used to work with Black Betty when she ran the department up there, saw the vacancy in the city and thought I'd see the big smoke." He turned back to the front of the elevator before continuing, "Got a wife and two kids, a mortgage. I'm a Gemini and I enjoy recreational fishing. You might not have noticed, but I also claim Aborigine status."

Harris possessed a skin colouring akin to the depths of night, a dark, gun-metal black. His nose was wide and splayed, the mouth twisted upward in a slightly mocking smile, ready to deal with life's knocks on his terms. His eyes shone with intelligence and life, he was a man of value in the world.

Isaac blinked before replying, straight-faced, "Is that right? Hard to spot really."

"It's subtle," replied Harris, "but the signs are there." A pause, "Anything else you want to know?"

"No, I'm good," said Isaac, "What about you, Sally, got any questions for the detective?"

Sally had only been half listening to the conversation, she recognised the wry humour when Harris replied but was not prepared to be a part of the talk. She stuttered, "Uh, no." She again felt like a schoolgirl, what was it about these secret men's conversations? Feeling the need to make a mark she asked, "Your partner is this guy, Albert?"

A brief chuckle told her she had mistakenly read the signs again. "No," said Harris. "The morgue's in Albert Street, my partner's Patricia Lee."

"Patricia Lee!" exclaimed Isaac, "Get away, you got teamed up with Short and Twisted?" The elevator pinged, doors opened and they walked to Isaac's car. Opening the doors, they climbed in, Sally taking up a position in the rear seat.

As the car moved off, the two men continued their talk, "Yeah," said Harris. "Me and Patricia, cultural stereotypes gone mad. Who says Black Betty doesn't have a sense of humour."

"Patricia's all right," said Isaac, "Good to have around when you're down in Chinatown, blends right in."

"No, she's good. I'm getting to know my way around a Chinese menu pretty well by now. God, that girl can eat. Met her family once, she's got more relatives than me and I know most of the Northern Territory."

Sally leaned forward, "Why is she called Short and Twisted? Is she little or something?"

Isacc gave a small snort, "Short! She's six foot three, thin as a rake and has several black belts in a variety of martial arts."

"Yep," continued Harris "Short and Twisted can spin kick a spring roll out of your mouth at twenty paces." He looked across at Isaac, "Did it last week again with Flannery, he reckoned she was getting too old and withered. Lost fifty bucks."

"Dill," said Isaac.

Sally thought about the mental picture of a tall, lissom woman flying through the air. "She's not short?" she asked, the implication for Patricia's nickname hanging in the air. "And she's not twisted?"

She could feel the silence grind into the front seat. Neither man looked at each other, they had not communicated in any way, yet she knew they were both thinking the same thing. She had asked a girl a question about men's brains. When would she learn?

Finally, Isaac spoke, "Yeah, you're right, Sally, bloody stupid name."

They travelled on in silence.

Chapter 13

After a twenty-minute drive, the car pulled over to the curb. Across the short stretch of footpath was a large, old structure. Not the modern glass and steel of the new structures on either side but the dilapidated architecture of another time. A large sign announced it as a municipal building, a wide entry driveway allowed ambulances and large vehicles to enter the nether regions of the city morgue.

Harris unbuckled his seat belt and turned to Isaac, "You know what Black Betty wants?" he asked.

Isaac sighed, "Yeah, I guess."

The black man extended a hand, "Take care, man."

They shook, eyes meeting in a greater communication, "No worries," said Isaac. "Say hello to Patricia for me."

The car rocked slightly as Harris exited, Sally watched him enter the dark building. When she turned her eyes back to Isaac, she saw he was looking at her, "Want to jump up here in front?' he asked. "Don't enjoy feeling like a chauffeur." Sally moved into the now vacant front seat and buckled up as Isaac pulled into traffic.

"Where to?" he asked.

"I'm in Liverpool, 'Sunrise Apartments'. Know them?"

"The Great Wall, eh?" he chuckled, "You really must be broke, I thought only the truly desperate lived there," said Isaac.

Sally felt offended but knew the truth of the remark. Her apartment was one of many in a long grey building, never rising more than eight floors. It snaked around in a giant horseshoe embracing a flat concrete common. The passing years had streaked the building with dirt and grime, the common was discoloured with a variety of fungi and the tenants moved with quiet resignation. But the rent was cheap and there was always a vacancy. She lived in a small, one bedroom apartment, bed in one room, everything else in another. It wasn't a home, it was a den, a lair, a cave. The doors stuck, the sun beat in through unprotected windows and no one was comfortable.

But it was a place to rest.

"I am desperate," she said, turning to look out the window, cutting off any more conversation.

Isaac drove.

The mechanical actions of guiding the vehicle through familiar streets allowed his mind to wander. He reflected on the conversations with Leonardo, the references to clues. One was his name, 'Leonardo'. The only Leonardo that came to mind was Da Vinci. Isaac recalled he was a great mind, an artist and an engineer. Because Isaac liked to read, he had come across the name in reference to secret societies, the Sistine Chapel, and several novels used his work as a basis for conspiracy plots.

But nothing came to mind that had significance to multiple murders. Isaac was sure he would have come across some reference to a charge of murder against Da Vinci in all of his readings. Was there another Leonardo? Leonardo the Lion, perhaps? Was the killer saying he was a king?

Isaac's mind ground to a halt. The killer said his name was not Leonardo; just that he could be called that. What did it mean? He gave up and shelved the word.

Cresting a hill, he caught sight of the Great Wall, ugly as ever. There was little traffic in front of the concrete common, a few people loitered on the scattered benches under dying trees and broken lamp posts. He stopped and turned to his passenger.

"Here's my number, Sally, call me anytime. I'll come."

She looked at this crumpled detective holding out a business card. Having gone through what felt like an entire lifetime with him she knew he meant his words. He would come if she called, he would be a rock for her. She appreciated his trust, smiled at the big man and took the card. "I can take care of myself, copper," she said, and punched him lightly on the shoulder before exiting the car.

Isaac watched her hunch her shoulders and walk towards the main entrance, she was indistinguishable from the many other dwellers in this lost city of despair, yet Isaac knew she was special. She had courage. She didn't give up easily. He decided he liked her, wished her well.

Pulling back onto the road he let his mind wander again, driving aimlessly as his subconscious tried to make sense of recent events.

What was the next clue? 'School days are the best days of our lives – discuss'. What was that all about? Sounded like a question in a test, one of those awful ones which had so tormented the detective at school. How could you discuss such a statement, and why wasn't any answer correct? After all, a discussion was just the exchange of ideas, you can't grade a discussion! It wasn't until he was at university that a kindly tutor showed him the hidden meaning behind the question. He discovered other words like it: compare and contrast, justify, and debate. Isaac's mind rebelled against the discipline needed but he struggled with his temper until he finally achieved success and a bachelor's degree.

What was he supposed to do here? 'School days are the best days of our lives", what did that mean in relation to these crimes?

His phone rang as he waited for a set of lights to change. Watching the red glow, he flicked open his case, "Howard," he said into the handset.

A whispery voice, "Isaac? Is that you?"

"This is Isaac. Who's that?"

"It's me, Sally. I'm outside my door. I think there's someone in my apartment."

EVIE WATCHED JOSHUA greet another man, they treated each other warily; she was impressed to see Joshua treat another human being with any sort of deference. Still and mouse-like behaviour seemed to be called for around these two men.

"I've got this spare LifeChip for the trial, Jimmy," said Joshua to the other man, "complete with a viable personality - one from my earlier collection. Not a terribly valuable acquisition, one I had gained before applying my current selection parameters."

"You are one messed up dude, Joshua," said Jimmy, "you're always coming up with such interesting glimpses into your private life. Are you saying you have a collection of viable LifeChips? Ones with a complete personality stored away?"

Joshua stared deadpan at Jimmy, "I do." The silence hung for a few moments before he asked, "Do you have a problem with my collection?"

Evie managed to insert herself closer to the wall and found a small shadow, the negotiations were not going well, she thought.

Jimmy stared at Joshua, the stillness grew, tension climbed. Neither man moved.

Then Jimmy guffawed and pointed a finger at Joshua, he mimed pulling a trigger, "You mad bastard! What a hoot!"

Joshua had also relaxed and play punched Jimmy's shoulder, "Sick turd! I thought I had you going there."

Both men relaxed, Evie stayed where she was, more comfortable in the darkness away from these two dangerous men.

"Righto," said Jimmy, now all business, rubbing his hands as he outlined the procedures. "This is what we do. I take our contestant's LifeChip from you and upload it into my system – that gives us an electronic copy of ... who is it anyway? Might have been a friend of mine?"

"No-one important, an annoying little man who ran a numbers game some years ago. Little weasel called Charlie Knox, he upset me by winning my money."

Evie saw Joshua give a LifeChip to Jimmy. The technician then moved to a desk laden with several racks, each holding something electronic and complex. Jimmy inserted the chip into a slot, did things to a keyboard and looked at the screen. He announced, "Chip's viable, got all his data stored now, just in case we have to make a few more copies of the poor bastard."

Jimmy then took the LifeChip and placed it into another container, this one was attached to some well made machinery emblazoned with the logo of LifeCorp. Evie would normally have been interrupting two ordinary men to ask what was happening, but not this time. Now was the time for restraint in the cause of self-preservation.

"Bring one of the clones over here," Jimmy instructed.

Joshua wheeled his trolley over to the LifeCorp apparatus and helped Jimmy position various attachments to the body. "Pretend this LifeChip of yours has been extracted from the original host after some accident or whatever. Notice these two thin wires I'm attaching to it?" Joshua nodded agreement. "Good," went on Jimmy. "They take the data and run it through my newly stolen LifeCorp regeneration machine."

"How long will the clone live once we kick it into gear and get it off the slab?" asked Joshua.

"If we took our time and did it right, he could go on for weeks. The upload will eventually reject the body and he would have a helluva heart attack as the brain realises it's in the wrong body. Could be very entertaining, I reckon we could sell tickets – imagine the looks that go across the poor bastard's face as his brain tries to work out why the bits don't fit."

Jimmy paused and wiped an eye, "I love a good laugh, I really do."

"Of course," he went on, "I'm not going to do it right, I couldn't care less about his longevity or comfort. We just want it to survive long enough to get some new memories implanted on the LifeChip. Then when I extract it, I can demonstrate my brilliance by combining the two sets of memories, the original LifeChip and the stuff we take from this clone."

Jimmy moved to a control panel and looked over his preparations; he caught sight of Evie "Hello, darlin'. Want to come over here and watch Uncle Jimmy be clever?" Evie froze, both men were now looking at her, she felt like a deer moments before a car made roadkill.

She sauntered over as casually as she could. Casting a glance at the clone on the trolley, she noted the thick, red cable from the LifeCorp machine snaking into a small hole in the clone's chest.

"What's the red cable for?" she asked. The macabre nature of the scene and its participants had to be combated somehow, she realised, so she decided to focus on the details of the procedure. If she stayed just as an observer, she believed she would be picked off by Jimmy as a plaything. Or discarded by Joshua as baggage. She could not afford to be either simple observer or unnecessary baggage, she had to get into the game.

She walked a fine line between self-preservation and staying a halfway decent person.

Jimmy smiled, "Not just a bimbo, then, eh, Joshua?" the milky eyed man remained silent and passive, gaze still following Evie.

"The doctor has already inserted blank LifeChips into these clones; very forward thinking of her. All I have to do is transmit the personality data from the original LifeChip down the red wire into the clone."

"Can we get on," said Joshua, "I'm easily bored."

Jimmy winked at the other man and manipulated various controls on the main machine, after a few seconds five small beeps sounded.

"Data uploaded. Now it does a system check," said Jimmy. The trio watched the clone for a few moments before another five beeps sounded followed by one long, three second beep. "All done, baby's ready to come out of the oven. Shall we wake the poor little tyke?" asked Jimmy.

"Wait a minute," said Evie. She shrank a little as both men looked at her; Joshua's gaze caused her mouth to dry up and her brain stuttered.

"Tread carefully, dearie," he said. "You do not give orders here." He did not move but transmitted violence with a look.

Evie quailed but she had decided on her course of action, she had to be a participant in this event, not an observer. "What about his new memories, the ones we want to try and combine with the original personality? Have you thought what it should be or how it happens? Does it need to be something significant, after all we don't store every little memory on those LifeChips." She swallowed and went on, "What's the plan?"

"Hoo, boy," said Jimmy, "she's good, Joshua."

Evie watched Joshua, he was the key to her security, her chance of surviving this episode rested with him. She realised that he had told her many secrets, and by allowing her in to witness this procedure he had given her more information than was safe. As she watched him her mind came to the inevitable conclusion – she wasn't critical to the success of the doctor, she was not a key player. If Joshua was showing her all this stuff it must mean she would not be around long enough to be a future threat.

She was bargaining for her life, she realised. She had to make herself useful to Joshua. She couldn't use sex, her usual weaponry didn't work on him, all she had left were her brains. And a desperate desire to survive.

"Give the clone a significant memory," she said, her brain making it up as she went along. The next words came out of her mouth without conscious thought. "Joshua, when he wakes up – kill him again."

She was stunned by her words. How could she do that? How could she so casually instruct this demented man to take another's life?

Jimmy whistled, "Damn! That'd do it, Joshua. I'll bring him around and you do him again, but different to the first time. Give him another set of death memories."

Evie and Jimmy both looked at Joshua. Evie waiting for him to make the decision about her usefulness. If he accepted her suggestion, she might make it out of this room alive.

Joshua moved to stand in front of the trolley, "Last time I killed him I used a gun, blew his brains out." He extracted a clasp knife and extended the blade, "Let's introduce a bit of variety."

Evie stood still and watched the scene unfold, her brain kept yelling, "My God! My God!" over and over in the stillness of her mind but her body remained rigid. She didn't even blink as the clone's eyes opened and consciousness came over the face.

The Knox/Clone saw Joshua standing before him, fear blossomed over his face, "Joshua! What happened?" Silence hung for a few moments, Evie could almost see the memories being inserted.

"You shot me!" said Knox, raising a hand to his head. A surprised look came over his face as he realised he was sitting in a new body, his hands moved over his face and chest, his mind exploring its new home. "I've been regenerated? How? Something's not right." He stopped and Evie saw confusion and fear move across the face.

"Joshua," he said, "help me."

"No problems, Knox, you little weasel." Joshua brought his hand up and showed the seated man the knife; he held it still before Knox's eyes, waiting for the sight to register in the clone's eyes. As Knox opened his mouth to speak Joshua slashed the thick knife across his throat and stepped back.

The blow was deep and powerful, Knox died within seconds, the body falling back onto the trolley. Blood fountained for a few moments covering the corpse and floor with the thick, red liquid.

"Damn," whispered Jimmy.

Evie agreed.

Chapter 14

Jimmy burst out laughing, "Did you see his face? Talk about surprise!" he moved forward to the corpse, in his hand was a small circular device. "Now to get that new LifeChip out." He positioned the device over Knox's chest and depressed a button. A small click sounded followed by a wet, punching sound. "Don't you just love these? Got one for just such an occasion."

"What is it?" asked Joshua as he cleaned his knife on the dead man's coverings.

"It's a LifeChip Extractor. Bit new, it allows the Rescue people to easily extract a LifeChip – neater than your knife and it does have a wonderful sound to it. Did you hear that slurp?"

Both men seemed oblivious to the carnage over which they stood, Evie had degenerated into her own world of horror. She had done this, she had initiated what lay before her. What sort of person was she?

She watched as Jimmy cleaned the newly extracted LifeChip and placed it in his first machine. As her mind tried to deal with the shock of such eloquent violence, she temporarily lost track of events. She was brought back to the moment by Jimmy saying her name.

"Evie, how do you want to do this next bit?"

She focussed on the scene before her, the last clone was now hooked up to the regeneration machine; both men were looking at her, expecting an answer. Jimmy seemed to accept her role but she sensed Joshua was still assessing her status. She needed to keep her course, to retain the initiative.

"You can't revive him in the same position," she said, "spin the trolley around so that he'll wake up facing a new wall. And move it out of that blood pool." Jimmy followed her instructions, Joshua stood and watched her.

Evie decided to risk it all, "Joshua, you need to keep out of sight. Stand behind Knox when he revives. I'll question him about his memories, see if his recent death has been integrated with his original chip." A thought struck her, "Jimmy, how do we know that you've integrated the two sets of memories, you could try to fool us by uploading just the last chip again."

Joshua's gaze finally left Evie, she breathed a mental sigh.

"Good question, Jimmy," he said. "Got an answer?"

Jimmy held up a blood smeared LifeChip, "this is the one from the dead clone," he stated. "And Joshua, I know better than to dick around with you and the doctor." He looked from Joshua to Evie, "Now, are we going to do this?"

Evie nodded and stood before the trolley. As before, the clone revived and tried to focus, fleeting spasms of panic jolted across his features before he finally focussed on Evie standing before him.

"Oh, thank God," Knox groaned.

"Mr. Knox? Mr. Knox?" asked Evie, using her best matter-of-fact voice.

"Who ... who are you?" asked Knox. "Where am I?"

"You're in a Police Revival Unit," said Evie. "I'm Detective Amy Johnson, I need to ask you some questions about your death. Are you up to talking to me?"

Knox let his head fall back onto the pillows, he rubbed his face with a strange hand before staring at his unblemished skin in wonder. "I'm dead, I was dead. Again."

He sat up sharply "Oh, Christ! Joshua! Where's Joshua?"

The man was terrified, Evie deduced. "Calm down, Mr. Knox, you're quite safe, we have Joshua in custody. Now I need to ask you about the circumstances of your death. Can you tell us anything about it?"

Knox seemed to settle a bit, "He shot me. Bastard shot me in the face." Again the man fell back to the pillows, eyes closed. Evie looked over his head at Jimmy and raised her eyebrows in a question, the newer memory didn't seem to be present. Jimmy mouthed, "wait."

Knox opened his eyes slowly, "Shit! He did it to me again."

Evie leaned forward, "What did he do to you again?"

"Killed me," Knox groaned. "I remember being regenerated and seeing him standing in front of me." He ran a hand over his throat, "I think ... I think he cut my throat." Confusion seeped over his face. "What the hell is happening to me, detective?"

Evie signalled to Joshua before patting Knox's shoulder, "I'm afraid we've been a bit cruel to you, Mr. Knox."

Before the clone could speak Joshua stepped forward and looped a wire over Knox's head. He pulled the garrotte snug and leaned back until the struggling stopped. Evie watched the murderous act, a gentle sadness seeping over her as she farewelled her last vestiges of innocence.

"I like a bit of variety," said Joshua. "Some people, eh?" he indicated the dying man, "No luck at all."

Quiet descended into the room, its three living occupants facing the remains of Charlie Knox, dead three times over.

"Who's for a coffee?" asked Joshua.

SALLY CLICKED THE PHONE shut and stepped backwards towards the stairs, her front door was unlatched and slightly ajar. She never left her door unlocked. With eyes fixed on the small vertical slit between door and wall, she placed her right hand against the wall and took another backward step. Her left foot felt space, the top of the staircase.

She was unwilling to take her eyes off the doorway, afraid of what might come out. Stepping down two steps she waited, leaning against the wall, one foot on the step above.

"You all right, lady?"

The voice was deep, a profound bass. Sally started, jumping back into the wall as she tried to find her new terror. Below her, on the small landing as the steps doubled back on themselves, stood a tall, dishevelled, swarthy man. A newspaper would have referred to him as a person 'of Middle Eastern appearance'. He was dressed in old and stained jeans and a sleeveless football jersey, his torn and dirty sandals failed to protect his large feet. The man carried a small shopping bag, the clink of glass coming from within as he set it down on the floor.

"You look a bit worried there. Everythin' all right?" he asked again. From within a pocket, he extracted a small bottle, unscrewed the top and dropped a tablet in his hand. He reached into the bag pulled out a soft drink container, opened it and drank a measure of the fizzy liquid with the tablet.

Sally's heart climbed back down from her mouth, she leaned against the wall, shoulder bag dropped at her feet. "I'm... uh...," she waved her hand vaguely in the direction of her apartment. "There's someone in ...."

The man had a small coughing fit, doubled over as the spasms swept his body. He straightened up, wiped his mouth and said "Sorry, got a bit of a cold. Be right once that tablet kicks in." Straightening up he continued, "You were sayin'? There's someone in, what..."

She sat on the top step, back against the wall. Opening her bag, she searched for and found the Taser. "I think there's someone in my apartment. I've called the police and they're on their way. Everything's fine. No need to trouble you." Please go past, she thought, please don't stay and talk to me. Sally's upbringing had left her with all the prejudices, things she would never admit, feelings she rejected over a glass of wine or a lively dinner party. But on a run-down staircase, talking to an unkempt Muslim brought her unconscious feelings to the surface. She was ashamed of herself.

"Bloody cops are no good, they'll never come here for that. Come on, lady, let's sort that bugger out." He stepped quickly up past Sally, she had a clear view of one large foot as it was placed on the step next to her hand and then the man was at her doorway.

She jumped to her feet, this was going too fast. "No, wait..."

But the man had already pushed his way into the apartment, the door swinging back with a loud crash followed by a bellow. "Who the hell are you? Get out of this lady's place, quick smart! Bloody squatters!"

Sally reached her door in time to hear the sound of breaking glass, another voice raised in protest "Hey, mate, settle down...." She entered the main room, the front door opening directly into the living room/kitchen. Another man was sitting on the floor, he had fallen from a chair which was now overturned behind him. On the low coffee table was a can of beer, a saucer holding several cigarette butts and some snack food wrappers. Her champion was standing over the fallen man, one fist clenched, veins on his neck very evident and a look of fire in the deep-set eyes.

Sally groaned, the man on the floor took his eyes off his tormenter and switched to the young woman. A look of relief spread over his features, a smile giving his face a jauntier expression. "Sal! How are you?" he said.

The Middle Eastern man never changed his stance, remained a tower of rage, a frozen threat. Suddenly he relaxed and slumped on the couch with a guffaw, "Got you a beauty, didn't I, Al? Jeez, mate, you shoulda seen your face."

Standing in the small entrance way, Sally looked at the two laughing men, around them was the strewn debris of empty beer cans, juice bottles, chip packets and cigarette butts. All accompanied by the stale smells of tobacco and sweat.

"Mokti," said the man on the floor as he climbed to his feet, "this is my wife, Sally. Sally, this is Mokti. He's a mate of mine." Alan sat on the couch next to his friend, reached for the beer and leaned back, sipping the can.

Both men turned smiling, expectant faces to Sally. No guile, just two little boys saying hello to Mum.

Sally exploded, "I am not your wife, Alan! We finished two years ago. We are divorced. Look at this place! A pigsty! Clean it up and get out. And take your drunken mate with you!"

"Steady on, Sal...," began Alan.

"I will not! You keep doing this to me. You keep coming back! Please leave me alone, I have my own life and I want you out of it!" Both men sat frozen, Mokti with mouth agape, Alan holding a slowly burning cigarette. "And put that bloody thing out! I've told you and told you. THEY KILL PEOPLE! God, you are such a dinosaur." Sally ground to a halt, her eyes had found a few more tears and squeezed them out.

Mokti stood up, embarrassed and ashamed. "Come on, Al, you never told me you were divorced. You said she knew we were coming." He started cleaning up the mess, moving around the table, picking up the saucer full of cigarette butts. "I'm sorry, lady, we'll get out of your hair."

Alan leaned back and placed one possessive arm across the top of the couch, the extended hand holding a cigarette. He took another sip from his can and shuffled into a more comfortable position, "Are you happy now, Sal? Look what you've done. You embarrass me in front of my friends, I come by to say hello and you just humiliate me, just like you always did." His voice was calm and conversational. Almost unconsciously he flicked his hand and ash tumbled onto the floor behind the couch. "This is Mokti Setiawan, I met him on the bus from Perth and thought I could show him some of the town. You've done a good job of that, haven't you? Extended the hand of friendship. God, you're amazing."

Another sip of beer, Mokti was rinsing things in the sink, pushing rubbish into the bin. Alan continued to sit comfortably, holding his little court, "And look at the state of you, is this how you live now? Staying out all night, tomcatting around the town? You look like you haven't been to bed. Or worse." Sally could feel her face burning, sensed Mokti's gaze on her dirty clothes, she pulled a wisp of hair into place, hating herself for the gesture.

"You call me names," went on Alan, "but you spend all night on the town and stagger back to bed to sleep it off. Did you pick up some stranger? Who'd you spend the night with, Miss High and Mighty?"

A voice from the doorway said, "That'd be me."

Chapter 15

Isaac stood in the doorway, weapon pointed past Sally, aiming at the seated man. The big detective moved in and held a hand up towards Mokti, "Stand very still, sport. Do not move, do not budge an inch." His eyes had not left Alan, maintaining the link with the seated man he stepped beside the woman and asked, "You all right, Sally?"

Alan was terrified into immobility. The pistol aimed at his head sucked out his will, his mouth dribbled. Mokti stood motionless, unsure what to do. He was at one end of the small kitchen area, bench down one side, cooktop on the other; behind him was the refrigerator. He could see a set of drawers under the bench top to his right and thought there might be a knife in one of them. The big man with the gun looked like he had done this before, Mokti decided to stand still and hope for the best. So far, his trip to Sydney had been full of surprises, Perth was definitely quieter.

His father had warned him, told him to stay in the west. Now he wished he was still there.

Sally calmed down as soon as she heard the detective's voice, "I'm fine, thank you, Isaac; you don't need the gun. This is my ex-husband, Alan Lassiter. My very ex-husband. He likes to drop around unexpectedly sometimes. Alan, this is my friend, Detective Isaac Howard, we're working together."

Isaac holstered his weapon, turned to look at Mokti. "And you are?" he asked.

"I'm Mokti, Mokti Setiawan. My friends call me Mok." He stepped forward, palms up, trying to be as non-threatening as possible. "I didn't know this visit was going to be an issue. Al didn't give me the full story." He looked at Sally, "Look, I'm sorry, lady, I just met him on the bus, didn't know anyone over here, thought it was a good opportunity to make a few friends." He turned to the still seated Lassiter, "You're a dropkick, sport" he judged. "You can't treat your friends this way, especially women."

The three of them stood together, all looking down at the seated man. "Hey, when did I get to be the bad guy?" exclaimed Alan. "Bloody hell, Sal, you're doing it to me again, you always wreck everything!" He got to his feet, took a last pull on the cigarette before standing tall and erect, "It's not fair," he said, pushing through them to the open doorway where he stopped.

He turned side on and pouted, "After all I've done for you..." Then he left.

There was a moment of pause, of utter stillness as the three stood looking at the now empty doorway.

"That was Alan Lassiter," said Sally "I used to love him, but the drink and mood swings killed it. He should be on medication, definitely no alcohol. But he never sticks out a program, never finishes." She sagged a little, "He still haunts me, shows up every few months. Just assumes we can continue our conversation where we left off like nothing ever happened." She placed a hand on Isaacs's shoulder, "Thanks for coming, when I saw the door open, I thought the worst, thought it might be Leonardo." She moved into the room, continuing to tidy and wash, her body on automatic.

"Who's Leonardo?" asked Mokti, an innocent to the big city. Sally stopped wiping the bench, looked up at the dark man in surprise. "Sorry," he said, "none of my business."

Isaac took in the room; saw the smallness of a human life. He had almost taken an apartment after Mary's death, almost sold the house. He thought he needed to move away, get on with his life and not be held down by the anchor of daily reminders of lost happiness. But this room, this apartment of Sally's was far worse than memories. This place stared you in the face each day with an empty message. On the end of the bench was a pile of Sally's business cards, her smiling face shining up, all full of hope. This place wasn't a home, never was. The walls contained too many past memories from too many different people, other tenants lost and hidden. Broken marriages, tired people, mournful lives. He could have ended up here so easily.

Mokti had moved to the doorway where he picked up an old duffel bag, slinging it over one shoulder he knocked on a framed photograph on the wall near the door. Straightening the picture, he said "Look, I'll shoot through. Sorry about this, lady, your ex has a good way with words." He stopped, had a good look at the photo, "This you, is it? You in the army or something?" The silence that returned his question was deafening, he searched for something else to say, some piece of verbal magic. "Anyway.... sorry...." A lame finish, he thought as he turned and stepped outside.

"You right, Sally?" asked Isaac. She had stopped cleaning and now stood, slumped and worn against the bench. "Better get some sleep, I'm going to ask a few more questions, try to find out about this Leonardo." He stretched his neck and rolled his shoulders, trying to ease the stiffness and fatigue. As he moved to the doorway it was again filled by Mokti, he had come back up the stairs and the two men bumped gently into each other.

"Sorry, mate" said Mokti "But look, I could use a lift. Al hired a car at the bus station and we used that to get around, but now I'm stranded. Any chance of dropping me a bit closer to the city? I'll never get a cab out here."

Isaac was astonished by the brazen request, the sheer effrontery of the man. He took a moment to study him; early twenties, unkempt appearance but something in the face. He pondered a moment before realizing it was a lack of guile, an absence of selfishness. This young man was indeed what he appeared, an innocent abroad.

And Isaac knew this area, knew there weren't any taxi ranks out here. Uber drivers avoided the area, too many had been hit on the head, they might drop someone off, or come out for a fare but no one in their right mind cruised these streets looking for a fare.

"Yeah," he said, "no worries." Both men moved outside and began heading down the stairs. Sally watched them disappear, rinsed the cloth out and draped it over the tap to dry. When she looked up, she saw her life reflected in the dingy apartment. She couldn't face it alone again, at least not for a while; picking up her bag she paused for a quick look at the photograph. There she was, back row, second from the left, just one of the gang. Army Reserve, such a mix of people, such a joyful set of friends, it was where she had met Alan all those years ago. Happier times.

She ran down the stairs, catching up with the two men as they were getting in the car.

"Wait!" she called. Isaac stepped back out of the car, Mokti was already in the front seat. Standing at the passenger window she spoke to Isaac over the car roof, "I want to come with you. I need to...," she stopped. "I need ..." Another pause, "I...I..."

Mokti kept his gaze fixed through the front windshield. He was grateful the passenger window was up, he did not want to be too close to this woman with her bared emotions. Perth was looking better and better, maybe his father had been right.

Isaac looked at the young woman, saw the lines under her eyes, the thousand-yard stare. If he drove away now, he would be abandoning her to that awful apartment, she would have to walk back up those stairs and confront the memories of a failed marriage and the slippery slope of her future. He couldn't do it.

With a sigh he opened his door, "Get in" he said.

Sally entered the back seat, feeling more at home there than in her own room.

The silence in the car was heavy with tension, fatigue and confusion. As Isaac drove, Mokti decided on some gentle chat to ease the mood, "So, you guys are working together, eh? Got a big case on?"

"Mass murderer," said Isaac.

"Four bodies first time through, another four last night," murmured Sally.

"Oh," very quietly from Mokti.

Sally went on in a conversational tone, "Cuts them up, rips their guts out."

"Right," whispered Mokti, looking out the window.

He definitely should have listened to his father.

EVIE SIPPED HER COFFEE, grateful for the opportunity to be alive and in a crowd, but strangely alone. Next to her Joshua gazed at the screen of his laptop, a latte quietly cooling on the tabletop as he accessed the data from the chip given to him by Frankie in the gaming lounge.

"So, Evie" he murmured while he worked, "looking for a move up the pay scale, are we?"

She decided not to play dumb around this man, "The doctor might appreciate some of my other talents. I have a brain, I'm not afraid to use it." Her chance of survival rested on convincing this man that she was useful, that perhaps she shouldn't just be discarded like a worn tool. Or like Charlie Knox.

Her companion grunted but otherwise did not acknowledge her presence. Joshua scanned through the names on his laptop, the small data stick had generated an interesting group of addresses for the selected people and he sought locations within the city.

He had decided to let Evie live a bit longer, she had demonstrated an admirable ruthlessness during the earlier part of the day and such people were rare in his circles. She was scared of him, a sentiment of which he approved; but she could see a task through and perhaps he would take her on as one of his staff.

Yes, his staff. He liked the idea of staff; yes, employees meant that he was improving. Getting better. Mother would be impressed.

Back to the job in hand, he decided. Time to select someone else for his newest collection.

Joshua scanned through the names on his laptop, the small data stick had generated an interesting group of addresses for the selected people, and he sought locations within the city. Many of the names showed locations in other states, these he deleted; he also sent to the recycle bin any addresses on the other side of town. Eventually, he settled on a short list of eight names, eight women who lived within reach. His reach. His women.

The other file holding information from the police informant was short, a duty roster, locations and the emergency code for the afternoon's foot patrols. Perfect.

After minimizing this data screen, he opened a link to the internet ready to begin the next stage of his search, a few keystrokes sent him online to his favourite sites.

Evie maintained her silence, her eyes followed Joshua's movements but she tried desperately not to show him her interest.

The laptop's screen lit up to show a familiar website, a way for people to keep in touch with friends, a mechanism for finding those who may have drifted in and out of a person's life.

"Hello, ladies" he murmured.

After a short search, he found one person who fitted his criteria, Mary Ichku - a small photo displayed a pretty brunette in her maid's outfit, one of the "House Angels" employees, ready and willing to clean up after the big party, wedding or other celebration. Reasonable rates. He placed a phone call to the number and began requesting the maid's services but was told that company policy did not include a customer requesting a particular person for a first time visit unless they came with a recommendation from someone else.

"I'm sorry, sir," said the House Angel receptionist, "but we don't want to put our people at risk. There are some very unsavoury people out there."

"I quite understand," sympathized Joshua. Perhaps he would have to go to the next person on the list.

"That's not to say that you are in any way such a person," continued the receptionist.

"I understand completely." Joshua looked at his list and began researching another name.

"Besides, Mary called in sick today."

"Really?" responded Joshua. "Nothing serious I trust?" He accessed the police files again and saw Mary's address. The Great Wall Apartments, how depressing.

"Just a cold. Now, what sort of cleaning do you require?"

A sudden thought struck Joshua, a chance for a shaft of humour to penetrate his world. "I'm afraid I need someone to clean up a particularly messy bathroom left by a previous tenant." He gave out Isaac's home address.

"No problem, sir, I'll send someone over within the hour. And don't worry about Mary, I'm sure she will be back on deck tomorrow."

As Josua hung up the phone he said to himself, "I rather think not."

On a whim, he entered Sally's name into the search engine and wasn't too surprised that she had a profile, complete with a photo. Most of the information was standard and, to his mind, boring. But one line stood out; next to her photo was a single line entry proclaiming an 'Interesting titbit" as the site called this section. Sally's birthday was the second of February.

"How very interesting" he whispered, "Any other surprises, Sal?"

The section on hobbies piqued his interest, Sally was a member of the Army Reserve. Perhaps she was worth a visit, he looked up her address from the online telephone directory, grimacing when he saw the location, "Oh, dear, Sal, is that the best you can do? Still, must be nice to have a neighbour like Mary.

"Evie," he said, "I fancy a bit of a drive; how about you bring the Medical Van around here and take me for a spin. Off you go, petal."

He stayed looking at his screen while Evie collected her bag and began to move off. She looked at Joshua and tried to fathom his thoughts before realizing that his instruction allowed her to leave his presence. She could just walk away and disappear.

And yet.

And yet she decided to comply with his wishes; the afternoon's activity had let her see another world, a darker, more dangerous world. And she realised she was not horrified by what she saw; her instructions had led to violent death of a man who was unknown to her, a stranger.

"Back in a minute," she said.

Joshua whistled as she walked away, he was happy in the service.

Chapter 16

The car pulled into an empty parking space at the shopping mall, Isaac opened the door and stepped out into the strong sunlight. When Sally exited, they both started moving towards the pedestrian strip, the detective pointing back at his car with the remote locking device. They reached the strip and paused, Isaac still holding the remote. Eventually, he lowered his arm and squinted, he was unable to lock the vehicle because Mokti was still in the car, dithering with his seat belt. Very deliberately the young man placed it back in the stowed position and then opened the car door.

Isaac couldn't believe someone could be so slow, he was only now getting out of a car, after all! Mokti placed one sandaled foot on the ground, swivelled his body and carefully placed the other foot beside the first. Placing his hands in very definite positions, he eased out of the car, then turned and looked back inside.

"What are you doing, Mokti?" asked Isaac. Sally had zoned out, the gentle beat of the sun was making her feel warm and cosy.

"Just checking I haven't left anything in the car, mate. You haven't seen my sunnies, have you?" He straightened up and held the door open while he spoke to the detective.

Isaac blinked. "They're on your head." Mokti reached up and located his sunglasses, gave the big man a smile of gratitude. He carefully lowered them onto his nose, wriggled them a bit and then seemed satisfied all was well. He gave all of his pockets a final pat before shutting the door and standing before the other two like a kid who had just won a school prize.

"All set," he beamed.

Sally nudged Isaac into action. She had watched the little episode and could sense Isaac's impatience. Mokti moved to a different drum than the big detective.

Clicking the car doors shut, Isaac turned on his heel and walked down the path to the main doors leading into the mall. Sally stepped brightly beside him and Mokti sauntered along behind. "What's the go here, Isaac?" asked Sally.

"There's a coffee shop here and I need coffee in a big way," he answered. In a lower voice, he continued, "How can someone take so long to get out of a car, for God's sake!"

Sally looked back and gave Mokti a smile; he returned it with a little wave. When she turned around again Isaac had reached the counter of a Gloria Jean's. He pulled out his wallet and handed the waitress a loyalty card. "Long black, please and a ..." he looked a question at Sally, "flat white?" Sally nodded.

Before he could turn away Mokti appeared over Sally's shoulder and said, "Love a cappuccino, mate."

Isaac amended the order, gave his name and then asked Mokti to find a table. As the man drifted off Sally asked, "What are we doing here, Isaac?"

Keeping an eye on Mokti Isaac said, "Remember the first murder I told you about?"

"The schoolgirl?"

"Right," he confirmed. "Her father owns this shop. Just before I got back to your place, he called me. I'd left my number with all the next of kin, kept hoping something else might turn up."

They watched Mokti saunter through a selection of empty tables, he would pause from time to time as if he had made a decision but then move on.

"What did he want?" asked Sally.

Eventually, Mokti seemed to have found exactly the right table. He looked over at them, gave a little wave and then pointed at his selection with raised shoulders. Isaac muttered, "He can't even pick a bloody table without making a big deal out of it."

They both gave Mokti weak smiles and nodded; the young man grinned and shook like a puppy before sitting down. He clasped his hands together on the table and drifted into people-watching mode.

"He said," continued Isaac, "that he had an envelope for me. An express delivery post had arrived this morning at the shop. It makes sense. His first victim was a schoolgirl and that ridiculous clue he gave us referred to 'school days'." They exchanged meaningful glances. The waitress called his name and

Isaac stepped down to the serving area. He and Sally collected the coffees, then Isaac leaned towards the barista and called, "I understand there's an envelope here for me. Isaac Howard?"

The barista wiped her hands on a cloth, reached under the counter and passed it over to Isaac. "Tom says hello," she said. With the envelope under one arm, they made their way over to Mokti and sat down. There was a bit more fuss as he retrieved spoons and sugar, Isaac liked a lot of sugar in his coffee.

Mokti ceremoniously ladled the chocolate laden cream into his mouth. "What's in the envelope?" he asked.

Before he could answer Sally stood up, "Give me a minute, I want to enjoy this coffee. I need to go to the restroom. Back in a flash." She moved quickly through the tables and disappeared into the crowd.

Isaac opened the envelope, Mokti leaned over to see the contents and was met by a look of frost. He sank back into his seat and slurped his drink, big eyes fixed on every action the detective made.

Inside the envelope was a picture, a printout of a building, nothing else, no note, no other paperwork. Placing the envelope carefully to one side Isaac turned the picture around; he recognised the building immediately, most people would.

Cradling his coffee cup, Mokti spoke over the brim as it rested against his mouth, "Who's sending you pictures of the Leaning Tower of Pisa?"

Isaac looked intently at the picture, trying to find a clue. Absently he answered, "Probably Leonardo."

"That's one cool dude," said Mokti, "Leonardo of Pisa."

SALLY DRIED HER HANDS, picked up her bag and left the restroom. As she turned into the corridor leading back to the main concourse, a man stepped up behind her. He was dressed in a heavy black coat with "DEATH SUCKS" emblazoned on the back surmounting a flaming skull. With the collar turned up and a black cap pulled low over his eyes it was difficult to see any of the man's features.

He moved in close and whispered in her ear. "Don't turn around. I have a knife in your back." The voice was gravelly, croaky and deep. "Walk forward, head out to the parking lot. If you try to run, scream, or attract attention in any way I will cut you. I also have a gun. After I have killed you, I will open up on anyone else I see. Preferably women and children. Nod if you understand."

Sally nodded, her shoulder bag suddenly grew in weight, pulling her hand down. She gave in to the impulse and let the strap fall to the floor, the bag tumbling open. Her whole body seemed heavier, it seemed that every time she moved, wherever she went, she was assailed, attacked and beaten down. She didn't know how much more she could take.

"Pick it up. Start walking. Don't look around," said the voice.

Bits had fallen out of the bag, old tissues, scraps of paper, she let them lie and shouldered the bag. As Sally walked, she saw the people around her. There were so many of them. All innocent and all potential victims. Up ahead, on the left, a woman stood over a baby in a stroller while beside her a two-year-old demanded attention. On the other side was a group of prepubescent girls, looking in windows and giggling. All were dressed in clothes far too old for them, beneath the poorly applied thick make-up Sally could see they were just children. There seemed to be children everywhere. How had she not noticed this before?

"Keep walking," rasped the voice behind her.

Exiting the mall they crossed the car park, weaving in and out between cars. Finally, the man said, "Stop. Close your eyes."

Standing with her eyes shut was probably the most terrifying thing that had happened to Sally since this whole nightmare had begun. At least with Isaac and the big pistol she could see what was going on, could see the bulk of the large detective. But now, standing, trembling in between a row of parked cars with a knife-wielding maniac behind her, she felt in the grip of total and numbing terror.

She felt thick tape go over her eyes, quickly fastened. Then a cloth was pulled over her face, thick and woollen. "Pull the beanie down so it covers your eyes. Leave your nose and mouth free. I don't want anyone to see you blindfolded and raising the alarm. If they do, believe me, I'll know." She did as instructed, finally standing in a darkness she had only ever experienced in nightmares.

"Into the car." She was guided into a car seat, hands were taped to her sides and then she was strapped in. More tape held her still. "Better hope I don't crash, you'll never get out."

"Please...," she said, in a small voice.

"Shut the hell up!" The voice snarled now, losing some of its depth, replacing it with venom, hatred, and rage. She felt a fist punch deep into her side, knocking the wind out of her lungs, forcing her forward in pain.

"Sit up!" commanded the voice, slightly calmer, struggling for control. "Sit up, breathe normally, in and out, in and out. That's better. Now, no talking."

She felt the car start and begin to move.

Help me, Isaac, she pleaded silently. Please save me.

"WHO?" ASKED ISAAC.

"Leonardo of Pisa." Mokti was startled by the detective's reaction. "Hey, settle down, man. It's just a name." He put the coffee on the table and thought how well he could get on without his duffle bag. Just in case this big man got too excited and he had to run for it. He thought Isaac was all right, but the detective's posture was all over the place. He didn't seem to have any consistency; his eyes looked like raw eggs, clothes a mess. And he could do with a bath.

"Who... what..." Isaac forced himself to calm down. "Tell me about this Leonardo of Pisa character. Is it Leonardo Da Vinci?" he asked.

Mokti saw the iron control clamp down on the detective. This was one impressive guy, he thought. "No, Da Vinci was another Leonardo. The guy from Pisa was a mathematician, did stuff with rabbits on an island."

This wasn't making any sense to Isaac. "Rabbits? Island?" He looked again at Mokti. "What are you talking about? How do you know this stuff?"

"Hey, man, I'm over here to do my Masters at Sydney Uni." He leaned onto the table, settling into a good yarn, "Dad didn't want me to go but I said 'Dad, Sydney Uni is where I have to be if I'm going to get one of the top jobs.' Perth's great and I got my bachelor's degree there but you can't do your postgrad at the same place you do your undergrad. You'd have no cred. Anyway, Dad and I got into a ......"

Isaac had leaned over and clamped a hand on Mokti's arm where it lay on the table. "Shut up!" he said through clenched teeth. Squeezing the limb hard he went on in a low growl, "Shut up and tell me about Leonardo of Pisa."

Mokti looked blankly at the man opposite, too many things were going on in his brain. How could he talk and shut up at the same time? And his forearm was being squeezed, it was starting to throb.

"Uh," he began, waving his free hand in the direction of where Isaac had his death grip, "hurts...."

The big man released the arm and sat back in the chair. "Sorry, Mok, it's been a long day. I don't think I've had more than two hours sleep in the last thirty." He drank the last dregs of his coffee. "Please, please just tell me about Leonardo of Pisa. Imagine I don't know anything."

Mokti rubbed his bruised arm, leaned back and began to speak, "Guy was big with numbers, did a lot of good work. Best known for his Sequence, it was named after him."

"What, the, er, 'Leonardo Sequence'?" asked Isaac, feeling completely out of his depth.

"Yeah, that'd be a good one. Nah, we don't use first names, mate, doesn't sound classy enough. How'd you like 'Albert's Theory of Relativity', "Charles's Origin of the Species', or "Steve on the Nature of Time'? We call Leo's stuff the Fibonacci Sequence since his last name was Bonacci."

"Why not the Bonacci Sequence? Where does the 'Fib' bit come in?" Isaac was struggling.

"It's Italian, mate. 'Fi' means 'son of'. His real mane was Leonardo, Son of Bonacci. Pretty cool, huh?" Mokti was enjoying himself, he liked the history of numbers, always felt excited when he could put a human face on some obscure theory or equation.

"Okay," said Isaac, "I think I get it. This Leonardo character came up with a special set of numbers and it was called the Fibonacci Sequence. That right?"

"Got it in one, mate. That wasn't so hard, now, was it?"

The big detective looked at his slightly rumpled companion. Now he didn't see a person on the edge of vagrancy, he saw a university student. "You're really a clever bloke, aren't you?" he said.

"Too right, Isaac," he said smugly. The two men looked at each other, each recognizing the birth of a possible friendship.

Mokti looked at the third cup of coffee on the table.

"Where's Sally?"

Chapter 17

Sally sat in darkness, the sound of her breathing loud in her ears. Her body rocked as the car turned corners, moving through traffic. Occasionally she heard a muttered curse from the driver. His smell was heavy in the car, a mixture of sweat, breath and dust.

A car horn sounded, she turned her head towards the passenger window. Would someone see her? Would someone guess she needed help? Then the car moved on and her chance of salvation was left behind. After a few more minutes the vehicle stopped and the engine noise ceased. She felt hands rub over her limbs, patting the tape, ensuring she was still secure. After a final tug on her beanie, she felt the car rock and then the sound of the door shutting. Moments afterwards there was the beep of locks being activated.

The silence began, except it wasn't pure silence. With the engine noise gone and the absence of the wind moving over the car, she was able to hear more and more sounds. Strange sounds, sounds near and sounds far away. Far, far away. She concentrated. She listened.

Very faintly a voice cried out, it was somewhere in the distance, the fullness of the sound evaporating into the open air. The car rocked, was he back? There was no click of locks or opening of doors. What had happened, why was the car rocking, gently rocking? A voice, a conversation outside. Someone was sitting on the hood. Couldn't they see her? Couldn't they look through the window and see a victim?

Another voice, angry, a snarl. Commands snapped, muttered responses, and then the car moved again, the weight coming off the hood. More snarls, one voice staying strong, the others moving away, becoming fainter. The doors were unlocked and she again felt someone move into the car. A voice from in front of her spoke, "Bloody vagrants. Shoot the lot of them."

Sally realized she was not in the front seat, she had assumed she was, but she was wrong. She must be in the back seat, but still, couldn't people outside see in and notice her? The car started again, she felt terror rekindle in her heart. The short stop had given her hope, an unreasonable hope that was now shattered. Please let this stop, she begged silently.

This drive was a short one, the car stopping after a sharp right turn. She felt the driver exit and, after a few minutes, another door opened, a closer door. Her limbs were freed and a strong grip pulled her out of the car; a hand firmly wrapped around her right bicep made any chance of escape a forlorn hope. Each time she found her balance the grip would wrench her again and she stumbled; they mounted a set of stairs. The heat of the sun disappeared from her back and she sensed she was in a room, sure enough, a door behind her slammed.

"Home, sweet, home," was whispered in her ear, the mouth stayed beside her head for a few more moments and she both felt and heard her captor's hot breath.

There was no respite, no chance to stand and consider her plight. Again, she was tugged and pulled, twisted around and shoved. Her legs hit something and she fell back onto a seat. Tape wound around her body, tying her to the chair. Earphones were jammed into her ears and heavy metal music blared uncomfortably, almost painfully.

Sally's captor straightened up surveying his victim. She was now secure, a few more minutes of work had taped her legs and arms to the chair, she was immobilized. Stepping back the jailer checked the blinds on the window ensuring only minimal light could enter.

Strapped to the chair Sally, could feel her arms and legs numbing, the sounds in her ears prevented thought, her eyes were still covered, her mouth taped shut.

In her awful prison, into her forced silence, she screamed and screamed.

ISAAC STRAIGHTENED up from the small pile of debris outside the restrooms. It was from Sally's bag, he was sure of that because, amidst the pile of tissues, was one of her business cards. He put it into his pocket and looked around, she was nowhere in sight.

What to do, what to do, he mused. Mokti had a perplexed expression, gazing at Isaac for the answer, the key to this strange and scary city.

"What's going on, man?" he asked. Other shoppers brushed past the duo, elderly females gave them accusing looks. Hanging around the doors to the female restroom was not an accepted spot for a pair of men. A single male could do it, as long as he looked worried and helpless, waiting for a wife. These two did look worried and helpless but they were together, it just wasn't done. A stern matron bumped into Mokti and apologised in the tone of voice that women use when they want the man to go away. More and more, Mokti felt guilty.

"Come on," said Isaac. He led the way back into the main concourse, checked the signs and strode off in the direction of Centre Management. Mokti still felt there was a chance for his bag and so continued after the big man.

Isaac knocked on a door marked 'Security' and waited. When it opened, he showed his badge and identified himself as a police officer, explaining there was a chance a young woman had been abducted from outside the restrooms. A uniformed security guard ushered them into the central control room where two other guards were stationed. He introduced himself and made a call to his supervisor. Shortly, a tough and competent looking female arrived, checked Isaac's ID again, then looked at Mokti.

"He's with me," said Isaac. "Less than twenty minutes ago a young woman went to the restrooms, and when she didn't return, we investigated. I suspect she has been abducted, we are working on a serious crime and it is vital this woman is found. Her life may be in danger. I need to see any CCTV records of the corridor outside the restrooms. I presume you have camera coverage there?"

"You betcha, that's where the creeps like to hang out," said the female. She looked at Mokti as she spoke, and he wished he hadn't gone so fully into impoverished student mode when he dressed earlier.

She gave a few short commands and the uniforms quickly obeyed. This was a unit that functioned well, looking after the security of a large mall was a demanding task, not one for the casual rent-a-cop. These people were professionals and she was their boss, there was no mistaking the hierarchy.

A side screen fuzzed with static and then lit up with a view of the corridor. After a brief interchange and a fast rewind of the footage, the camera quickly found Sally. Isaac and Mokti both yelped, "There she is!" The operator slowed the backward motion until it showed her emerging from the restroom. He stopped the video and began to run it forward.

The control room watched, saw it all, the coated man behind Sally, her stiffness, the dropped bag, both moving off.

"Can you follow them, any other cameras, see where they went?" asked Isaac. The woman nodded, she and the guards spoke in rapid shorthand, flicking between records and cameras. Isaac and Mokti kept quiet, these people knew their craft, the clever thing to do was shut up and let them get on with it.

After ten minutes they stopped and looked at each other, "I'll need a copy made of all that video," said Isaac "From the time the guy in the coat enters until he leaves the mall with Sally. When we get him, it will become evidence." The woman nodded. "Are you sure there's nothing in the carpark, no cameras?"

"Sorry, detective," she replied "We look after the mall, only up to the front doors and that's it. Once they exited through the west doors, they could have gone anywhere. Look, are sure it was a kidnap? She didn't just leave with this guy?"

Isaac thought about it, was it possible Sally had been leading him along all this time? Was this when she finally cut the ties? He rejected the idea, a tired mind and a tired body made clear thinking difficult. "No," he said, "She was moving under duress, I'm sure of it."

The woman nodded, "I agree, but I had to raise the question." She was convinced Sally had been taken, too many years of watching people in malls had given her the ability to read body language. Sally had been stilted and unnatural in her movements. Besides, what woman drops her handbag and then just leaves all the debris on the floor?

"I need to make a call," said Isaac "I have to phone this in. We'll need help if we want to find Sally before Leonardo kills her."

SALLY FELT A SLIGHT movement in her bonds, a looseness. Even blindfolded, with arms restrained and legs strapped to the chair, she was able to wriggle. Her bonds were loose. She had screamed and writhed, pushed and pulled, twisted arms and legs, her body had rebelled. From deep within her, a beast emerged, a snarling, ravening thing of spirit and fire, her inner core had decided that enough was enough and it wasn't going to take it anymore. Her screams kept going but were no longer screams of fear and terror; they were the guttural snarls of rage.

Her rage fuelled muscles, gave her legs and arms the will and strength to extend, to stretch.

And her right leg moved.

Surprise made her still, her voice ceased the screaming, and her brain snapped back into focus. What had happened? She was bathed in sweat, the last period of time had just disappeared, she did not know how long she had spent in her fugue. Something was different, what was it?

She tried to move her arms, with no effect. Then her legs. Again, her right leg moved, just a little. But enough to give her hope.

She could deal with hope.

Time again began to move, but this time it was with a difference. Sally would count her kicks, do twenty, rest and then do another set. After one hundred kicks she started doing twists, again and again. Bit by bit the tape gave way; it continued to hold her with a grasping stickiness until the moment came when she could pull her foot from the hateful binding.

Her right foot was free!

Sally felt elated; the heavy metal music kept pounding into her head, the earphones taped into place. But she could ignore the insistent beat because she had a victory, and she was determined to have another.

She kicked her right shoe off and then used her bare foot to remove her left shoe. With that foot now freed she was able to gain leverage and wiggle the bare foot up between the tape and the chair leg. It took some time, many tears and the loss of some precious skin but eventually she sat, sweat-soaked but triumphant, with two legs free.

Sitting in her blindfolded prison she was elated but the discordant barrage of heavy metal music still drowned out all other sounds. A chill ran through her, a sudden thought. What if she wasn't alone? What if her captor was still in the room, watching her pathetic attempts to escape? Perhaps she had made too much noise herself and he had entered the room to watch her stretch and strain, sob and cry her way to the pitiful freedom she now enjoyed.

Would he even now stride over, laugh at her and then retie her sweat-soaked legs back to the hateful chair?

Where was he, her tormented mind demanded.

ISAAC FELT FRUSTRATED and angry, frustrated he could do little to find Sally and angry at himself for letting her be abducted. Rationally, he knew it was not his fault, but she had become a part of his team, they both were on the trail of Leonardo and shared a common bond. He had let her down.

"You reckon this Leonardo fellow has her?" asked Mokti. They were sitting in some spare chairs at the back of the control room. The female supervisor was having a backward search on all cameras, trying to spot Leonardo. So far there had been no success, the strange man had exited the male restrooms wearing his coat and hat but there was no trace of him entering.

"He must have gone in and changed," she said, talking back to Isaac and Mokti. "We aren't allowed to have cameras in the restrooms, breaches too many privacy laws. We're printing out pictures of all males fitting his physical shape and carrying bags. That coat would have taken up a bit of room, we don't sell them in the mall. Could have come from the Salvation Army shop outside."

The big detective leaned back into the chair and let his head rest on the wall, a great fatigue enveloped his body. He heard the noises in the room, Mokti's voice blended into the soft susurrations lulling him to sleep, his eyes closed.

"So tired," he murmured.

Mokti watched Isaac drift off. He was interested in the room, the comings and goings of messengers, the concise managerial style of the supervisor. She treated her people well, he decided, gave short instructions without being terse and abrupt. The room had a very businesslike feel to it. She brought over a sheaf of photographs printed out from the CCTV records and gave them to Mokti, he felt quite excited about the assumption he was a detective.

"We'll finish making the copies in another ten minutes, is there anything else you need from us?" she asked.

Mokti stood and tried to think of something policemanlike to say, the supervisor was looking at him expectantly. The door opened and two uniformed police officers entered, followed by Sergeant Harris and another female with a detective shield clipped to her belt.

"I'm Detective Sergeant Harris, this is my partner Detective Patricia Lee. We're here to collect any evidence pertaining to the abduction. These uniformed officers will be taking statements from everyone here."

The supervisor indicated Mokti and said, "I was just giving some photos to this detective."

Harris and Lee both turned to a very embarrassed Mokti. Harris raised an eyebrow and asked, "Dress standards seem to be falling, Detective ...?"

"Yeah, well, I'm not really a detective," said Mokti, shuffling a sandaled foot. "I was just, you know .... me and Isaac ..." He eventually trailed off and stood silent, wishing this moment would end.

The female detective said, "Isaac's been collecting strays again, Bill. Where is the big goose?"

Mokti stood to one side and indicated the sleeping man. His mouth was open, head back against the wall, slow and deep breathing came from his chest.

"A thing of beauty is a joy forever," said Detective Lee. She sat down beside Isaac and tickled him under the chin, "Wakey, wakey, Mr. Detective Man."

Isaac snorted, shook his head and sat up. After a moment he focused on Patricia, "Short and Twisted, thank goodness, I thought I was having a nightmare." Looking up at Harris he said "G'day, Bill. What are you doing still up? I thought your shift finished this morning."

"I love my work," said Harris.

"Want to tell us about tall, dark and untidy here?" asked Lee, gesturing at Mokti.

Isaac struggled to his feet, "This is Mokti Setiawan, met him when I took Sally back to her place. Looks like a no-hoper, but he's actually very cluey. Been a good lad, told me all about Leonardo of Pisa."

Harris said, "Fibonacci Sequence."

The female supervisor joined in, "Rabbits on an Island."

Isaac looked at them all in some amazement, "What, did I miss a memo or something?"

The supervisor answered first, "I've just finished a course on Number Theory at College. These computers don't write their own code." She left them and returned to the rest of her team where the uniformed police officers were conducting interviews.

Looking at Harris, Isaac asked, "What's your excuse?"

"Had a good maths teacher at school, some things stick," responded the black detective.

Mokti interrupted the conversation, "Hey, Isaac, these photos..."

"What about them?" asked Isaac.

Mokti held up one of the pictures, "Do you reckon this looks like Alan Lassiter?"

Chapter 18

Sally pulled her will into a ball and used it to quell the fear. If her captor was in the room then so be it, but she would not let her fears rule her life. She had been doing too much of that, the events she had witnessed since meeting Isaac had shown her how unfair and cruel life could be. She was determined not to add to those circumstances holding her down.

At least she could control her fears and hopes.

She placed her bare feet out to each side of the chair, spreading her base and giving more leverage. Then she began to lean against the bonds, first to the left and then to the right. Her spread legs prevented her from toppling over, her arms objected, especially when the tape began to cut into her flesh. When she could take the pain on one side no longer, she would lean over to the other. Back and forth, back and forth.

Her arms were strapped to the sides of the chair, straight down the back and finishing with hands taped to each leg. As she leaned, she gradually worked some movement into the tape, bit by bit she was able to move to freedom. The heavy metal noise in her head continued unabated, whoever these groups were, she was not a fan.

Finally, the adhesive on the tape began to release, after the first bit of movement she could feel the tape compressing, pulling together. Two songs later she was able to slide her hands up and down the chair legs, they were still held by the tape which was now more of a rope than an adhesive.

Now she was at an impasse. The tape would not break, by compressing it she had made it stronger. Less likely to break. All she had gained was the ability to slide her still restrained arms and hands up and down the chair leg.

But it might be enough. Throwing her weight to one side she toppled the chair over, she tucked her chin into her chest but the knock on her head was painful. As a small bonus, one of the earphones was slightly displaced. Her left ear was still subject to the dreadful music but at least it was from an earphone bud some millimetres from her head. She was grateful for small mercies.

By twisting and turning, by cursing and swearing, by force of will, she was able to slide her still trapped hands down each leg. First, her right hand slid over the bottom of the leg and was freed. Then the left.

She was now able to reach across her body and pick away at her bonds, searching for the end of the tape in her painful darkness.

And then she was free, just her head remained covered by the tape.

She stood up from the chair and found the earphone buds, pulling them free with a sharp tug.

The silence was almost physical, she slumped, the cessation of noise giving her a huge sense of peace. After a moment she took a deep breath and reached up to uncover her eyes.

"Who's a busy girl, then?" asked a voice behind her.

ISAAC GRABBED THE PHOTOGRAPH, "Can you show me this on the screen, please?" he asked the supervisor.

She gave instructions and shortly the bit of footage showing Sally's ex-husband was on the display. The detectives gathered around, Mokti peered over Harris's shoulder. The operator let the footage run normally, Isaac recognised Alan from his gait even though his face was slightly blurred. "That's him," he said. "Freeze it there." The screen showed Alan Lassiter with one hand on the door into the restrooms. In his other hand was a carry bag.

"Fits the scenario," said the female supervisor, "He's going into the restrooms with a bag big enough to hold other clothes. Run it forward, Jim, see if he comes out."

The seated security guard increased the speed of playback; men darted along the corridor, the restroom door flapped back and forth like paper in the wind. When the coated kidnapper emerged, the picture was slowed back to its normal pace.

"There's our bad guy. Leave him and keep looking at the vision from that door. We want to see if that Lassiter fellow comes out. Speed it up a bit."

A small counter on the top right corner of the screen showed the time, after another twenty minutes of elapsed time flipped over, Isaac called a halt. "Either Lassiter was the guy in the coat, or he's eaten a lot of curry. He went into that restroom nearly thirty minutes ago. I reckon he's our man."

The others agreed. "I'll keep scanning the records just in case," said the supervisor. She gave appropriate instructions to her crew as well as dispatching another guard to conduct a search of the restrooms. "There's an outside chance he's still in a cubicle, might be a victim, could have been mugged and had his clothes stolen."

Isaac grunted, he turned away, leaving her to coordinate her team. If Lassiter was the kidnapper, why had he done it?

"Why would Al want to kidnap Sally?" asked Mokti.

The big detective looked at the lanky student, surprised to find his thoughts echoed. "Not unknown," he said. "I get the impression he didn't really believe the relationship was over. If he has psychological issues, maybe he just ignores the bits of reality that don't fit."

Harris and Patricia asked a few questions about Alan Lassiter. Isaac told them of confronting the man in Sally's apartment. He described the man's demeanour as he left the apartment. "You know," he said "it's possible he took Sally because she was not accepting his truth. She may have needed, in his opinion, some time to see the error of her ways."

"Where would he take her?" asked Mokti, he stood in the huddle with the other three detectives, an equal partner in the discussion.

Patricia looked up from the floor where she had been examining her shoes for inspiration. "And just when did you become a copper, handsome?" she asked of the young student.

Mokti stammered, Isaac thought he spotted a blush, but it was difficult to see with the man's dark skin colour. "It's all right, Mok. Pat terrifies everyone." He rubbed a hand over his face, brushing the sleep out of tired eyes. "Bill, can you check out the databases and see if he's got a residence here? I suspect not, he didn't strike me as a bloke with a lot of money. I'm going back to the Great Wall, have a look around Sally's apartment to see if there's any clue to Alan's whereabouts."

Patricia collected the visual records from the supervisor, blew Mokti a kiss and left with her partner. "You coming?" asked Isaac, looking at Mokti.

"Too right, this is better than sitting on the couch watching TV." The two men made their way back to the car. Mokti's gait had changed, he was now walking with purpose, striding beside the big man. "Look, Isaac, on the bus Al and I got on pretty well. It's hard to see him as the type of bloke who'd do this sort of stunt. He seemed to be just a normal person. Wait a minute!" He stopped, Isaac continued for another step before crumpling to a halt.

The tall youth gazed into the distance, "We were talking at night, you know been on the bus for ten hours already with another twenty still to go. The brain just hibernates and the mouth wanders along by itself. He said...," Mokti's eyes lost focus as he dove into memory, "... He said he was going to be staying with his wife, said he was going to surprise her with a big place. Make her see he was successful. Then he said it was right next door." He looked at Isaac, "Right next door, mate!"

The two men ran the rest of the way to the car, Isaac pulled away from the mall with a screech of tyres. He drove with one hand while the other reached beside the steering wheel and pressed a blue button. Immediately a siren sounded, and a set of blue lights began to flash from the sun visor, a shield prevented the driver and passengers from being blinded by the bright lights.

"Cool," gurgled Mokti.

THIS VOICE WAS DIFFERENT, yet oddly familiar.

"Please leave the tape over your eyes, there's a good girl."

Sally stood still, one hand half raised to her head. The darkness was now a friend, she did not want to see who was standing behind her.

"Leonardo?" she asked, nerves stretched, fear running again through her battered frame.

"Sal," said the voice, "after all we've been to each other, I think you can call me Leo."

She felt him move behind her, her body rigid with terror. A hand gently embraced her shoulder, the warmth of his palm burning through her skin. "Stay very still" he whispered, voice close to her ear.

Her body was now trembling, she was afraid her legs would begin to spasm, and she would collapse. Sweat beaded her top lip, all the knocks and bruises of her struggles screamed for attention. It seemed as if her body was demanding a stop to all of this, no more shocks, no more panic; her mind was gazing at her slowly crumpling physical form, unable to assist, barely able to stand by and watch.

"There's a chair behind you, a wheelchair. Sit down in it, please." The hand on her shoulder pressed down gently, guiding her into the strange, padded seat of the chair. "Feet up." She followed the various instructions, could hear clicks of metal, felt flaps being dropped, "All done," the voice concluded.

The chair was pushed in a circle; Sally could feel she was leaving this room, entering another part of the apartment. "We might go for a little walk, Sal. This place has some bad Feng Shui, floor's a bit sticky underfoot. Hold on a minute."

She did not know what this strange man meant, why would the floor be sticky? A stinging pain in her arm made her give a little yip of surprise.

"Sorry, my dear. A touch of medication was called for, I believe. Have a little nap." She struggled to stand, writhed against the unfairness of her tormentor but the drug pulled her into its warm embrace, her head lolled forward, consciousness left.

Leonardo pushed the wheelchair out the door, humming a little tune.

ISAAC PULLED INTO THE parking lot of the Great Wall; he was out the door before the car had fully stopped. Mokti ran after the big man, sandaled feet slapping the pavement, fear and determination across his face.

Isaac pushed open the glass doors leading to the small foyer and the stairwell. Sally's apartment was on the first floor, he snatched his pistol out of the holster and mounted the stairs two at a time. He reached the small landing halfway up the flight where the stairs turned back on themselves and continued to the first-floor doorway. His shoulder slammed into the wall and he used the bounce to propel himself up the last flight. Mokti was leaping up the stairs, pulling himself up with a hand on each banister.

Both men reached the doorway onto the floor at the same time. Isaac thrust the handle down and used his momentum to shoulder the door open, he and Mokti burst through, entering the external balcony which gave access to all of the rooms on this floor.

The Great Wall was a utilitarian structure. Tenants did not have the luxury of protection from the elements for the length of this balcony. Wet weather allowed rain to drench any person scurrying to reach the limited sanctuary of their doorway. Glancing over the balcony rail as they ran Mokti, saw the rear of Isaac's car jutting out below him. The big detective reached Sally's apartment and did not pause. He shoulder charged the door, smashing it inwards, entering her home with the fury of an avenging angel.

Isaac was almost beyond reasonable thought; his sense of failure over losing Sally had fuelled his innate duty and rendered him into a rampaging beast. Entering the apartment, he shrugged the remains of the door to one side and thrust his pistol out, ready to shoot any threat. The first room was empty, a moment's glance was enough to show it was still in the same condition as when they had all left earlier.

Caution and training lost the battle with his sense of urgency; he barely slowed his momentum as he ran into the only other room, the bedroom.

It was empty.

Standing in the room, gun by his side, he felt bitterly powerless. Helpless, another woman who depended on him had been taken. His sense of futility spiked into his already over-wrought brain, telling him again and again of his failure. The gun in his hand twitched for a moment as he unconsciously debated using it on himself, such was his sense of despair and remorse.

Mokti's voice called to him from the balcony.

"Isaac! Got someone here you should meet." The big detective left the apartment and walked back onto the baloney, looking to his right he saw Mokti several yards away.

"Look who I found, he just ran out of the next apartment." Mokti spoke from a seated position; under him, stomach flat against the dirt-streaked floor, hands outstretched and mouth grimacing in pain was a man.

Alan Lassiter.

Chapter 19

Isaac pulled the fallen man to his feet and thrust him against the wall. The back of Alan's head hit the brickwork with a smack.

"Where is she?" demanded the detective.

Mokti watched the interplay, he realized Isaac was in a vengeful mood, capable of doing great harm if he was thwarted. "Steady on, Isaac," he counselled.

"Keep out of this, Mokti," snarled the big man. He pushed his face in close, nose to nose with the now thoroughly frightened Alan. Sally's ex-husband could feel the detective's hot breath. The knock on his head, combined with the terrifyingly close proximity of the enraged Isaac, produced a nausea-generated fear.

Alan waved a limp arm towards the apartment door next to Sally's own small home. Tears flooded his eyes, shame over his conduct fought with outrage over the treatment he was receiving from Isaac. "Can't do this, man," he said. "Can't just hit me."

Isaac pulled him off the wall and, retaining a firm grip on Alan's shirtfront, shook the smaller man like a puppet. "Shut your face, maggot." Stepping to the doorway he propelled the helpless man against the half-closed door to the new apartment. The door slammed back against the wall with Alan still being pressed against the unforgiving wood.

Standing in the doorway, Isaac could see the legs of a body lying on the floor, the upper part of the body hidden by the kitchen bench. A woman's body. Both he and Alan could easily see the pool of blood spreading from her torso to lap against her ankles. Alan spasmed with incredulity before Isaac punched him hard and low, the full weight of his body pressing his clenched fist deep into the quivering man's torso. Isaac's face never changed expression as he let the moaning, puking body slide to the floor.

He spun to the woman, entering the lounge room and stopping, face slack, brain trying to make sense of the sight before his tormented eyes. Was it Sally?

Mokti had entered the room, witnessed the savage blow that levelled Alan Lassiter and then saw the corpse. He stepped past the fallen man, briefly considering kicking him before coming to a halt beside Isaac. Looking at the corpse he felt ill, a physical nausea which threatened to spill out of his mouth and cover the already defiled corpse.

Not Sally.

The woman had been cut open, her maid's uniform split and torn where the knife had slashed her torso revealing the pick wetness of chest and stomach. Isaac pushed past Mokti and grabbed Alan by the hair. He dragged the man into the lounge room and threw him down beside the woman's body.

"You bastard, Lassiter," said the detective. "Or should I call you 'Leonardo'?"

Alan Lassiter was a victim, he knew it, had always known it. Life seemed to always destroy his plans, crush his dreams, and laugh at his every success. What had he done to deserve this fresh assault? They just didn't understand.

"Leave me alone, man," he said, lips muttering into the carpet. If he kept his eyes squeezed shut, then all of this was a bad dream. "Go away, I didn't do anything."

Moments passed, the room watched the four occupants, three living, one dead. Walls looked down at the destroyed life on the floor and the whimpering man huddled with knees held up to his chest. A quiet, broken only by the deep breathing as each man sought to live with mayhem and grief.

Mokti sank heavily into a cheap lounge chair, collapsing back into the faded upholstery. He moved a small coffee table to obscure the woman's body; he was experiencing the unreality of momentous occasions, the futile wishing for the bad things to go away. But his mind, his intellect dragged him along the path of awareness, moment by moment he realized this was real life and would never go away. Never leave him.

Alan Lassiter felt himself grabbed by an arm and pushed into a chair, he let himself be limp, not wanting to accept any responsibility for his movements. Life could just keep pushing him around, it always had treated him so unfairly.

Isaac finished bundling Lassiter into the chair and then, using some standard issue quick ties from a coat pocket, he secured Sally's ex-husband's hands to each chair leg. The man's head just lolled against his chest while he murmured his mantra, "Not my fault, you got no right..."

The detective phoned for more support, asked for detectives Harris and Lee to be informed. As he spoke his eyes moved around the room, looking anywhere but at the mess on the floor. He saw a standard, low-rent apartment; this room served as a combination lounge and dining area, an incredibly small table for meals; a tiny kitchen nook nestled near the front door. The solitary bedroom would be behind the only other door in the apartment. In every way, it was a duplicate of Sally's accommodation, one of several hundred identical, featureless caves for the lost and lonely who made up the population at the Great Wall.

After replacing the telephone, he opened the bedroom door and looked in, it was important to intrude as little as possible until the forensic team had swept the place, they always bitched and moaned about the stupidity of policemen in a crime scene. But they were never the first into a place of violence and disgust, they always turned up knowing that someone else would be having those nightmares. Someone like Isaac.

Standing in the doorway he saw the bed had been pushed onto its side and placed against the wall. Bits of electrical tape lay strewn about the centre of the room; an overturned chair, probably from the dining table, was the only other piece of furniture. Under the cheaply draped window Isaac could see a small bag, next to it was a crumpled black coat bearing the motif "DEATH SUCKS". Isaac agreed. He moved back into the main room and sat on the couch seat closest to Alan Lassiter.

"What happened, Lassiter?" he asked.

Raising his head meant that Alan could see the maid's body, he jerked away from the corpse and said, "Jeez, man, can't you cover her up or something? Or move me." His neck muscles stood out with the strain, stubble-flecked chin thrusting with bony intensity. "That's an awful sight."

Bill Harris and Patricia Lee arrived moments before the forensic team and a host of uniformed officers began performing the minutia of crime scene investigation. The Medical Examiner arrived, a different man from earlier that morning, he looked at Isaac, looked at the body and sat down on the remaining dining chair. "I dunno, Isaac, you keep Frank busy with an early morning autopsy, we got bodies coming out our ears down the lab and now you go and find more. What's going on?"

Mokti found a kitchen stool and pulled it into a corner, he sat to watch the unfolding drama. By being still and quiet he could almost imagine he was watching a movie, one of the crime shows on TV. But they never communicated the awful smell of a crime, the background hum of traffic and flies, the scent of violent, sudden death.

"We have a mad, cruel sicko out there, cutting people up and taking their LifeChips," began Isaac. He paused, "Calls himself Leonardo. This makes five murders, probably all by the same person: four women, one man. Two of the women had their LifeChips taken, not the man, and two of the women still had theirs. One was extracted but left on the side of my bath. The other was just dumped back into the body." His brain teased out some questions, but his body just wanted to sit. "Don't know about this one," he nodded towards where the maid lay.

"Why take some chips?" asked the ME, "Why not all of them?"

"We'll have to ask the man himself." Isaac nodded towards where Alan Lassiter sat on the end of a couch. He had been placed there by a uniformed officer who now stood behind him and to one side. The officer kept one hand near his sidearm and was watching Lassiter carefully. Beside the miserable man sat Detective Bill Harris, he was having a whispered conversation with Lassiter who, from time to time, shook his head violently.

"Why not take all the LifeChips, Lassiter?" asked Isaac, raising his voice so it carried clearly through the room.

Sally's ex-husband started a little at the question, looked up to meet the big detective's eyes. "I didn't do this, Howard, I took Sally but ... this..." he stopped and choked a little. "I just wanted Sally to see things from my point of view, to stop being so selfish. She never considered my feelings, never thought about the hurt she was bringing into my life. She just needed to give me a few moments alone and let me talk to her. That's all I wanted to do, talk. But she would never even look at me. That's why I took her, she needed a jolt, needed to see how much I loved her and how she needed me. Then she would have understood and loved me back. It's all her fault, she never gave me a chance."

Mokti could see the other members of the room listening to Lassiter as they worked. Even he, who was more comfortable with numbers than people, could tell that every other occupant of the room, both male and female, was beginning to loathe Alan Lassiter. He lived in a different world to everyone else. In his world, Alan Lassiter was always the central figure and any random act anywhere in the world was only seen as another detail in his life, its importance was only realised by how much it impacted him.

"Bill," said Isaac, "Can you handle the little snot, if I come over there, I'll rip his guts out." The big detective then folded his arms across his chest, lowered his head and closed his eyes. The ME got to his feet and bent over the desecrated form on the floor.

Across the room Bill Harris was joined by Patricia; Mokti could hear them batting Lassiter's mind back and forth between them. He couldn't hear the words, but their tone made for interesting theatre. At no time did they touch the seated man but there were moments when a comment made the prisoner react as if struck. Their voices joined together in a delicate dance, a pavane between three people with Lassiter spinning between each of his interrogators. His voice would raise a querulous protest and then degenerate into sobs and adamantine refusals. Finally, he sank back into the chair, focused on the opposite wall and spoke at length in a monotone. Mokti thought he may have witnessed the breaking of a man's will followed by a fatigued surrender of the guilty conscience. Certainly, the tone of the two detectives' voices changed, there was no longer the sense they were playing off against each other. Now they merely interrupted the steady flow of Lassiter's monologue with an occasional brief phrase, sometimes a question.

Finally, Patricia Lee stood up and signalled to the uniformed officer to take Lassiter away. Mokti watched a small procession as first Lassiter and two officers left the room, then the corpse of the maid was encased in a body bag before being placed on a gurney and wheeled through the front door.

The Medical Examiner paused as he followed the gurney, stopping by the table he spoke to the detectives, "No LifeChip."

He looked a little longer at the sleeping Isaac before nodding and walking out the door.

The room seemed almost empty.

Lee and Harris came and sat down at the table with Isaac, Patricia looked over at Mokti and said, "Why don't you join us, clever man? Time for a bit of a yak to see what we have. You get to wake ugly drawers up."

Isaac grunted, "I'm awake, Lee. Just resting my eyes." He sat up, stretched and asked, "What have you got?" Mokti moved into the last vacant chair.

"As you heard," began Harris "Lassiter admitted to kidnapping Sally. His story tallies with what we saw on the CCTV. His plan, if you can call it that, was to put a scare into her and then leave her in this apartment. She was tied with tape to the chair in the next room, blindfolded and deafened by earphones. He thought this would make her feel vulnerable and scared."

"Struth," said Mokti, "that'd make anybody scared. Sally probably thought she was taken by that Leonardo character."

Isaac interjected, "Maybe she was." They looked at him. "Well, come on," he said, "It makes sense, doesn't it? And we find him with another body. He'll do me for Leonardo."

"Don't think so, mate" replied Harris. "I heard Leonardo on the phone, and I can't see that Lassiter has enough brains to talk the way that nutcase spoke to us. I'm willing to bet he was on that bus from Perth when the earlier murders were committed. And Mokti here will be his alibi."

They all looked at Mokti who quailed a little under the gaze of three hardnosed detectives. "Here, steady on, fellas, I'm just an innocent bystander."

The big detective stood up and stretched again, ran his fingers through his hair before resuming his seat. "Yeah, you're right, Bill, Lassiter isn't Leonardo. Just an idiot. But an idiot who kidnapped his ex-wife. What did he plan to do? Untie her here and expect that she'd be willing to listen to him. Sally would have clocked him with the nearest blunt object."

Patricia joined the conversation, "I've had boyfriends like that. When you break it off, they think if they can talk to you then you'll see sense and take them back. They never accept that it's over. Even after a few conversations, they talk themselves into believing you've not understood the situation fully. So, they hunt you down for yet another intimate conversation. Helps them with their self-delusion that there is a relationship. Happened to me a couple of times."

Mokti had to ask, "What did you do?" The idea of hunting Patricia Lee down when she did not want to be pursued seemed incredibly dangerous.

She gave him a smile and rubbed his leg with her foot, Mokti jumped. "My dad had a little chat with them." All three men contemplated that interview for a moment. The silence hung.

"Right," coughed Harris. "Anyway, Lassiter figured he'd leave Sally here for a bit and then make a performance of 'rescuing' her. He was on his way back to carry it out when you blokes came by. The officers outside interviewed some of the neighbours who said Lassiter had knocked on their doors saying he had heard a woman screaming in this apartment. He planned to kick the door down after establishing this bit of groundwork, leap in and untie the poor girl. She would then fall into his arms, sob and see him in his true light."

Isaac snorted, "Bloody idiot."

"Too right," said Harris. "The neighbours can't hear anything here, that's one of the blessings of living in the Great Wall, the soundproofing is amazing. When the government built them as cheap accommodation they just churned through the concrete. Walls are thick as. So, there's Lassiter, trying to convince these people he's heard someone screaming and they knew he was off his tree. Thought he was one of the many dope heads or drunks around the place and told him to push off. Without anything else to do, he decided to come in and finish his plan anyway. Tried kicking the door open and damn near broke his foot."

Mokti looked over at the front door and saw a steel plate near the lock. Patricia looked in the direction of his gaze and said, "These apartments were built by people who didn't want to keep repairing kicked in doors. They've all got a steel inner and those reinforced plates. Lassiter's been watching too many action movies. When we come here, we get the keys."

"And that's what he did, eventually," continued Harris. "He'd rented this place, so he already had the keys in his pocket. Probably didn't think ahead about this if Sally ever asked him. Another self-delusion. Picture this - he's hopping around on one foot, fishing for his keys, unlocks the door and heroically limps in to find the maid's body on the floor. Has a bit of a turn, looks into the other room for Sally and she's not there. His plan, his life has all come unstuck and so he does what most people do, He panics and bolts out the front door."

Patricia again rubbed Mokti's leg and purred, "And that's where you came in, sweetie." She sighed and fluttered her eyes, "My hero."

Mokti was terrified.

"Go easy, Pat, he's new to the city," said Isaac. "But Sally is still gone, if she freed herself, we would have found her by now. Those uniforms take up a lot of space, bit hard to ignore. Where is she?"

They each knew the answer, but none wished to be the first to speak it aloud.

"Bugger," said Isaac, finality bearing down on them all. "Leonardo."

They all lapsed into silence before Isaac went on, "What I don't understand, is why he takes some LifeChips but not others. Is it a coincidence that only one of the victims was male, or is that another pattern? I dunno." He stood up, patted his pockets the way men do when looking for their car keys. "Right, I'm going over to LifeCorps and see if they can help, maybe there's something the chips have in common, a brand or something." He looked at Mokti, "Want to come? Help me keep awake, might be some more numbers in it for you."

The young man leapt to his feet and stood behind his chair, he stuttered and felt his face grow hot as he tried to avoid Patricia's gaze. "Yeah, that'd be good, Isaac. Uh, I'll wait for you at the car," and he bolted out the door.

Harris rose to his feet and gave Patricia's shoulder a squeeze, "Come on, Tex, you can put another notch in your gun belt. Poor guy, are you going to give him a chance?"

Patricia rolled her eyes in exasperation and then stood up, "What is it with you men and a self-assured female? You run a mile if a woman shows any interest."

"That's because we're all such shy and retiring types, not used to aggressive Asian women with their inscrutable practices." Harris spoke while scanning the room for any further evidence.

She snorted, "Inscrutable, me? I was born in Balmain, not Taiwan. See what I have to put up with Isaac, getting relationship advice from the Last of his Tribe. Look," she changed mental gears, "we'll head back to the station and see what's turned up. Do you know anyone at LifeCorp?"

"Yeah," replied Isaac, "I met one of the vice presidents when they were receiving threats from some Onelifers. His name's Brodie, Jim Brodie. Good bloke, he'll help."

A SENSE OF CONSCIOUSNESS returned to Sally, not full awareness but the impression of awareness was there. Deep in her mind she felt herself, felt a returning idea of who she was. Time passed.

There was no real point at which she could say she was awake, sometimes she thought she was becoming alert and then nothing, only to realise that some time had again run through her life. She was not even aware she could not receive any sense impressions, no smell, no touch, she was not even aware she could not feel. More time passed, she floated.

There was a moment when she realised she was a person, that she was unconscious. At the next point of awareness, she began to feel she was a human being, and then she began to swim. Like a diver who sees the surface of the water so far above and begins to swim upwards, Sally slowly rose to consciousness. High overhead, it seemed to her, was a light and she must rise to it, she must break the surface.

And she did. Not with a cough and a splutter, not with a great intake of air, but with a dawn. The sun of her true self rose over a horizon of blackness and she saw she was alive, she was real.

She was trapped.

As the cotton wool receded from her mind, she was able to make better judgements about her condition. Her mouth was dry, her tongue lapped against the inside of her cheeks, trying to summon some moisture. Her eyes were closed and blocked, perhaps a mask or blindfold, she hoped. She did not want to be blind forever. And then a strange feeling crept into her core, her inner self. She began to feel discomfit from her body, first her chest, then her arms and finally her legs and feet. She almost wept with relief and gratitude, she was alive! The pain, the tingles, the lumps under her body all proved to her that she was capable of feeling. She was not lying in a cold, strange room with her chest cut open. She was not dead.

This moment was fleeting, this sense of relief. It was quickly submerged by her discomfort, her battles to regain consciousness were soon forgotten, fading into that part of the mind where dreams go on awakening. With each moment that passed she became more alert, each moment she thought that she was fully awake, only to rise more fully to realization and then decide anew that she was now awake. These moments chased each other through her mind until they finally slowed and stopped and she lay there thinking; "Now I'm really awake."

And she was.

Time passed, her discomfort grew, swelled up and receded, pain washing through her like a wave. She realised she was prone, lying on her back. Arms and legs were pushed against her body by some form of restraint. A gag filled her mouth, small tendrils of cloth enticingly fluttering in her airway. After a brief struggle, she forced herself to lay still, fearful that her movement might force the cloth down her throat and she would die a horrible, painful death.

Her bed moved, it had been moving all during her struggle. The sway and rock eventually made sense when she realised she was again in a moving vehicle, this time she was horizontal. By the way she was pressed against her bonds and then released she understood that she was not across the back seat of a car. More like a station wagon or van with her head to the front. The deceleration would force her body to push against her head and it was at these times she felt the gag creep down her throat.

Bit by bit her world became focussed on the finger of material slowly reaching through her mouth and into the airway. In her darkness, she fought for calm, pressed her panic down deep, forced herself to be relaxed, and please, oh please, not die.

Some battles are epic, on a large scale. Defending the bridge, charging into massed ranks of the enemy. Some are tussles of will, the prisoner and torturer issuing challenges and confronting each other with pain.

Some struggles are on life's broad canvas, open for the wide world to see.

But some are carried out in the dark places of the mind. Some battles we fight with ourselves, we fight a pain, a loss, a betrayal. Or we fight the battle that can never be seen by others, never understood when recalled and retold. These battles we forget, for when they are over, we look at the bright face of a new day and feel the fight could not have been that hard, we have made too much of it. We put it away.

But these battles are still majestic, the battles we fight in the fields of our mind, in the loneliness and darkness of the night.

Sally fought such a battle. Every bump in the road, every change of direction pushed the cloth closer to her air. She lay still, forced calm, her life was focused on a space of a few millimetres.

Please, oh, please, she prayed, don't let me die.

Chapter 20

As Isaac drove, Mokti was able to glance across at the big detective from time to time. He was just a big, ordinary, lumpy bloke, Mokti thought. I'd pass him in the street in a minute, just another cipher in the ranks of the grown-ups.

And now I'm sitting in his car and he's talking to me, asking for my help. This is so weird, he thought.

"What's on your mind, Mokti?" asked Isaac, navigating the city traffic with ease, sliding into side streets, muttering soft curses at other drivers. All automatic.

Mokti started, was this guy a mind reader? "Sorry, what?" he replied.

"I said," repeated Isaac, "What do you think, any ideas?"

"Me? Isaac, I'm a student, numbers, you know. You're the copper. I got no idea."

"I'm not asking you as a copper, you dill, I mean about the numbers and the clues. You're my expert, Mokti. Can you see any link between these deaths and what you know of Leonardo Fibonacci?"

Mokti had to think about that. He'd never been called an expert before, a nuisance, a waste of space, a drain on his father's wallet. But never an expert. "Look, Isaac, the Fibonacci sequence is about numbers, not people. Give me some numbers and I might have a shot at it but all I've seen is a body."

"Tell me about the sequence," asked the detective.

"Okay." Mokti spoke into his mind, the outside world receded as he explained. He saw the whiteboard, the computer screen, ran calculations as he spoke. From this other world, he spoke, "You start with two seed numbers, then add them up. This gives you the next number in the sequence. Then you add that number with the second number and the result is your fourth number. Each number is generated by adding up the two previous numbers. Once you have the two seed numbers you can go to town."

He stopped and looked at Isaac. They were pulling into a parking lot, a large sign dominated the entrance, the sign of LifeCorps.

"What's it good for?" asked Isaac.

The question puzzled the student. "What's it good for? Well, it's just neat, you know. Pretty cool, huh, the way it just pops along. Elegant."

Turning the car off Isaac turned to Mokti and said, "I think you mathematicians have way too much time on your hands. Come on." Before leaving the car Mokti grabbed his one piece of luggage, being around Isaac it seemed like a good idea to be prepared to move on quickly.

Entering the foyer Isaac tried once more, "You mean to say this sequence is just a game, it's got no real use. You just do it, for," he struggled for the right word, "for fun?"

They reached the main reception desk as Mokti replied, "Of course it's fun, mate, it's maths. Real maths." Isaac looked at his companion and waited for more explanation. Mokti stood gazing happily at his friend.

The receptionist cleared her throat, feeling she was the one who was intruding, "Can I help you, gentlemen?"

After one final look at Mokti, Isaac realised nothing more was coming from him. He turned to the receptionist, identified himself and said, "We're here to see Mr Brodie," Isaac saw the name tag, "I called earlier, Elizabeth, I think he's expecting us."

Elizabeth had enough people skills to recognise this man had made an effort to identify her as a human being, not a faceless clone. Even knowing the technique, she felt warmed by the effort and smiled up at the big detective, "Certainly, Detective, if you would just wait a moment, I'll give him a call."

Very soon afterwards an elevator chimed and a fit looking man emerged, walking towards where Isaac and Mokti sat on a comfortable lounge. He was dressed in a lightweight suit, well cut and wearing an expensive shirt and elegant tie. When Isaac saw him, he nudged Mokti and they all stood up for the introductions.

"Jim," said Isaac, "this is Mokti Setiawan, he's helping with the case. I've asked him along for his expert opinion, maybe he can spot some clues I miss."

Mokti felt embarrassed standing in the foyer talking to this expensively dressed man. He managed to say, "Um...yeah...g'day," before sliding to a vocal halt. He wished he had worn shoes instead of sandals, wished he had put on some good clothes, wished he had the chance to clean up properly after his bus trip. He wished life would give him some warnings about situations so he could be better prepared. All this went through his mind, thoughts fleeting through his subconscious. When his mind got to the last point he smiled inwardly, relishing the irony of his conclusion; life doesn't give warning, it just happens. Some of his thinking made its way to his face and he broke into a gentle smile.

Jim Brodie was good at reading people, being responsible for the welfare of several hundred employees had made him a specialist. He saw the smile on the young man and felt warmed, here was someone who had a good heart. "How are you, Mokti?" he asked, extending his hand, "Always happy to see someone giving Isaac advice."

The handshake was warm and genuine, no sense of caste or status, no hint of superiority. Mokti relaxed, "He's a bit of a worry," he said.

"Let's go upstairs and you can tell me all," said Jim. Together the three men made their way back to the elevators and rode upwards; standing side by side within the small box, the three men made small talk - at least Jim and Mokti spoke, Isaac just leaned against the side wall and wished for bed. "Where did you meet Isaac?" asked Jim.

Standing between the two men Mokti again felt the unreality of the situation, "I'm just off a bus from Perth, Jim, been on it all night. Anyway, the bloke I yarned to on the way over, turned out to be a bit of a ratbag. When we arrived, we went to his place to freshen up, have a drink, you know how it is. Turns out it wasn't his place, belonged to his ex-wife but this dropkick couldn't accept the finality of it all. She comes home, sees us there on the couch with ex-hubby drinking beer and dropping cigarette ash all over the place and goes ballistic. Next thing I know the big fella here comes through the door with a military-grade cannon pointed at me. Since then, I've been with him chasing some psycho nut job who's killing people and cutting them up." When he stopped there was silence in the car as it continued to rise.

Mokti had listened to himself relate the events of the last few hours, remembering some of the phrases for later. He was sure there would be a later; this was a story he was going to have to tell a few times. The folks back in Perth would want to know; his mum was going to have a heart attack when she heard about her baby boy and the big city.

Jim Brodie continued to stare at the closed elevator door, facing the front as all travellers do, Mokti's voice had told his story with strange inflections, as if he was hearing it himself for the first time. He sounded surprised, surprised to be in such events.

"Isaac's a fun guy to be around, that's for sure," said Jim. The elevator pinged quietly and the doors slid apart. "Come into the office, I'll see about some coffee." The three men walked through another entrance space, complete with a reception area. Behind an expensive workstation sat a competent looking female, well dressed and calm; just the sort of guardian an executive needs to filter out the constant stream of demands for his time. At a smaller console to one side sat a young man, gazing into a computer screen and glancing from papers to keyboard. All was subdued, quiet and workmanlike. "Alice," said Jim, stopping at the desk, "this is Mokti." He placed a warming hand on the young man's shoulder, "He's wrecked. Needs a shower and some breakfast. Do you reckon you could organise things for him?"

Mokti had a sense of disbelief, a shower, food! Sounded like heaven. Alice looked up at Jim and then to Mokti, "Dear me, you do look done in. Edward and I will look after him." She looked past them both to where Isaac stood, "Is that you, Isaac?" she asked.

"Hello, Alice. G'day, Ted," mumbled the big man.

The young man at the terminal had stopped working and greeted Isaac with a smile. Alice continued "Edward, pop along and get some towels and soap. Mokti, if you follow Edward, he will show you where you can freshen up. Do you need a change of clothes?"

What sort of a world was this? thought Mokti. He could feel the expensive tone of the room, the wall colours, the decorations, everybody here moved in a far different world from him. He shrugged to indicate his bag and said, "No, I'm right. Got some gear in here." He turned to look at Edward who was giving him a warm smile, a welcome.

"We'll look after you, mate," said Edward.

As Mokti moved off after a smiling and chatty Edward, he heard Alice start in on his companion, "You're a menace, Isaac. Look at you, heavens, are they working you too hard down at that police station? DO you want me to ring them and give them a piece of my mind? Don't they know how to look after people, heavens above!" The voice trailed off, mumbles from Isaac reminded Mokti of a small boy coming to dinner with a dirty face. Isaac moves in interesting circles, he thought.

"In here, mate," said Edward as he opened a door into the executive washroom. It was a large, clean area, with discrete doors leading to rooms for showers and other bodily functions. Edward moved passed him, opened a cupboard and pulled out a large towel, soaps and shampoo. "This is how the other half lives," smiled the young man as he held out all the necessary ingredients for a welcome shower. Mokti was beyond being stunned. He took the offered equipment, his brain turned off.

"Come on back to the reception area when you're done, I'll organize some food. Any dietary requests?"

"No pork, stuff like that. I'm a Muslim," Mokti replied, dazed. Edward left and Mokti moved into the shower, rehearsing another conversation he could have with his father.

> Hello, Dad, got off the bus all right. Caught up in a domestic dispute, had a gun pointed at me, saw a woman who'd been cut up, watched the police interrogate a bloke I captured. Now I'm in the executive suite of a big corporation having a shower, then I'll pop out and have breakfast with one of the bigwigs and a new mate, a copper.

How was your day?

HE REJOINED ISAAC AND Jim in a large office. On a small table was a range of breakfast foods, coffee and juice towards which he moved with the anticipation of the hungry young. The other two men were looking at a screen on Jim's desk and having an intermittent conversation. As Mokti sat eating the food he watched Isaac move to a printer and retrieve several sheets of paper. The big man looked at it, then said, "I've filled Jim in on the background, these are the details of each of the deceased, both men and women. Everyone who has a LifeChip has their data recorded. Have a look at this and see if anything makes sense, Jim thought we should look just at the data stored on a LifeChip. The information on this sheet would easily be retrieved by anyone with a Chip Reader.

He kept a page for himself before handing one of the sheets to Mokti who asked, "Isn't this sort of stuff confidential?" His mouth chewed a mouthful of croissant as his eyes moved casually from Isaac to Jim, "You know, privacy and that stuff?"

Jim Brodie answered while looking directly at Mokti, "Highly confidential."

Mokti stopped chewing, coffee cup paused halfway to his lips. He flicked his eyes to Isaac who had sat on the small couch, the big man returned his gaze without saying a word. A small pause developed. Swallowing a mouthful of food, the young man tried to regain composure; he looked back to Jim Brodie. The other man simply sat, waiting.

"Right," said Mokti.

From his couch, Isaac saw the young man struggle for sanity. He decided to rescue him from his moral storm. "It's all confidential, Mokti. When we need it for the courts, we'll come back with all the paperwork, but I need a head start. That bastard who took Sally won't wait. Jim and I have been around the block a few times, he trusts me." He levelled his best look at the young man, "And I trust you. You can't mention this situation to anyone, Jim's risking a bit here. Job, career, position." He waited a bit and then said, "Are you in?"

All the time, Jim Brodie sat watching the two men in the room, gauging reactions. From what Isaac told him, he was more than prepared to risk his own exposure to help another human being. Especially the sort of trouble that Sally was in. A life is worth more than a job and if Isaac trusted Mokti then that was good enough for him.

The young Muslim realised that yet again he was in a room with the grown-ups, and they trusted him. Him! He felt a surge of pride at being treated as an equal by these men, real men.

"No worries," he said.

Chapter 21

"Isaac says you think there might be a Fibonacci Sequence in there somewhere?" asked Jim.

"That's all I've got," replied Mokti. "If we can't spot some numbers then I don't know what use I'm going to be." He looked at the printout, "This is all names and addresses, date of birth and stuff. Nothing looks like a pattern."

"We need the seed numbers?" asked Jim.

Still examining the sheet Mokti replied, "I can't see any link, no straight run of numbers." On the sheet was listed each person's name, date of birth and date of implant. Someone had handwritten a word or two for ease of identification.

The list was:

Date of Birth Date of Implant

Sally Grant Feb 2, 2035 Feb 2, 2035

Beryl Wolters July 11, 2023 July 12, 2023 body in the bathtub

Ma'telle Caprisi Feb 1, 2019 Feb 5, 2019 Mama Luigi

David Mitchell March 2, 2021 March 3, 2021 man in alley

Mary Hodges Jan 1, 2017 Jan 1, 2017

Mary Ichku March 2, 2028 March 4, 2028 maid in apartment

Kim Nee Han October 22, 2030 October 22, 2030 nurse at Mama's

Isaac spoke from the couch, "I don't know what I'm looking for. What's a seed number?"

"A seed number starts the Fibonacci Sequence," replied Mokti, "two of them. The classic seeds are 1 and 1. To get the next number in the sequence you add the previous two numbers so the third number would be $1+1 = 2$. We now have 1, 1, 2. Make sense?"

"Yeah, right," said Isaac. Big deal, he thought. "So, the next number would be $1+2 = 3$? Is that right?" He scanned his sheet looking for any set of numbers representing the sequence so far. 1, 1, 2, 3. "Beryl Wolters has a date with the number 11. Is that any good?" he asked, "Could that be seen as 1 and 1 and the start of a sequence?"

"Yeah, sure," said Mokti, "now we need a 2. She's got another date for the implant, a 12, if you linked them up, we'd have 11, 12. Ignore the common 1 and we'd have the starting sequence."

Jim Brodie joined the conversation, "You're suggesting the day of birth and day of the implant are the common links. If you're right, then the next two numbers we're looking for would be 23 and 35." There was a pause as each man examined the data. "Anyone?" he asked.

"What about the years, there's a 23 in 2023?" asked Isaac.

"And there's a 35 in 2035," said Mokti. "No," he went on, "I don't like it. Too messy, not elegant enough."

Isaac was surprised, "What do you mean, 'elegant'? We're talking about numbers, not a fashion show!"

Jim stood up and began to pace back and forth, "Mokti's a real mathematician, Isaac. Numbers have their own beauty to some people, a certain grace. I'm willing to bet that Mokti is one of those folk." He turned to where the young man sat, "Am I right? You like a good looking equation?"

"Well, yeah, sure. Numbers are pretty cool, man. I mean, the stuff just sings when it all bubbles away. And you have to admit, the Mandelbrot Set is just it, I do so love that ol' Chaos Theory." He sat back with a smile, shifting his gaze from man to man.

A range of responses flooded through Isaac's mind, all with a common theme - this kid was seriously nuts. But looking into the transparently honest face of Mokti he could not bring himself to utter any of them. He sighed and asked, "So where does that leave us, are we looking for any old number or has it got to be good looking?"

Mokti had been scribbling on his sheet of paper, without stopping he said "I'm transferring all of the dates into a numeric format. But even so, they don't all feel right, I get a sense that some of them are linked but then these other numbers come and muddy up the data. Do we need all of these people?"

"LifeChips!" Jim surprised himself, the word leaping unbidden from his lips. "Isaac, didn't you say that only some of them had their LifeChips taken? Others were left behind?"

"That's right, Jim. LifeChips were taken from Mama Luigi, my Mary and the maid in the apartment today. The others were either left in place or removed and then dumped." Isaac didn't like to think what sort of mind would cut a LifeChip out and then casually drop it back into the body cavity, discarded as refuse. "Righto, cross out these people", he consulted his notebook. "Beryl Wolters, David Mitchell and Kim Nee Han – they all still had their chips."

Mokti had been making more marks, "If we just look at the missing LifeChip people, including Sally, then we have a subset of our original data."

"Subset, yeah. Right" murmured Isaac.

Both men watched their younger companion. Mokti would write on the paper, suck the end of the pencil, then his eyes glazed a little as he looked up and saw things only in his mind. This happened a few times before he finally leaned forward, his lips pulled back in a grimace. "It's almost there," he said through clenched teeth, "What's wrong... too much...Sally, you're the problem..." Then he sat up, "Got it!"

"We leave Sally out," he said, "and line the data up in the order of their deaths."

"That's Mary, Ma'telle Caprisi and the maid," said Isaac.

Mokti moved to Jim's desk where he grabbed a piece of notepaper and scribbled:

Date of Birth Date of Implant
Mary Hodges 1/ 1/ 2017 1/ 1/ 2017
Ma'telle Caprisi 1/ 2/ 2019 5/ 2/ 2019 Mama Luigi
Mary Ichku 2/ 3/ 2028 4/ 3/ 2028 maid in apartment
Sally Grant 2/ 2/ 2035 2/ 2/ 2035

"Now, if you just look at the dates of birth, we get 1, 1 for Mary; 1, 2 for Ma'telle Caprisi and 2, 3 for the maid. Of course, you have to use the European convention for writing dates, not the American method which puts the month first. It all makes sense, now."

Isaac had taken up a position that allowed him to look over Mokti's shoulder, the scrawl of numbers on the paper looked decidedly uninspiring. "But that's not the sequence, the Fibby thing," he said. "It starts with a 1, 1 from Mary but then it's all weird. You've got 1, 1, 1, 2, 2, 3."

"Ah, but" interposed Jim, "if we drop out the repeated numbers after the first two, we have 1, 1, 2, 3! The Classic Fibonacci Sequence! Well done, Mokti, I think you've cracked it!"

Mokti sat looking at the numbers, seeing them dance their weave in his head. "The repeated numbers are the link between victims, the next number would be 2+3=5. So, we have the repeated 3 and the new 5! Leonardo needs to find someone with the right date of birth, someone born on May 3rd!"

"And a woman," said Jim. "Look at the man's date of birth, 2nd March - he could be a contender with a 2/3. Do you think that's it, Isaac? Do you think he only targets women?"

"I dunno," replied the big man. His day just seemed to stretch on and on. Up all day yesterday on the job, then last night the confrontation with Sally in his house. Just last night! Impossible, he thought, couldn't have been just last night. The discovery of the bodies at Mama Luigi's, Alan Lassiter, the Great Wall. Sally missing, and the dead maid, still in uniform.

Uniform.

"There's more, all of his victims wore some sort of uniform. They're female and they wear a uniform" he said.

"What about Sally? What was she wearing?" asked Jim.

Isaac sagged, "Just ordinary clothes. No uniform." Damn, the link wasn't there after all, he sank back into the couch.

"But she does!" exclaimed Mokti, "she does wear a uniform. The picture, Isaac, the picture on her wall! She's in the Army Reserve!"

Isaac sat up. Was that it? He teased the idea around his head, running it through his Bullshit Detector, the one built by years of police work, by countless observations, by making a lot of bad judgements. "I think you're right, Mok," he said.

A pause developed, finally broken again by Isaac, "But I just don't know what good it does."

Mokti drew some more numbers, "If we're right about his sequence then we can predict the birth dates of all his next victims. They'd be the ones I just said, the 3rd of May and the 5th of August. After that, he has to stop because he'd need a set of numbers matching 5 and 13, but we don't have a thirteenth month. I suppose he could make the 13 be 12 + 1 and just roll over to the next January; go a bit longer but eventually, he'll run out of this sequence. The numbers will be too large. Could take a while, though."

"If he tips over into January for a victim, we'll be wall-to-wall bodies" muttered Isaac.

"I don't think he will, though," commented Mokti, "I don't think he'll keep going with this sequence."

"Why not" asked Jim.

"It's not elegant, almost cheating. No, if he's going to keep on looking for victims, he'll have to start another sequence, I don't think he'll just repeat the first one, that'd be mathematically boring."

The three men sat in silence for a while, each pursuing his own pathway through the problem. Jim stirred and said "But if Leonardo killed these women and left their bodies to be discovered, why did he take Sally? Why not just kill her and either take her chip or leave it like he did the others? And why did he kill the others, the man, the woman in the bathtub, the nurse?"

"Some of them would have been just in the wrong place at the wrong time," replied Isaac. "Murder motives are generally simple, aside from the psychopaths like Leonardo, most victims fall into two broad categories. Innocent bystander and victim of passion. I suspect that the man and the nurse at Mama Luigi's were with her when Leonardo called. He just killed the man, but he did check the LifeChip of the nurse."

"Was she in uniform?" asked Mokti.

"Yes," responded the detective, "but her date of birth didn't fit his pattern, the Fibonacci thing. He probably checked it and then just dropped it back into the body."

"Cold blooded bastard," murmured Mokti, "what about the woman in your bathtub?"

"Beats me. He'd obviously set it up beforehand, must have come during the day," replied Isaac. "Bill and Pat have sent some uniforms on a door to door in my area to see if anyone saw anything."

Jim spoke from behind his desk, "Bit hard to hide the fact you're breaking into a person's house and then taking a body inside."

"Not if it wasn't a body," said Mokti. The other two men looked at their young comrade with growing respect, they nodded for him to continue. "I mean," he went on, "it would have been easier to have the woman walk into the house and kill her there, rather than risk being seen dragging a corpse across the front step. He probably had her walk in under her own power – maybe it was by coercion, or he just tricked her."

Mokti couldn't believe what he was saying, calmly discussing the method of perpetrating one of the most violent acts one human being can do to another. "Am I a sicko, or what?" he asked the others.

"A human being has to be able to view some of the most appalling acts from some distance, otherwise the person would go insane," said Jim. "That's what your mind is doing, Mokti, it's thrown a mental lifejacket around your personality. We see it frequently downstairs in the recovery room, the next of kin viewing the growing clone of their recently deceased dear one. Until the LifeChip is uploaded from the deceased's body, the clone is just a blank slate; we used to let husbands and wives view the extraction of their spouse's clone from the final vat, but we were forever calling on counsellors. Tears, anguish, loud cries, resentment – and then there was the follow up feeling of rejection for the clone. They'd seen it 'born' and it obviously couldn't be their own dear husband or wife."

Jim shook his head, remembering his own second life and the subsequent reuniting with his wife and two boys. A difficult enough time already, how were we ever so stupid as to add more distress to people, he mused.

"A lot of marriages failed before we came to our senses."

"So, you're not a 'sicko', Mok," said Isaac. "Just normal."

Mokti looked across at his detective friend, how do you do it? he thought to himself. How do you see the sort of sights I've seen in the last few hours and stay sane? He gave Isaac a small smile, the big man saw it and recognized it for what it was. The friendship deepened.

Rubbing his face, Isaac asked the big question, "Back to Sally. If I'm right about the uniform thing then I want to go back to the Great Wall and check her clothes, see if her Army Reserve gear is there." He looked at Mokti, "What do you want to do, mate?"

"Can I come? I think I know why Sally was taken, I also believe she's still alive" said Mokti.

Jim reached into his desk drawer and pulled out another mobile phone, he gave it to Mokti and said, "Use this to call me, my private numbers are in memory, also this office. If you need any more numbers, any more data - just call me. Now, what about Sally?"

"Her birth date," replied the young man. "2/ 2. When he finishes his first run of victims, he'll use Sally to start the next Fibonacci Sequence. And then he'll start another with 3/3 and another with 4/4." Mokti followed Isaac out of the office.

"Lots of bodies still to come."

Chapter 22

The vehicle slowed and stopped, Sally continued to fight her war for calm, the threads of the gag tickled her throat, and her discomfit was extreme.

After a short pause, she felt the car slowly move forward, there was a slight jostle as it passed over a bump. Probably a speed bump, she thought. By casting her hearing into a wide net, she was able to distract herself from the unpleasantness of the gag, she was intrigued by what she sensed.

The vehicle moved slowly, far slower than previously. She felt they may be in a driveway or some parking lot. Someplace which needed a slow speed and gentle turns. Occasionally the car would stop and then move off again.

It came to another halt and she heard the door open and close, there was a subtle shifting of weight as someone left the vehicle. Leonardo, she thought, he's probably coming around to get me now. Her terror began to surge again, the darkness and physical distress combining to vault her once again into near panic. Another battle.

The minutes ticked by, and she was left alone.

And then she changed. Lying there in her world of anguish, she changed. Some part of her mind, her inner self spoke up. She was fed up with riding this rollercoaster of emotions, she had had enough of being the victim of her fears. If Leonardo killed her then so be it, there was nothing she could do about that. She had no control over his actions, all she could control was herself and her reactions.

So far, she had not done a good job of that, she thought. Isaac, Alan Lassiter and now Leonardo had subjected her to situations in which her emotions ruled her body. Her apprehension had magnified the event.

Right, she thought, that's it. I've had a gutful. You can do what you want, she told the world, but I'll decide how I deal with it.

The gag still tickled, the bonds still hurt, but her mind calmed. She knew she had not transformed herself into a warrior woman, knew that she had not suddenly acquired the ability to go hand to hand with Leonardo, that was for the movies.

And it wasn't resignation, she wasn't lying there like a limp rag, all wrung out and forlorn. No, dammit, I don't like it and I will not give in, not to Leonardo, Alan or even bloody Isaac. Bring it on, dipstick, she thought.

She heard her door open and felt her small room expand, noises from outside were different. She decided not to panic.

"How de do, Sal," said the voice of Leonardo "All well?" The vehicle rocked as he moved to sit beside her. "Let's get you sitting up, see what's what, shall we?" After some moments of pain as circulation returned to bound limbs, she had her hands shackled behind her back.

But she was now sitting, and the hateful gag had been removed.

"Got some water here, old thing. Open wide and I'll squirt a few drops in," said the voice. She did as instructed and luxuriated in the blessed wetness, the cool liquid flowing down her tortured throat. "I'm leaving the blindfold on for now but I'm happy to forgo the gag. That is if you promise not to scream. Not that anyone would hear you, of course, but I'm sitting right beside you and I'm sure I would find the experience both uncomfortable and annoying. What do you say, Sal, gag or no gag? Lord, I sound like a game show host."

"No gag, please," said Sally.

"And manners, too. Well done, Miss Grant, now I wonder if you could indulge me a little. Were you really born on the second of February?"

Sally was surprised by the question. She paused before replying, trying to fathom the reason for it. "Yes," she slowly answered.

"Jolly good," said Leonardo, "bit of a stroke of luck. And you're in the Army Reserve? How very militant of you. Tell me, Sal, are you a Leader of Men with rank or just a grunt, a footslogger, one of the Great Unwashed?" She felt the capital letters embedded in the slightly mocking voice. A voice she was beginning to detest.

Sally shifted her posture slightly, wriggling her toes and fingers to keep the blood flowing. What was the point of these questions? She wondered. Was there a pass/fail mark? "Everyone is trained as a rifleman, but I'm also a driver," she responded. "I'm just rank and file."

"Excellent, well done, that man." A slight pause before Leonardo spoke again, "Uniform at home?"

She nodded her affirmation while her mind sought to understand the reasons for his strange questions. Deciding a straightforward approach was the only way she would find out more she asked, "Why do you want to know?"

"Ah, Sal, let's keep a bit of mystery in our relationship, shall we? Don't want to reveal all just yet. And you picked up another musketeer for your gallant band; saw him as I was driving off with you. Isaac must have an extra dose of charisma to be able to attract such followers. A gentleman of colour, as they used to say. Well, bring 'em on, Sherlock, I say. And what's his name, my dear?"

"Mokti," Sally replied, immediately regretting telling this evil man anything. "What are you going to do with me?" She was scared beyond anything she had ever known, a fear that didn't go away, it just went on and on. She wanted her mum. But now her fear was crashing against a new rock, the rock of her rejection as a victim. It crashed, and was quieted.

"Please, Sal, try to be a bit more creative in your line of questioning. Can we please skip all the usual drivel – "Where are we? Are you going to kill me?" – B grade melodrama at best."

She sensed Leonardo move a little and then felt a small prick in her arm. "Time for beddy-byes, I have a few errands to run. When I come back, we'll see what we can do to make your stay a bit more comfortable. Perhaps a change of clothes is called for."

The anger surged despite her earlier deliberations about self-control, then it was washed away as the drug swept through her body, plunging her down, back into the abyss.

But this time it was a silent scream of rage, not despair.

ISAAC AND MOKTI PULLED into the car park at the Great Wall, got out and held a brief conference. Mokti looked long and hard at his companion, noticing again the tiredness, the fatigue that seemed to emanate from every pore of the big detective.

Gesturing towards a small cluster of shops that serviced the tenants of the housing estate, Mokti said, "I'm going over to that pharmacy, Isaac, and get some painkillers. Hanging around you can give a man a major headache. You want anything?"

"No, I'm good," replied the detective, leaning on the car. He looked at the grey and sullen sky, the overcast blanketing the day in a bleak overcoat. Aren't I the cheery one, he thought. Heaving himself erect he shook himself into alertness, rearranging his mind to be ready for the next round of surprises.

I'm so tired, he thought, then he straightened and had a good talk to himself. Smarten up, dopey, people need you. Besides, you can always rest when you're dead.

He watched his young companion saunter across the road to the shops, again marvelling at Mokti's ability to stroll. He drew his pistol and began to climb the stairs to Sally's floor.

As Mokti stepped from the road back onto the footpath, he sidled through a gap between two parked cars, both vans. One sported a sign indicating it came from the pharmacy and was willing to do home delivery. Very willing, judging by the size of the letters and signs covering every surface. The other van was a Medical Transport Vehicle with a pretty girl sitting in the driver's seat; Mokti tried to gaze at her without being blatant and like so many other young men before him he tripped on the kerb. The girl ignored his embarrassed look and weak smile; and again like so many young men Mokti wasn't sure whether he preferred to be ignored or to have a beautiful woman see him as a clumsy oaf.

When he reached the self-opening doors, Mokti collided with another man exiting the shop. They stumbled together and did that little dance people do when trying to work out which way to go around each other. The small collision had dislodged the man's sunglasses.

The other man was of middle height and dressed in some sort of white uniform top. Because Mokti had his eyes down – looking at his feet, as usual, his father would say - he noticed that the man's hand holding a pharmacy bag had three of its fingers fused together. He looked up and said, "Sorry, mate."

The two men drew apart and rethought their passing strategy. Their eyes met and Mokti looked into two filmy pupils, both eyes were almost opaque. He pulled his glance away in embarrassment, sensing a flash of something cross the man's face. The stranger seemed to be surprised at more than just the collision with another pedestrian. Mokti's gaze hit upon another physical defect - the man's left ear. It was only half formed, as if the flesh had melted into the skull. The man bent down and retrieved his sunglasses.

Mokti stepped to one side to let the man pass, horribly ashamed of himself and the way he had dealt with another human being's deformity. The man stepped out of the shop, moving to the van with the red light. Before unlocking the door, he paused and turned back to the open doors of the pharmacy and spoke to Mokti.

"Oh, Mokti," he said, "be a good chap and give my regards to Isaac." He opened the car door, entered the vehicle and looked out the open passenger window towards the young Muslim. Mokti had still to enter the shop who had still to enter the shop. "By the way, Sally says 'hi'." The pretty girl had started the van's engine and the vehicle accelerated away.

Mokti was stunned, frozen into immobility. Watching the van drive away, his mind drew the threads together and realised what or who he had just seen. He had one final look at the departing vehicle before running back across the road yelling. "Isaac! Isaac!"

The detective had only just reached the floor containing Sally's apartment when he heard Mokti calling his name. Looking over the exterior balcony he could see the young man running back across the road, calling his name. The big man was interested to see that Mokti could move quickly if he wanted to, and that led to an intriguing question.

What had made Mokti so worked up that he broke into a run?

Leaning over the balcony he called down, "What's up, Mok?"

"The van!" Mokti called up, "The van!" Isaac followed the outstretched finger but could see no van, except for the one parked in front of the pharmacy.

"I see it," he replied. "What about it, do you want a home delivery?"

Mokti leaned over and rested his hands on his knees, the brief sprint and yelling had taken away his wind. What was Isaac talking about? Home delivery? Looking back, he saw only the van outside the shop, the one carrying the stranger had disappeared.

Straightening up he cupped his hands over his mouth and called out "I think I've just seen Leonardo!"

BY THE TIME ISAAC HAD bolted down the stairs, Mokti had recovered his composure. He told of colliding with the man at the shop, adding the physical deformities of hand, ear and possibly eyes to the description. The detective had already called for support and it soon arrived in the form of two marked police cars and an unmarked vehicle containing Patricia Lee and Bill Harris.

They came up as Isaac was questioning Mokti, "Can you describe the van, make and model, colour? Any markings?" No response. "Come on, Mokti, you must remember something!" the detective spoke with a fierce heat, with the unforgiveness of those towards people who should know the answer. "Use your bloody brain, man!" he finished, stress making small flecks of spittle fly from his mouth.

"Steady on there, Big Fella," murmured Harris. "Isn't he on our side?"

But Mokti agreed with Isaac, he should know stuff like that. He was a man, wasn't he? Can't all real men identify a car down to its make and year level, just by looking at its brake lights? He was useless.

"I'm sorry," he kept saying, "I'm so sorry, it just happened so fast. The man, what he said, the van. I couldn't take it in. I'm sorry." He should have crash tackled the guy before he even got in the car, he should have grabbed him, punched him, thrown him to the ground. He should have done something! But all he did was stand and stare, mouth open, totally useless. What sort of a man are you, he questioned himself. Call that a reaction, you just let him laugh at you and walk away. All the time in the world and you just stood and watched.

Patricia had been around men enough to recognize the signs, and she also knew there was nothing she or anyone else could say to make it better. Saying anything to console him would only make it worse, he would feel he was being treated like a child. So, she put her arm around his shoulders and just sat still; she was with him, she was a friend.

"Yeah, you're right, Bill. Come on, Mok, go over it again for these two. One more time," said Isaac.

So Mokti spoke, sitting on the bottom steps of the apartment block. Patricia beside him, Isaac a brooding presence just off to the front, pacing up and down, and Bill Harris, standing over the seated man, asking soft questions, teasing out information.

Uniformed officers stepped around them and through them, Isaac asked some to check for any signs of entry into Sally's apartment, others he asked to look for her army uniforms and to collect the photograph on the wall.

After going over the events for what seemed the hundredth time, Bill asked "What about the number plate on the van? Did you see any part of it?"

"Sure," replied the young man, "I saw it all. Clear as a bell, but I can't remember it. It had three letters which could be anything and then three numbers. Don't know them, either."

Patricia spoke, "So, our mystery man is in a white van, number plate ABC 123." She was trying to lighten the mood, but it was like fighting a bushfire with a water pistol.

"No, couldn't be 123," muttered Mokti, absently.

"Sure it could, kid," said Harris. "Could even be 666, the devil's number."

"No, not 666" said Mokti, a little life creeping into his voice, "but the first number could be a 6. Can someone give me a pen and paper?" he asked.

Patricia dug her notebook out and passed it to the young man. Mokti turned to a blank page and started writing numbers, three to a pattern. Looking over his shoulder Patricia asked, "Whatcha doin', sweetie?"

He mumbled his reply as he wrote, "Looking for the right pattern... the right shape..."

After a few moments, he stood up with the pad in hand, stretching it out at arm's length he squinted at the sheet and decided, "I think this is it. I think the numbers on the plate were 647. No idea what the letters could be but I'm pretty sure that these are the numbers. Probably." Pause. "Possibly."

"How do you know?" asked Harris, "You've just gotten through telling us you couldn't remember anything."

"Nothing specific, but I remember the feel of the numbers, their shape. And these numbers feel right," responded the young mathematician.

"They feel right?" queried Harris, exasperated beyond comprehension. How can numbers feel?

Mokti couldn't explain it, living with numbers the way he did gave a person a sense of the flow of forms, a 3 did not look like a 6, 7 could never be an 8. Even though he had not seen the number plate he had subconsciously picked up the shape of the three digits. But how to explain it to a non-mathematician?

Isaac stirred, moving forward he held a hand out to the Mokti, helping him to his feet. "Elegant, Bill, the numbers were elegant." He said, smiling at his young friend, "That right, mate?" he asked.

"Got it in one, Isaac," Mokti replied, relieved and grateful for his friend's understanding.

They both smiled at Bill Harris who mumbled, "Idiots."

Patricia was on her phone, she closed it and said, "I've asked for a motor vehicle search. Any white van with that license plate, with those lovely numbers." She hugged Mokti from behind, squeezed him and gurgled, "My clever, clever man."

"Let's go eat," suggested Isaac, "Bill, bring the lovebirds."

Chapter 23

The local shops boasted a small café and the group headed for a booth; Patricia picked up the uniformed officers' reports before they left the Great Wall. The café was a long and narrow room with a serving bench running down the left-hand wall. The booths ran down the right-hand side and complemented the row of stools bolted to the floor in front of the serving bench. Menus in hard plastic cases sat erect on each table, clustering with a group of condiments for mutual protection.

When the three detectives and Mokti entered, the five customers on the stools flicked a glance in their direction. One of the seated men stood up and exited the café, avoiding brushing past the police, head down.

Mokti felt the looks, he was used to strangers examining him, but usually it was from a sense of prejudice and bigotry. Everyone these days, it seemed, wanted to check his terrorist credentials. He was even used to people getting up and leaving the way the recent departee had left the room, but again, there was a difference. When he was alone, he would often overhear a derogatory remark, just a mumble but enough to hurt. People leaving would brush past and sometimes jostle. Young white men were the worst, although anyone with a southern Mediterranean completion always gave him a cause for concern.

But that was not the feeling from the room today. Today, when they entered, his social radar picked up the scanning, the judgements. But there was a very healthy presence of wariness in the reactions. People lowered their profiles, pulled into themselves, sent out the message that they were just sitting there, not doin' nuthin'.

Sliding into a booth Patricia also felt the room's assessment of the group. She asked Mokti "Feel it? Even though we're in plain clothes there are parts of the city that can smell a copper. Might as well wear a big sign." She reached down and held the young man's hand, squeezing it, sending a very clear message to the room. The message said, "He's with us, one of us. Not a prisoner."

Bill and Isaac missed it all, they'd hit too many rooms to feel anything different, but they heard and saw Patricia's words and gestures, were grateful that one of their team was on the ball. They slid into a booth, picked up the menus, Isaac again slumping against the wall.

"Looking a bit crook there, Isaac," said Harris, "How long since you slept?"

"Woke up at six am yesterday, did my shift. Haven't seen a bed since." The big man yawned prodigiously and gazed at the menu without seeing anything.

"Oh, Isaac," said Patricia, "you must be exhausted. Poor man, why don't you go home and put your head down? You're not as young as you used to be and these sort of days can take it out of you." Mokti was impressed by Patricia's care of her colleague, she had looked directly at Isaac as she spoke, her face full of concern.

Harris joined in, "Pat's right, mate. We're a lot younger and fitter, we can handle it. Just look after yourself, get a good hot meal into you and then head off."

"Maybe have a long hot bath," suggested Patricia.

"A glass of warm milk will help you sleep," murmured Bill.

"Tuck yourself in, snug as a bug in a rug."

"You need your rest, poor old fella."

Mokti had lost track of the conversation. Was Isaac really that old? He did look a mess but Mokti knew he was still a threat to bad people, he remembered how easily the big man had handled Alan Lassiter. Isaac's next words let him in on the secret.

"Piss off. Pair of bloody wankers, leave a man alone."

The two other detectives burst out laughing, Harris said, "You big girl's blouse. Anyone'd think you were doing it tough. Come on, let's eat."

As they ate, Isaac and Mokti filled in their comrades on their deductions about the Fibonacci Sequence, uniforms and Sally's predicament. "Is that why you wanted to know about her uniform?" asked Patricia, "Do you think he wanted to dress Sally up and start the next sequence with a 2, 2 female in uniform? That's why he came back here?"

Isaac bit into his burger, "Makes sense to me, it would mean Sally is safe until he runs out of his current batch of victims. Did you find out what he bought at the pharmacy?" A trickle of juice ran down his chin, so he put the burger back on the plate and wiped himself with a napkin.

"Sedatives," replied Patricia, "He had ID with him, and a prescription for painkillers and some heavy-duty knock-out junk. We're checking the ID, but I wouldn't bank on it being for real." She was eating the café's version of a Caeser salad, picking disconsolately at sad lettuce swimming in a sea of bottled dressing. "Who's idea was it to come here, anyway?" she muttered.

"But why uniforms?" asked Harris, ignoring his partner's question "And why females?"

The big detective shrugged, "Beats me. But the guy's a nutcase; maybe he had a bad experience with a nurse when he was a baby. Matron smacked his bottom too hard."

"He sure looked a mess," put in Mokti, "fingers glued together, no ear and those milky eyes."

Isaac looked at Harris, "Bill, what about Flannery's hand? It's fused because he's on his last life. Reckon this guy's in the same boat?"

Harris thought back to the morning's interchange with the big desk sergeant; it was true, he thought, fused fingers were a very common outcome from a second regeneration. "We could check that, too. Reckon your mate at LifeCorps can get us a list of second regeneration clones with that list of deformities? Sounds like Leonardo won the lottery for regen deformities. I know a guy with the ear Mokti described but that's all he's got. Never heard of the eye one, though."

"And how does he know what women have the birthdays that he wants, especially ones in uniform?" asked Patricia.

They continued eating in silence, condemned to play catch up with the bad guys, frustrated by their inability to predict his next move or fathom a pattern.

And until they could do that, more people would die.

YVONNE STOOD ON THE edge of the footpath watching the front door of the hotel. Her partner stood on her right, tall and gangly; they made an interesting contrast for the evening patrols. Streetlights were beginning to come on, the open door to the public bar began to develop the welcome glow so beloved of publicans. Darkness hid the poor carpets, bad paint jobs and sad atmosphere of a daytime drinking hole. The night allowed for shiny lights, flashing neon and the perception of noise and excitement needed to attract the casual drinker looking for a haven from a stressful day.

"Let's give it half an hour then swing back," suggested her partner, the senior member of the team. "We'll stroll through the bars and see if any underage kids are trying to sneak in."

"Yeah, righto, Josh," replied Yvonne. The two police officers turned and began their regular beat, one of the city's night areas, a place for people to be. A place for predators to hunt. She scanned the people around her, noting those who smiled a greeting, ignoring those who gave her a look of hate and suspicion. Being a police officer carried with it the dislike of a large sector of the public, you either learned to live with it or got out. Walking a beat was not the place for someone needing their self-esteem boosted. So, she ignored those who glared, concentrating rather on those who looked away or the smaller number whose greeting was a bit too hearty.

SALLY AWOKE ON A LOW cot, her hands secured by strong rope and intricate knots; the rope led to metal shackles embedded in the concrete of the floor. Looking up, she saw a figure dressed in white, sitting on a stool, hunched over, back towards her. Her awakening caused small noises, a foot scuffing the concrete floor, a rustle of clothes, sounds both small and loud. The figure went still, her mouth dried. She could not avert her eyes from the white clad back as it straightened, slowly becoming erect. The head came into view, then the hair, brown and slightly mussed.

Sally lay with her head pulled off the cot, her neck muscles stood out like cords, shoulders pushed up, eyes unbreakably fastened to the other figure in the room. His head turned, the entire body swivelling on the low stool – not once during all of these movements had Sally moved, she wasn't on the cot, her concentration was fixed on the slowly revealing figure, she lived on the edge of her vision.

"Evening, Sal."

She twitched, causing the shackles to jingle; she realised her right leg had every muscle tensed, trying to drag the body to freedom. She relaxed the limb, breathed again and asked "Leonardo?"

The figure smiled. "Bit of a hoot, that name, don't you think? No, my name isn't Leonardo, old girl, it's Joshua. Very biblical." he said. He stood and stretched, yawned and spoke again, "I'm about to head out again, old girl, got a thousand things to do. Must see a man about a dog, that sort of thing. Do you think you'll be all right here by yourself for a while? Won't be too long but there's this absolutely faaabulous young policewoman I simply must see."

As he spoke the man was collecting some items from the workbench and placing them in a small brown shoulder bag. He lifted it and said, "Pinched this idea from you, so useful, isn't it? Do you know, I've never been happy with carrying a briefcase but where does a man put those odds and ends he needs for a day's work? You know the sort of things I mean - pens and papers, lunch, gun, sharp knife, that sort of thing. Then I saw your shoulder bag and thought, 'the very thing', so I popped out and bought this jazzy little number. You like?"

Sally sank back onto the cot but kept her head turned to Joshua, "What are you going to do to me?" She regretted the question immediately, he ignored her.

He closed the lid of a small laptop, looked at it in judgment before coming to a decision. "Might just leave that here," he muttered, pushing the computer to one side of the work desk. "And really, Sal," he said, "this? This is your weapon of choice?" He was holding her wand-shaped Taser, waving it the air as if casting spells. "It just won't do, child." He took the wand in both hands and snapped it in two, throwing the pieces to the floor.

"Joshua!" Sally cried.

He moved to the door and gave Sally a little wave, she noticed the fused fingers. "You'll be fine, old girl," he said, "there's even a change of clothes over there – we'll tidy you up when I get back." He opened the door and stepped through.

Sally looked over at the pile of clothes, stacked neatly on a chair was an army uniform.

The door opened suddenly and Joshua's head reappeared. "Just a thought, Sal, feel free to scream and generally carry on. There's no one around for miles and I've done a great little job on the soundproofing – picked up some DIY tips from the web. Don't you just love YouTube? Toodle-pip."

The door shut, Sally was alone again.

PATRICIA THANKED THE uniformed officer and dismissed him. She returned to her seat in the café's booth and said "The drugs he bought could be used to keep a person sedated, maybe Sally's just in storage for a while. Her uniform's gone, but no sign of a break-in."

"He would have used Sally's keys," said Isaac, draining the last of his water. "Now we need to find a woman in uniform who was born on May 3rd. "

"Good luck with that," said Harris, standing up. A hopeless search, he believed, hundreds of women would fit that description. "Come on, Pat, let's head back to the station and try to find a match to Mokti's description of Leonardo." To Isaac, he asked, "What are you going to do?"

The big detective looked over to Mokti, "Dunno, got any bright ideas, clever dick?"

Mokti was a bit surprised at the nature of the question, it seemed Isaac was having a go at him. Then he realised the detective was treating him as an old friend. "Can we go back to LifeCorps and see Jim Brodie? I've got an idea of how Leonardo finds out which women are in uniform, but he would need to know specifically which women to research. For my idea, he would need to know the woman's birth date already, birth date and name. How would he find that out? Maybe Jim can help us."

Patricia was placing money on the plastic table in payment for the meal, when she had finished counting, she said, "Next meal's on you, Isaac." She turned to Mokti, "So how does our killer find out which women are in uniform, sweetie-pie?" Her voice was a low purr, and her hand gently caressed the young man's cheeks.

The other two detectives rolled their eyes and Harris took Patricia's arm, "Let's go, Short and Twisted." They left the cafe, Patricia play acting the parting from her heart's desire. As she reached the door, she changed persona again and put an arm over Harris's broad shoulders, giving her partner a gentle pat.

"Good question, Mokti, what's your idea?" asked Isaac. The two men moved outside and headed towards his car.

"Tell you back at Jim's place," replied the young man, he winked at Isaac and slid into the passenger seat. Isaac raised his eyes to heaven and prayed for deliverance from smart-alec students.

YVONNE NOTICED THE man standing near the pizza delivery van. Another jerk, she thought, wearing sunglasses after dark was such a pose. He looked up and saw her watching him. Rather than look away quickly as she expected the man gave her a small wave. He started walking towards her.

Yvonne glanced around until she saw her partner, Josh. He was speaking to a small group of teenagers, across the street, the group were all dressed in the standard goth colours of black with metal accessories. Feeling safer she stood her ground and waited while Mr. Sunglasses came up, "Good evening, sir" she said.

"And a good evening it is, Officer Armstrong," said the man. He halted about a metre from Yvonne and stood easily, feet apart, hands in pockets, jacket unbuttoned over a designer shirt.

Yvonne was unreasonably annoyed over the use of her name, she knew that people could read her name tag and she was used to being called by name. Nonetheless, for some reason, she was a bit miffed by this stranger and his familiarity. "Can I help you, sir?" she asked.

The stranger smiled and took his hand out of his pocket, it was holding a gun. "You most certainly can," he said.

Chapter 24

Isaac pulled away from the kerb, desperately trying to think of some clue they might have overlooked. They passed the pharmacy where Mokti had collided with Leonardo and he jammed on the brakes, swerving his car off the road. Mokti jerked forward into his seatbelt, taken by complete surprise over the manoeuvre.

"You right, Isaac?" he asked. But his friend had already left the car and he was speaking to an empty seat. Looking back at the footpath he saw Isaac disappearing into the pharmacy. With a sigh he unbuckled himself and exited the car, by the time he entered the shop Isaac had begun questioning the clerk.

"The man we are interested in is wanted for questioning over a series of murders. Now, I understand he showed you an ID and gave you a prescription?" asked the detective.

The clerk, a woman of medium height with tired hair and motherhood on her features nodded. "That's right, but I told the officer this. And he recorded the details," she replied.

"What about the prescription, did he take that?" asked Isaac.

"No, but I showed it to the policeman and he took the details."

Hope flared in Isaac, "Do you still have that prescription?"

"No, the uniformed officers took all that. We kept copies," the clerk bent down and opened a drawer under the counter. "Here we are," she said "We've still got the details of the ID." She produced a small set of documents and laid them on the counter.

"Did he sign for the drugs?" asked Isaac. The woman nodded in agreement.

Isaac pulled on a pair of thin latex gloves before picking up the small pen attached to the counter by a thin chain, "Has anyone else handled this since he left?" he asked.

"Just the pharmacist and me," she replied, watching as the detective opened a small plastic bag labelled 'Evidence' and placed the pen inside. She was interested in what was happening, intrigued by the process of detection. Realisation dawned on her, "Are you thinking of fingerprints?" she asked.

"We might be lucky," muttered Isaac, writing the details on the evidence bag – description of contents, location and so on.

"Sorry, hon," said the woman, "but your bad guy was wearing gloves. He was dressed in clinical whites like you see people wearing at a hospital, and he had come from his little van with the light and sign. He looked like he was a health worker doing pick-ups and deliveries, we get them from time to time. A lot of them have to wear gloves when handling prescriptions, according to their company policy. I don't think you'll find anything except our prints."

Isaac deflated a little, he had hoped for a break, but this wasn't it. Mokti had watched the entire scene, had been excited about the prospect of identifying Leonardo but now that possibility evaporated.

"Can we use your computer, please?" he asked of the woman. Unsure of his status he glanced at Isaac before continuing, "It's police business."

The woman looked behind her at a younger woman standing behind a higher counter deeper in the shop. This was the pharmacist, seated ready to dispense all manner of pills and potions from the stacked shelves around her. She had heard the exchange and the question so when the clerk looked to her for permission she spoke up, "Sure," she said, "Come back here and you can use my terminal."

Mokti stepped through the gap in the front counter and, followed by Isaac, moved to the back part of the shop. He could see the shelves and displays from behind and a sense of childish delight crept over him. I can see all the secret places, he thought to himself.

Grow up, he groaned.

The pharmacist vacated her seat for the young man who sat at the terminal. The screen displayed the menu page for the dispensation of drugs. Mokti saw shortcuts for printing labels, stock availability as well as several keys that linked to various databases describing the effects of the entire pharmacopeia.

The young pharmacist leaned past him and pressed a few keys to exit the program and reveal the generic desktop. Mokti accessed the internet and then typed a short entry. Moments later the screen cleared with the home page of his selected site.

"You've got to be joking," said the pharmacist. "This is police business?"

Isaac stood behind his friend and looked at the screen, he trusted Mokti and so kept quiet despite agreeing with the misgivings of the woman beside him.

"This is just a guess, Isaac," said the youth, taking out the sheet of paper containing the names of all the victims he had been given at LifeCorps. "But if I'm right this is how Leonardo knows who wears a uniform." He typed in the name 'Sally Grant', and her birth date and pressed the Enter key.

On the screen appeared a picture of Sally and a set of short, snappy statements listing her likes and dislikes. Hobbies included Sally's membership in the Army Reserve with links to some more photos of her and her army comrades.

Going back to the Home page Mokti repeated the process for each of the murdered women. In each case, there was a reference to their job or a photograph of the victim in uniform.

"Bloody hell!" muttered Isaac softly, "What is this site, Mokti?"

Both the pharmacist and Mokti spoke at the same time, "Facebook."

The pharmacist continued, "You don't get out much do you, big feller? Everyone knows about Facebook, Instagram, Twitter and Snapchat - it's called social networking. Got me through High School and Uni," she sniggered.

"Leonardo would search for details of women with the appropriate birthdate," explained Mokti. "If he had that information then he was assured of finding at least one of them on these sites, a bit of a search would give him the necessary info about uniforms and even a rough idea if they lived in this city. It's all there, man." As he spoke, he was scanning the pages for the deceased women and, using the mouse for highlighting, he lit up data for each of the women concerning uniforms, their city of residence, work habits and other useful identifying information. On Sally's page was her business number, soliciting PI work.

Isaac felt more and more out of his time, he had heard of these sites but had never used them. The online media would occasionally beat up a piece about them, either defending their right to exist or decrying the dehumanising and invasive spirit of the internet. Whichever sold more views for that day.

"But why would anyone put such personal information on the Web?" he asked. "Nutcases can find anyone, this is a stalker's wet dream." He shook his head, not coping with new ways of communication.

The pharmacist patted him on the shoulder, "Yeah, it's not for everyone. Mainly 12-year-old girls and bored housewives having a fantasy." She paused, hearing her own words, "Oh, and Uni students. And singles. Lots of people use it, I think you're in the minority, detective."

"You got a page, Mokti?" asked Isaac. A few more keystrokes brought up the student's details and the big man leaned in to read.

Beside him, the pharmacist whistled, "You're in MENSA? Cool, me too." They shared a grin and Isaac could feel the woman becoming interested in his young friend. She continued to read "Maths, eh?" She pushed her hair back and leaned a little closer to the seated man, "Very hard to find a clever man. My name's Janice." She waited a few beats for Mokti to respond.

But she waited in vain. Mokti was a good and decent man with little experience of women and dating, he was a mathematician and a Muslim. His social life had left him with the grace and skill of a fourteen-year-old boy, limited in recognising signals. So, he responded the way he had since puberty.

He grinned a dopey smile and almost dribbled before giving an embarrassed chuckle.

Isaac rescued him, "Janice, this is Mokti, he's a consultant to the police department. That's me, the police department. Do you have a card or something in case we have to get back to you?"

Janice scribbled her name and number on the back of one of the pharmacy's cards and gave it to Isaac. She appreciated his sensitivity and grace, pity he was such a dinosaur, she thought.

Back in the car, Mokti reviewed his conversation, reliving the interchange with the pharmacist. Each time he did so he thought of witty comments, charming asides and sparkling conversational gambits. In his mind the pharmacist was swept away by his charisma, impressed by his intelligence and hanging on his every word. Mr. Cool, he thought.

But what did I do, he told himself, I sat there like a goof. Mr. Cool – ha! – more like Mr. Dork.

Turning to Isaac, he studied his companion. And he just cruises in and gets her phone number for himself, slick as you please. When will I get to be that smooth, he asked himself, I'm just a boy, out of my depth.

While still facing ahead, Isaac gave Mokti the pharmacist's card. "Here you go, sport. Might be useful for you when you get some spare time. You could do puzzles together, you know, being as how you're both intellectuals." He wasn't thinking about Mokti and the pharmacist, he was picturing a young woman imprisoned somewhere, a woman who had depended on him. A woman he had sworn to protect and keep safe. Another woman he had let down.

Sally.

A CHILL RAN THROUGH Yvonne as she looked down the barrel of the gun. A large silencer dominated the end of the barrel, its black hole huge; her eyes were fixed on this emptiness and the fear it brings for company. Inside her brain, the mind tried to recall the training, but she was struggling; her emotions were gibbering, pleading for mercy. Outwardly she remained still, her mouth slightly open, the descending night had taken on a richer texture, the darkness seemed to have a flavour, the lights had sound.

Her world came down to this moment.

"Good of you to stand still, Yvonne," said the stranger. "It is Yvonne, isn't it?" he asked. The gun was held close to his waist and, with his back to the street, it would appear that they were just having a chat, another in the unceasing list of conversations that a police officer has with Mr Public.

She nodded in response to the question. Slowly her brain was regaining control. Training said to obey the man with the gun, avoid heroics and wait for hostage negotiation. That was fine by her, the last thing on her mind was the need for action, it was all she could do to stop from falling down in a pathetic pile. Performing some sort of brilliant move that disarmed her assailant and kept her alive seemed impossible, she didn't even consider it.

"Excellent," said the man. "Now, Yvonne, you're going to be just fine, I'm not going to hurt you, I have no desire to do that." She almost wept with relief and joy. He wasn't going to hurt her, she felt absurdly grateful to him.

He continued speaking "I have a parcel I would like you to deliver to one of your detectives. A parcel and a message. I know you will have the parcel checked by the bomb squad and all those other forensic sorts of people. No problem there, the parcel is harmless, but it is important. Now, if you take delivery of this little chore, I can send you on your way. What do you say, do we have a deal?"

Yvonne opened her mouth to reply but only managed a croak. Swallowing she tried again, "I could do that."

Her radio beeped, the voice of her partner checking that all was well. Josh had seen the pair from across the street and had a sense of unease; by checking in he was giving her the opportunity to call for his help, they even had a code word which they could use if being coerced. It changed each shift but was announced at the briefing before every patrol. Tonight's word was 'three-pointer', the shift sergeant was a huge basketball fan.

The man wasn't surprised by the radio call, the brazenness of his actions, the very open and exposed nature of this conversation combined to give him a huge rush. The prospect of being so close to capture was a high unlike any he had experienced before, he was determined to repeat the sensation. And repeat it he would, the concept of capture was not a notion he considered. This game was just such fun.

"Let him know you're fine," said the man. "I know about the code words so please don't say 'three pointer'. Your shift sergeant should follow a real game like football, not this Nancy-boy dribbling game." He watched the shock hit her face, enjoyed the sense of dominance he had and the consequent feeling of powerlessness from Yvonne. He knew things!

Yvonne's hand had begun to move automatically to her radio after Josh called in. When the man spoke and revealed his knowledge of their secret words, her hand faltered before resuming its journey to the transmit button. "No problems, Josh. I need a bit of privacy, though. I think this guy could be a useful informer about those underage kids. Better stay on that side of the road." She let her hand fall back to her side, brushing her holster on the way down.

The man noticed the movement and the nearness of her weapon. Oh, this was getting better and better. She had a gun! She could shoot him! His breathing became shallow, he felt his heart beat faster with the thrill. "Good thinking, Yvonne. Underage kids, indeed! Yes, I think you should get on top of that, and the sooner the better. Now, about your gun. Best leave it alone, don't you think? Any problems and I will shoot you first, probably several times in the stomach. What do you think are the chances of having kids with those sorts of wounds? That's if you survive."

Again, fear threatened to engulf Yvonne. She did want to have children, she loved the notion of raising a family. To lose that opportunity would give her life no meaning, leaving her desolate and barren. Barren. The very word was a chill, a cold and lonely place. She nodded her agreement and asked "Look, I'll do what you ask, no problems there. Now, where's this package? What do you want me to do?"

The man had known about her love of children, her desire for a family. Gotta love the internet, he thought. "Just around the corner is a car," he said "We need to go there together, and I'll give you the package. You will have to open the rear door to get it. After that I will ask you to handcuff yourself; this will stop you from using your radio and give me time to drive off. The car's stolen, of course, so feel free to give out licence plates and that sort of thing. Now give your partner a story, I like the informant angle, play that up."

Yvonne did as instructed and Josh watched them walk off together. He wasn't unduly alarmed, even though they shouldn't split up, the job sometimes meant there were times when they were out of each other's sight. He'd give it a five count and then start after them, just in case.

Around the corner, Yvonne was surprised to see a small pizza delivery van. Perhaps her package was just a pizza! Was this some sort of joke? She wondered. Was Josh setting her up? Pranks were part and parcel of the policeman's lot, and her current posting had placed her in the company of some very creative people. She generally gave as good as she got but she wouldn't be surprised if Josh was behind this prank, it would explain the knowledge about the code words. He was so going to die, she thought.

But it was Yvonne who died.

As she opened the rear car door, Joshua shot her three times, her body collapsing onto the back seat.

Chapter 25

Mokti put his new mobile phone into speaker mode, Jim Brodie's voice crackled between the two men as they sat in the front seat of Isaac's parked car.

"The fused fingers are a common syndrome for a second regeneration," said Jim. "And I have heard of the ear before; but the eyes, I'm not sure about them." He stopped talking for a few seconds before continuing, "Keep talking, I'm searching our system for any reference to those defects, especially in one regeneration."

Isaac looked out the windshield and asked into the phone, "How hard is it to get one of those LifeChip readers? Leonardo must have one, he's able to check the birth date of each of his victims. Chips that aren't suitable he just leaves behind. Bastard."

"Simple function readers are easily available, any electronics store would have one. Plugging a chip into one would say if data is present, the name of the person involved and a contact number if found." Jim's voice had the half-distracted air of someone bent on another task. "Hang on a minute, I'm getting some strange stuff out of the system." The moment lengthened. "The only reference to milky eyes comes from the early days of this technology, some pretty grim reading here. The company knew that there was a limit to the number of regenerations; each clone became more and more unstable before they settled on two regenerations as the safe maximum."

Isaac didn't like the implications. "Are you saying that Leonardo is a regeneration past the limit? How can that happen? You must have safeguards in place. I'm willing to bet lots of people would be willing to take the risk of milky eyes if they got another life."

"It's not a risk, Isaac, it's a certainty. Fused fingers are a sign of the second regeneration, a common syndrome as I said. The ear and eyes are reported as coming at random times up until the fifth regeneration and then they are a definite outcome of the process. But a clone only ever has one of these abnormalities, more than that and it isn't used. Not everyone gets their three lives, sometimes the clones just don't work out. The chance of an abnormality rises sharply after the second clone and becomes a certainty for the third try. But nowhere do we have any records of a clone picking up more than one abnormality at once. To have all three at once is a bit mind-numbing for me; if this Leonardo fellow is a regeneration, then he is a long way past his use-by date. He should not be alive."

Isaac closed his eyes and looked into the darkness of fatigue. "Again, I ask you, Jim, how can this happen? It's not just anyone who can rebuild a body and insert the chip." A thought struck him, "Or is it? What sort of skills do you need, Jim? To grow a clone body and then upload the personality?" He started the car and moved off into the traffic; seeing Mokti have a shower and looking all fresh and clean had made him aware of his shabby state. His breath felt hot and noxious, his eyes were dry and he was beginning to feel like he had not bathed in a week. He needed to go home, shower and change.

"The process is quite straightforward now, with lots of modular units and machines to monitor progress. Growing the clone body only needs the right equipment; it's not cheap and, of course, you need the critical ingredient."

"Which is?" asked Isaac.

"The cell, the starter cell. It has to be one of the two cells taken from the baby at birth. Each cell will generate one clone, and before you ask, yes, we have tried to take more cells but the organ we harvest the starter cells from is damaged with any greater loss. A young baby needs all the remaining cells to grow and develop normally. The early researchers found that out the hard way; I've read the case notes of those years and they're not pleasant reading."

"Didn't see you as a reader of horror books, Jim," said Isaac.

A noticeable pause developed before Jim spoke again. "Everyone who takes up a position on the executive team at LifeCorps is required to read these notes, Isaac. Everyone, even if you marry the CEO's daughter. Before taking up a position on the Board a person must sit for an interview and demonstrate a knowledge of those notes. We know where we came from and we don't want to forget."

Mokti sat and listened to the conversation, acutely aware of the personal issues being mentioned. He had read about the beginning of LifeCorp in an online magazine, knew of the early experiments and the dead ends until the process was stabilised. Knew of them in a clinical, detached way. Knew of them as something in the past, the impossible time of everything before his birth. History, not real time. But now he was hearing the unease in Jim's voice, becoming aware that those early experiments to find the safe number of cells to take from a baby must have had some implications. Implications for the babies when they took too many cells, implications for the parents and the researchers as they slowly discovered their error, their crime, their sin and shame.

Mathematics was looking better and better.

Isaac was also considering the implications of those early days when a random thought struck him. "I can't go home. Damn!" He turned left at the next side street and weaved in and out through traffic, his whole direction changed. "My house is a crime scene, I won't be allowed in. Bloody Leonardo!" he drove aggressively for a few moments before speaking into the phone again "Jim, can you send someone to the station with some data?"

"Sure, Edward's available for you. What do you need?" asked Jim Brodie.

"I need to be able to find lists of people, women, and their birth dates. I need to know which ones have got LifeChips."

"Steady on, mate," replied Jim, "our database would have every woman on the planet recorded. You need to refine the search."

Mokti spoke again, his mouth still not letting his mind know what it was going to do, "We have to cross reference those names with women living in Sydney, Leonardo is in this city."

Isaac grunted agreement, Jim said "Our data won't be able to help you there, a lot of people don't update their address details with us. They move house and tell everyone they can think of, but we know our last address is generally wrong. You have to understand that we collect our original data when the person is a baby. How many people live their entire lives in one house?"

"What about when they, er, die?" asked Mokti, "How do you link them with their clones, how do you know if they have a LifeChip?"

"Every hospital and morgue has a LifeChip Detector, it's just a simple machine which is placed on the chest of the body, if there's a chip present it registers on a small screen. The chip is then extracted, put through a Reader and we know who we are dealing with. The hospital contacts us and we do the follow up."

"Deaths away from hospitals and stuff? You know, off the beaten track?" Mokti was absorbed in the minutiae of death and rebirth.

"Not a huge problem, there's a single-use Chip Extractor in many First Aid Kits. Done any First Aid training, Mokti?" asked Jim.

"Er, been meaning to, but, uh, no," replied the young man.

"Okay, well, the kits have this little device, looks like a fat circle, about the size and shape of a tin of shoe polish" Jim didn't want to ask Mokti if he knew what a tin of shoe polish looked like, he had been young himself once. "It's got simple instructions, place it over the chest and it will do the rest."

Mokti thought about that for a moment, a body in the jungle, death by misadventure, heat, pain and confusion. Placing a small device on a friend's chest and watching it punch through ribs and flesh, down to the small chip which had been watching and listening for years. "Sounds a bit grim," he commented.

"Had one used on me once," said Jim "Fell off a mountain, the recovery team extracted my LifeChip in front of my wife. Not a good sight, I agree, but better than the alternative."

"Can we get back on track?" asked Isaac, pulling into the underground Police parking lot. "I can get addresses, I can have one of our techies cross-check your data, Jim."

"I'll give Edward a laptop with some specialized access software, he can log on from wherever you are, Isaac. He's a cluey lad, I'm sure he and your guy can match up names and addresses. Give him 30 minutes to get there."

Isaac and Mokti left the car and entered the police station, Mokti was beginning to feel right at home amongst law enforcement, vague thoughts of future careers strayed into his head, quickly dismissed. Hanging around Isaac was like mainlining adrenaline, he preferred the quieter life of academe.

The two men entered the main reception area and Isaac left Mokti in the care of a rather bemused female police officer while he went in search of technical support. By the time Edward walked through the main doors a space had been found for the team to assemble, complete with a communications technician seated at a side table in front of a generic departmental computer screen. After Edward was introduced, he sat beside the young police technician and unpacked a state-of-the-art laptop, both young men immediately fell to discussing the merits of the machine, its operating system and other allied topics.

Isaac grunted, the two shiny faces turned and gazed up at him, eager for instruction. "Give me a list of females living in the city with these dates of birth. Rule out children under the age of ten." Mokti passed over a slip of paper to the two men, they fell to discussing the mechanisms for linking their systems, a conversation liberally sprinkled with a jargon which defied Isaac's comprehension.

"I'm going to find a shower and a change of clothes," he said, "Mokti will give you any further info you need."

Mokti blinked at the departing figure of the detective, then turned back to the room. A room that had somehow grown in size and emptiness, Isaac took up a lot of space, a space he knew he could not fill. He hoped the big man hurried back before the two men looked to him for instruction.

The time passed slowly for the young student, Edward and the technician chatted in low tones before finally one of them said, "Here you go, Mokti, we've got a list of names: females living in the city born on 3rd May and 5th August."

Mokti moved to stand behind the seated pair, he gasped, "There must be hundreds of names there." The screen displayed two columns of names, each headed by one of the given dates. Edward then scrolled down to reveal more potential victims, as Isaac entered the room. Mokti groaned, "How do we start to work out which is going to be the next victim?"

"Is Yvonne Borovansky on that list?" the big detective asked from the doorway, he looked and felt fresher after the brief shower. Mokti scanned the names, a cold sense of dread sweeping through as he saw the name Isaac had given glowing softly on the screen. He nodded assent to the question.

Isaac spoke in a clear, low monotone, "Yvonne Borovansky was killed earlier this evening, her body was found in the back seat of a Pizza delivery van by her partner, Constable Joshua McIntosh."

"Constable?" asked Mokti. The other two men sat silently, death had just entered the room and they were strangers in this world.

"She was a police officer, she was seen talking to a man while on patrol with McIntosh and went around the corner with the stranger. When she didn't reappear, he called it in and went looking, found the pizza van in an alley a few minutes from where she was taken."

"Her LifeChip?" queried the young Muslim. Behind Isaac, the door opened and more people entered the room, one was a strong featured, dark-haired female police officer in uniform, her shoulders carried several badges which Mokti assumed signified rank.

"Chest cut open," replied Isaac, "LifeChip taken. He only had a few moments to do it, looks like he shot her, drove off to the alley, cut her open to get the chip and left the scene." The big detective felt the presence of others in the room, looked over his shoulder and saw the newcomers, nodded to the woman, "Hello, Inspector." Isaac was tired, the shower had freshened him but any gains he had made emotionally were shattered by the news of the killing of Yvonne Borovansky.

Black Betty stepped forward, "What are we doing here, Detective Howard?" she asked of Isaac. "Who are these people in my station?" She pointed at Edward, "What is that man doing with his laptop?"

She didn't sound angry, but Mokti recognized the steel and power in her voice. He was glad it was Isaac on the receiving end, he was having trouble thinking. The woman overawed him to such an extent he wanted to flee the room, apologizing for ever intruding.

"This is Mokti Setiawan, a young man who has given us the only real leads we have in this case. Edward here is from LifeCorps, he has been rendering technical assistance to Sammy; together we had hoped to be able to find some clues to Leonardo's next victim."

The room went quiet as all waited for the Inspector to reach a decision; Isaac had broken several regulations by bringing in outside help without seeking prior approval. Mokti could feel that he was in trouble, perhaps he would end his first day in Sydney by being locked up. His poor dad, he thought, and mum would have a fit. He'd be called back to Perth and never let out of the family home again. As these thoughts ran through his mind his face wore a vaguely imbecilic grin, trying to convey a willingness to do whatever he was asked. He was all compliance and good citizenry.

And they probably think I'm a terrorist, he considered.

Chapter 26

Detectives Harris and Lee entered the room, picked up on the tension and shrank into the corner, Black Betty was not a woman whose attention you sought.

"And what have you found, gentlemen?" she asked.

Isaac briefly sketched the details that led them all to being in this room, he explained how they had found a link between the deaths, the numbers that form the Fibonacci Sequence. With sadness, he revealed the two lists of names and informed the room that Yvonne's name had been on the first list.

Black Betty mulled over the conversation, "How many names are on the second list?" she asked.

Edward responded quickly, "Two hundred and twenty-six."

"How many of those are in uniform of some sort?"

"We don't know," replied the young man.

Mokti spoke up, "We have to check them on the Internet, see who has a web presence."

Black Betty turned her gaze upon him, he quailed and took a small backward step. "Thank you, sir," she said, with just the slightest pause before the last word.

She looked at Isaac, "You have brought civilians into my station and given them access to our resources. You have used information garnered under very suspect circumstances. I refer here to the database from LifeCorps. Are you aware, Detective Howard, that these acts of yours will endanger our investigation? Yes, you may have gathered some information, but at what price? Any competent lawyer will rip us to pieces. You have failed us, Detective Howard. Again, I might add."

The room had fallen into the silence of the doomed, the stillness of those caught in the act of wrongdoing. Before her steely gaze, the young police technician raised his hand attentively.

"What is it?" snapped Black Betty.

"Excuse me, miss," said the young man, falling back on the skills gained from his fearsome grade three teacher, "Uhm, sorry, Inspector. But your name's on the list."

"What list?"

"The second list" replied Edward. "Women with birthdays on 5th August."

A chill waved over Black Betty's heart, "That's my birthday" she said in a small voice.

"Elizabeth Blackburn," announced the young technician, reading from the screen. All in the room looked at Black Betty, now in a small space all of her own, a physical, emotional and distinct space that separated her from all others, a space she shared with dead women and a killer.

Isaac spoke first, "We'll find him, Inspector." A gentle voice in that now crowded room.

Black Betty shook the mood off, "Not standing here, you won't" she said. "Find links with this Leonardo, backtrack his victims. Do your jobs, and do them properly," she finished, pinning Isaac again, "without breaking regulations and making it easy for any half-baked mouthpiece to make fools of us." Black Betty did not relish the notion of being taken for a fool. "Howard, if you think this sequence of murders began two years ago then go and look at the information from that crime again. Go through the files, look at the photographs, visit the scene. Find out what kicked him off and why he waited two years to start again."

Isaac's face lost colour, he stood hearing the instructions like nails hammered into his heart. After the last command from Betty, he crumpled a little, fell into his coat, a shrunken version of the towering force Mokti had been with. After a moment he shook himself, nodded and left the room, Mokti followed his friend, aware of some hurt but unable to help.

"Detective Lee," she instructed. "See this man off our site," she indicated Edward, "escort him back to LifeCorps and warn him and his employer that we may be pressing charges against them, charges relating to their wilful breach of the privacy laws." Edward began to pack up. "Harris, go and assist Detective Howard."

"Sure," replied Harris, he stopped at the door and said to his superior officer "You know about the first victim in this sequence, don't you?" he asked, "Who she was?"

"What do you mean?" asked Black Betty, voice dismissive.

"The first victim, the one that started Leonardo on this spree," said Harris, "It was his wife, Mary." He wanted to shake this woman, generate some sort of reaction, maybe this would do it, maybe she would understand that she had ordered Isaac to go through the entire experience again. "Did you know that?" he asked, eyes fixed on her face.

She brushed past him, "Yes, of course I did," she said as she left the room.

Without the presence of Black Betty, the room regained its normal perspective, time reasserted its dominium, the occupants hurried through their tasks. The room soon emptied, only the dust recording another confrontation in a long history of anguish and betrayal.

SALLY AWOKE, HER WORLD was dark but not the dark of night, it was the dark of despair.

"Bugger that!" she said and opened her eyes, the room was as she remembered, empty of the loathsome presence of Joshua, empty of torment. But she was full of her own hope, her own abilities.

"Dammit," she muttered, "I'm getting out of here."

And she did.

It took pain, the loss of skin, it took time and patience. The sort of patience one acquires as you try to free yourself while waiting for a psychotic killer to return.

Sally surprised herself with her strength, she stood looking at the lonely cot on which she had been imprisoned; she held the pieces of rope dangling from one hand. With a flick of her bloodied wrist, she tossed them onto the cot and moved towards the workbench.

On the workbench was Joshua's laptop. What would one find, she wondered, if you looked into the mind of a madman?

Sometimes you look into the abyss, she had read somewhere, and sometimes the abyss looks into you.

She turned the laptop on, it had no password. She wasn't surprised. Joshua had no secrets from himself.

THE DEATH OF THE POLICEWOMAN had been delicious, Joshua decided. Delicious.

Ah, Evie, he mused, some potential there but too cluttered in her thinking, still in awe of her power over men. Since he had to leave the van, it only made sense to leave the young woman with it; she had looked suitably surprised when he injected her with the knock-out drug.

Quite a lovely look of betrayal on her face, coupled with the slightest suggestion that it was, in fact, expected. He now had some time to deliberate the path of her demise, perhaps a little experimentation with the new tech would be a fitting end to the young woman.

He glanced down at the small aluminium briefcase, Jimmy had done a fine job of installing his newest creation in so portable a package. So much to think about, he chortled. Ah, well, a busy life is a full life.

And now for some thinking, some decisions needed to be made about the next step in the sequence. There was one last woman in uniform to finish this run at the pattern; and he already knew who it would be. The evil bloody woman who insisted on dominating his life, she would never leave him alone – not even in death could he expect some peace. She had to go, and he wanted her to know the utter failure she had been in his life, perhaps she knew already.

Did she?

Would she be waiting? Would she know he was coming for her?

He writhed in the gorgeousness of it all.

ISAAC HEAVED THE STORAGE box onto his desk; Mokti pulled the lanyard holding his new visitor's badge over his head. The police badge looked very official, he felt a moment of betrayal, a frisson of becoming one with authority rippled down his heart.

"Am I becoming 'the man'?" he muttered to himself.

"What?" queried Isaac, opening the box.

"Nothing. What's in the box?"

The big man peered into the depths of a very unpleasant piece of his past. "Each case has a box like this," he replied. "It holds all the physical evidence, primary sources of information, anything unusual or too hard to store digitally." He stopped talking and looked inside the box, Mokti peered past the detective's shoulders, noted the small plastic bags, each sealed with a label. An open magazine of Sudoku puzzles gazed up, some completed squares displayed numbers, others were blank or smudged; in one corner was a neatly folded dress, sadly nestling, bereft of the life it once held.

"This was Mary," said Isaac. "My wife."

What do you say in a situation like that? Mokti was stunned into immobility, I'm just a kid, he thought, this is too much for me, I don't know what to do.

Standing there, feeling embarrassed and intrusive, he grew up a bit more. It's never nice, this growing up business, he thought. I don't want to be responsible. I want my dad to come and make it all right, to take away the pain.

Detective Harris spoke in his ear, "For God's sake, Isaac! Give me that bloody box. Kid," he said to Mokti, "go and get him a coffee or something, don't stand there like a stale glass of beer." Mokti almost hugged the man, such was his relief. He scurried away on his task, grateful for Harris to be the grown up in the room.

He stood at the vending machine, replaying the incident over and over in his head, teasing out his reactions, questioning his responses. Or lack of them. He thought about himself, his role in looking after people - and grew up. He returned to Isaac's desk with a small tray containing several steaming cups and a heart holding more wisdom.

Next time, Isaac, he silently promised the big man. Next time I'll be there for you. I'm older now. In the back of his mind, he caught a flickering image of his father, standing and smiling at him. Thanks, Dad, he thought, I'm good now.

Isaac sat immobile in his old chair, the ancient wood and plastic creaked as he shifted weight. Harris had the box open, some of the contents were scattered across the desk, he stood looking into its depths, seeking some clue which teams of investigators had missed. He knew it was almost futile, the box stared back at him, empty of hope.

Mokti placed the drinks on the table, then he sat quietly on a small stool observing the standing detective and the seated big man. Both were still, Harris with the silence of incomprehension, of a man staring at yet more blind alleys; Isaac was also still, but he had a sense of struggle. Fatigue, grief and guilt had conspired to drain him of energy, he had nothing there to offer.

Harris had taken the puzzle book out of the box and placed it on the table. Mokti picked it up and idly leafed through the pages, his mathematician's mind casually inserting numbers into blank squares.

The silence kept the three men company for a while, not one of those silences where someone feels obliged to make a noise: merely the silence of three men, each communing with their inner selves. Isaac shifted to sit at a keyboard, the room had a terminal linked to the main database, useful for checking up on information when needed. He wasn't looking at doing any searches, he just wanted to be out of the way, maybe crawl into a hole somewhere.

Mokti's inner self spoke up; he questioned the thought and then shared it with the others "Why did he wait so long?" he asked.

Isaac remained immobile; Harris looked up from his examination of the box, "What?" he asked.

"Leonardo," said Mokti, sipping his coffee, "I understand that it was some time after he killed...," embarrassment clamped his tongue, he waved a tongue-tied hand at the box "... er, before he killed again."

The seated detective stirred, "Two years. Bastard waited two years."

"Why?" repeated Mokti. He had no real line of inquiry, but the thought had come unbidden into his mind, and no one else was jumping up and down with clues.

"Who knows?" answered Harris. "Every sicko is different. Maybe it took him that long to work out his plan, you know, maybe he had to study up on his mathematics." The aboriginal detective's voice carried some sarcasm, he didn't like what he had just said, but he was tired too. Then he started to think.

They all thought. Mokti turned another page of the puzzle booklet, saw the new set of challenges, "I've got something here," he announced.

He turned the page around so that the other two men could read the text. The author had introduced a new puzzle, a new set of numbers; his introduction was in large type, the title in heavy black letters, "The Fibonacci Sequence". Some of the new puzzles had been completed, not all, but some. Mokti flicked back and forth a few pages before stating "The first set of pages are done in pencil, these new ones have been done with a pen. A different person did them."

"How could you know that?" asked Harris, he wanted to shield Isaac a bit longer from any unnecessary confrontation with some of Mary's effects.

But it was Isaac who answered, "Mary never used a pen for these puzzles, she loved them but knew she sometimes made mistakes. She could rub out a pencil and put the right number in, never used a pen. Said it was too final."

"The person who did these later Fibonacci puzzles was arrogant," said Mokti. "Some of the numbers are wrong, most of the questions are incomplete because they had inserted the wrong numbers early in the sequence. He didn't know what he was doing." He turned to the earlier puzzles in the book, "Look at these, all in pencil, all complete. Mary was a fighter, she didn't leave challenges unfinished."

"Too right, she was," said Isaac. "Smart as they come, loved a puzzle. Never gave up. Oh, damn..." He lowered his head and tried to swim through the sea of grief; some days it threatened to drown him. It was always there, the hole in his heart.

The other men stood silent and useless, Mokti was horrified he had caused his friend more pain. Again. Harris felt the impotence of most men when confronted with true emotion, he hoped the moment passed soon, hoped they could restart this conversation without having to deal with feelings and other emotional bombs.

Isaac swallowed and asked, "Could these puzzles have been done by Leonardo?" He answered his own question, "Hell, he probably did them while he waited for me to find Mary. God, what a bastard!"

"That's where he discovered the Fibonacci Sequence. It's all here" said Mokti, holding up the booklet. "A good overview of the topic, nice explanation. But he's not a mathematician, just arrogant and opinionated."

Harris asked, "Arrogant and opinionated? That's a bit much, isn't it? It's just a puzzle book." He was grateful for the chance to say something, anything to move the discussion on to less personally confronting issues. He would far rather have a gunfight than talk about feelings.

"Nah," replied Mokti. "He uses a pen for a number puzzle. A pen! Only someone who knows nothing about numbers uses a pen. Mathematics is about making mistakes, about being willing to get it wrong, and going back and starting again. Maths is not for wimps, detectives, you need guts to work in numbers."

Isaac spoke up, drawn back into the world by the interchange, "You are one weird guy, Mokti. Mathematicians as tough guys? Sure they are, my accountant is probably Superman in disguise." He chuckled, alive again, "Okay, where were we before Mokti started beating his chest? This seems to be where Leonardo got his ideas, his pattern. But we still don't know why he waited so long to kill again."

"He wasn't around," muttered Harris, thinking aloud, "Why wasn't he around? What was he doing?"

"Maybe he was working out his plan, his pattern. He got the idea from this booklet, but it was just the start!" said Isaac. "Bill, what if you're right." He leaned forward, life flooding again through his veins. "Maybe he was studying, maybe he was unavailable!"

"Like in prison!" finished Harris. "Yes, could be. Hang on, that's a standard line of enquiry, there should be a record of the search in here." He rummaged into the box again, exacting a sheet of paper.

"What search?" asked Mokti.

Isaac had fired up his computer, "This is a list of their searches," he said, waving the sheet of paper. "A standard search of arrests around the time of the crime, I'll cross check it with the database, just to see that it was all done properly. Whenever we are looking for a missing felon we check the standard places, hospitals and prisons are usually a good bet. Your average crim who drops out of sight for any length of time can often be found recovering from wounds in a hospital. They always get a surprise when we turn up with a warrant. Dumb plonks."

Harris chuckled, "I got one guy last year, went in for an appendectomy. They opened him up and saw some other scarring, consistent with a bullet wound. Found the slug lodged inside a rib. His appendix was fine, but he thought he was dying. We matched the slug to an unsolved robbery, searched his place and found large quantities of stolen merchandise. When he came out of the hospital, I was leaning on his car bonnet with a warrant. Talk about surprised!"

"Here it is," claimed Isaac, staring at his screen, "the list of searches." He was silent a moment, Mokti could see the big man's lips moving as he read the screen and flicked galnces to the sheet of paper.

"Anything?" asked Harris.

Isaac shook his head "They did it all. Checked everywhere. We could go back and verify their searches, but it would be a long shot. I don't think Leonardo was in prison, hospital, nursing home, overseas or any of the usual places."

"Like he dropped off the planet," said Mokti.

"Look, kid," said Harris, "you're bright, I'll give you that. But forget the outer space angle. I don't think we can pin a lot of hopes on alien abduction and anal probes for this one. Not if we want to keep our pension, anyway." He sat in yet another chair, "So, where did the bastard go for two years?"

Mokti slurped some more coffee, "Maybe he died," he said absently.

"Shit!" said Isaac, he leaned forward, "Maybe he did! Harris, remember the Sarich assassination? What happened to the killer?"

"The bloke who gunned down Ambassador Frederico Sarich? Sure.... oh, right. But he was caught in the act, shot while trying to escape."

"And he had a LifeChip," said Isaac.

"Did they clone him? Bring the assassin back to life?" asked Mokti.

Harris smirked, "Too right, they did. Landmark case. Cloned him, inserted his LifeChip and then arrested him for murder. The defence argued that he had already paid for his crime by being shot and killed. Lovely case."

Mokti was still puzzled, "What happened to him?"

"Got sentenced to twenty years, no parole." Harris chuckled, "If he gets killed in prison he will be cloned again and sent back to finish his sentence.

The process has put a hole in the life plans of your career assassin. If they want to do it, then they had better get away clean and that's hard. If we catch 'em, we put them away. Again and again. Sweet."

Isaac was typing at his keyboard, "All that happened about the same time Leonardo was showing his hand, he would have known what would happen to him if he was caught. So, the question is..." he said, triumphantly, tapping one final key, "who was taken for cloning at that time?"

Harris and Mokti moved to look over Isaac's shoulder at the screen. Two search screens appeared, each with names and numbers flickering through the results table. "All deaths are recorded, either at the morgue or through a LifeCorps link to Central records." Each window had a title, the first said 'Deaths at Morgue', the second said "LifeCorps Registry of Deaths."

Mokti whistled and said "Pretty smooth search parameters, Isaac. Lucky your system had them inbuilt."

"Whaddya mean, 'lucky'?" growled Isaac. "I just wrote 'em then."

The young man was impressed, the more sophisticated search engines required some gentle nudging to perform a refined sieve on data; they all had a simple user interface, but the retrievals were often huge. He still felt obliged to give his friend a bit of stick, though, "Must be a simple system, eh? Some clever programming running behind it all."

Both detectives gave him the look reserved for small boys who tell the adults how to do things, a mixture of pity for the unintelligent coupled with a dash of exasperation over the naivety of youth. "Yeah, right, kid," said Harris, "The police force invests a lot of money in cutting edge programming for us grunts. I wish."

Isaac shook his head, "Ahh, to be so young. Remember what it was like, Harris?"

"Nope."

"In answer to your childlike comments, Mokti," said Isaac, "I happen to be a gifted crafter of search parameters. I am known around the precinct – affectionately, of course - as 'The Intruder'." He chuckled.

Mokti goggled a little, "Really?"

"Nah," said Harris, "he's having a go at you, mate. Old clever dick here," he gestured with a thumb at Isaac, "is just a busybody. Bloody good with a search engine though; he's got a lot of nicknames – GrumbleBum, Lardarse,

Mr. Painful – but certainly not 'The Intruder.'" He guffawed and slapped Isaac on the back, repeating the title with a further laugh "Oh, lord, that's rich – The Intruder! I gotta tell Short and Twisted about that."

Isaac groaned and shook his head, "What have I done to myself?"

The search screens stopped flickering, each set of results glowed softly, two columns of names; a common thought ran through the three men, was one of these names Leonardo?

Chapter 27

S ally started, she thought heard a noise. A noise from the other side of the door.

Leaving the laptop, she quickly moved to the door and bent to listen but the sound did not repeat. She stayed for several minutes, craning her hearing, striving to pick up any hint that Joshua had returned. She finally decided she had been mistaken, no other sound came through the door. She stood and took stock of her mental state. Was she on the verge of panic? No, she was just listening for a noise. She was composed and calm.

She was surprised by her lack of terror, she seemed able to move and think without the frozen stillness of abject fear. She remembered that sort of fear, but it no longer had a hold on her, it was somewhere else. Probably still tied up on the floor, she decided.

She had to get out of this room, had to flee. But the laptop, it might provide some clues to the identity of this madman. She crossed back to the workbench, picked up the computer and packed it into a nearby padded carry bag; the fit was snug enough to convince Sally it was the correct transportation method for the laptop. She returned to the door, determined to get out and away.

The door was locked, a simple button secured the first lock through the handle; this, she depressed. She turned her attention to the main lock, a formidable looking piece of metal inset into the door; she recognized a serious deadlock. Heavy machinery for door security.

The big room might provide some tools for escape; she began searching while trying to remain alert to outside noise. What she needed, she decided, was something heavy like a hammer or crowbar. Something which she could bring down on Joshua's head.

Be nice if it could also break locks.

"SURELY THE ORIGINAL investigation did the same search?" asked Harris. "I mean, we just spoke about the Sarich case, it'd be a logical step to get the records from the morgue and LifeCorps. Is there any record in the case notes of them doing a search?"

Isaac typed some more, "There's probably a note in the box but let's just be doubly sure. I'll access Archives and have a look at their detailed Investigation Transcripts."

"Investigation Transcripts?" asked Mokti; some words just roll out with capital letters.

Harris replied, "The box has physical evidence and a running summary, but every major crime would have detailed records of every step of the investigation; the people questioned and printouts of every interrogation; minutes of each morning's briefing; a journal of the senior officers on the case; plus any other bits and pieces thought necessary. It's all backed up into archives, both electronic and hard copy. Pain in the butt to do but so very useful when you have to backtrack like today."

"Here we go," announced Isaac. He studied the screen for a moment, Mokti could see the detective had called up a series of split screens, one of which displayed the results of his searches. Time passed as each name was cross checked with the original investigation, finally the big man leaned back in the chair. "They did their jobs. All of the names checked out, they followed every lead to a dead end."

"The morgues, deaths in hospitals?" asked Harris.

"All accounted for, matches my list exactly."

"And LifeCorps, no discrepancies there?"

"Not a one. And I'll tell you something for free. Some dedicated plod from Unsolved Crimes has gone back in every six months and updated the searches."

"What do you mean?"

"I mean," answered Isaac, "that my original search was date specific. I looked at deaths for the day of Mary's murder and the week after. Thought I was being comprehensive." He stopped for a moment, "Anyway, Unsolved

Crimes did one better; they checked for deaths over the next two years after the murder. Very meticulous."

"Very anal," murmured Harris. "I know the boss of Unsolved Crimes, he runs a tight ship. Lots of very detailed procedures. Pain in the arse."

"Yeah, well," said Isaac, "we know for sure that no one died or was cloned who could be Leonardo. Any clone regeneration abnormalities are also listed here, nothing to match our boy. They all check out."

"According to the records," said Mokti.

"That's what I said, kid," answered Isaac.

"What if the records are wrong?"

"Fat chance," interjected Harris. "We know about data corruption, hacking and all that romantic stuff. Most of these checks would have been done by some poor slob pounding the footpath, knocking on doors, eyeballing teary relatives, examining bodies, accident scenes. Bit hard to fake that stuff. No, kid, the records only get put down when they're right."

"We could double-check," put in Isaac, "You know, just to be sure."

"Give it a rest, Isaac," said Harris. "Sure, you could go over it all again, but you know as well as I do that the chance of someone faking that data is pretty much nil, we certainly won't be able to do it in time to save Sally Grant. We only go back and check if we run out of other angles."

The three men sat in silence for a while longer, poking their minds into all crevices, looking for something extra; Mokti raised his eyes to the ceiling in thought, Isaac lowered his chin onto his chest, Harris gazed into an unseen distance.

"Leonardo is a clone, right?" asked Mokti.

Isaac grunted affirmation.

"But he's more than third generation, isn't he?" Mokti was becoming excited, "How was he cloned? LifeCorps keeps records of legitimate cloning, what if this guy wasn't done by LifeCorps?"

Harris snarled, "Don't be stupid, kid. No one else does clones and regenerations, no one can."

Mokti stuttered to a halt, he was empty, fresh out of ideas.

"Then how do we explain Leonardo?" asked Isaac. "Jim Brodie from LifeCorps says those sorts of disfigurements are a sign of multiple regenerations. If LifeCorps didn't clone that freak, who did?"

"You think LifeCorp is rotten?" asked Harris.

Isaac thought about it, "Anything's possible. I need to get back over to Jim and ask a few more questions. Him, I trust. Come on, Mokti."

The big detective moved towards the exit, Mokti ran a couple of steps to catch up. At the door, Isaac turned back to Harris, "Can you look after that evidence box, sort of ...tidy up?" The big man was embarrassed.

Harris smiled at his colleague, "No worries, mate. I'll take care of these things, treat them with respect, all proper like." He began replacing things in the box, "Might have a look at a few other things when I'm done, got a bit of an idea."

"Fair enough," responded Isaac. "Come on, Mok," he said, "you're the only one coming up with ideas on this case. Back to LifeCorp, and you keep being clever."

Mokti felt a glow of pleasure, a smile blossomed as his face lit up with pleasure, "Thanks, Isaac," he said.

"Now don't go all mushy on me, sport. Ring Jim and tell him what's going on," grumbled the detective as he led them both back to his car.

EDWARD MET THE TWO men at the ground floor reception of LifeCorps, after a brief exchange he guided them down several floors.

"Aren't we going back up to Jim's office?" asked Mokti.

"He wants to meet you downstairs, in the vaults," replied Edward. Inside the elevator, the three men were confronted with the usual mirrors and company notices. The staff social club seemed to be very active. The small bell chimed, and doors opened onto a large open room containing a desk, an armed guard watching a CCTV monitor of the elevator and two people in white lab coats. One of these was Jim Brodie, he broke off his conversation with the other person, a woman, and waved at the newcomers.

"Isaac, Mokti, come over here," he said. "I want you to meet someone. Thank you, Edward, stick around in case we need some more help."

Edward smiled agreement before moving back into a secondary position, he knew when a conversation was going to be above his pay scale.

"Detective Isaac Howard, Mokti Rahim," said Jim, "this is Doctor Michelle Glanville. Michelle is in charge of this facility."

Isaac turned his policeman's eye on the woman, late fifties, dyed brown hair with a slash of red pulled back in a bun, smart and expensive clothes under the coat. And shoes that no one in their right mind would call sensible. He stared at the delicate pumps, all straps, shiny colours and gaiety. "Like the shoes," he grunted.

"Aren't they gorgeous?" queried Michelle, "My one piece of me in this austere environment. Hello, Isaac. May I call you Isaac? And you must be Mokti." She shook hands with the men; Mokti found his mind had gone away again, unable to deal with more strong characters in his life. He mumbled an acknowledgement.

"Speak up, Mokti, I'm sure your mother taught you better than that," ordered Michelle, but any sting was taken out of the words by a sunburst smile.

Mokti almost said, "Sorry, mum" but caught himself in time; he settled for an inane grin and hoped someone would rescue him.

"Bit of a live wire, aren't you, Michelle?" asked Isaac. Mokti metaphorically slumped with relief.

"Oh, dear, have I done it again?" asked Michelle. "Jim, a little help here, please." Jim Brodie was smiling quietly at the scene, "And stop smirking, young man," finished Michelle.

"I wasn't smirking," replied Jim. "I was merely smiling, Michelle. Smiling, not smirking. It would be a far braver man than me to smirk in front of you. No smirker, I."

She tapped his arm affectionately and turned back to Isaac, "Now, Isaac, Jim tells me that you want to know how someone could be cloned illegally."

"I'll get to that in a moment, Michelle," replied the detective. "To start with, what is the 'facility' over which you reign?" Isaac knew Jim would not have brought him down here without a reason and he assumed it would unfold in time.

Michelle turned and gestured for the group to follow her, she led them to a very secure looking door at the end of the room; Edward tagged along to fetch and carry as required. Beside the keypad lock on the door was another guard sitting at a small desk, Isaac would be willing to bet good money it wasn't a flimsy little piece of office furniture. Probably a secure armoured point, complete with instant link-up to reinforcements, police, army, air force, whatever. He tapped the desk while Michelle typed in a security code at the door, he recognized the distinct sound of reinforced polymers and steel. The guard gave him a small nod, recognizing a professional and confirming his deduction. This place had some serious security.

"This way, boys," drawled Michelle in her best femme fatale voice. The men followed her into a large, clinical room. Not so much a room, thought Isaac, a cavern of aircraft hangar dimensions. The walls consisted of thousands of small, rectangular metal plates, about the size of a man's middle finger; each plate bore a small engraving, a series of numbers. Mokti'll probably wet himself with excitement, the big detective thought.

As he looked up each wall, Isaac gave an involuntary whistle, the rows of metal plates extended up to the ceiling, the very, very distant ceiling. Forget thousand, he reconsidered, maybe millions. His brain told him he was standing with his face up and mouth open and was this any way for a man of the world to behave? He pulled himself together and tried to speak in his best 'I've seen it all before' voice.

"Big place," he croaked.

Jim laughed, slapping his knee, "I told you, Edward, told you we could crack him. Ha! 'Big place'! Oh, that's rich." He wiped an imaginary tear away from his eye, "Tell him what he's looking at, please, Michelle."

Michelle folded her arms and tapped one foot, looking at each man in turn, "Well, hello, boys. Have your parents let you all come out to play? Honestly, Jim, if you didn't pay me some outrageous salary, I would walk out right now." The men shuffled their feet, Mokti and Edward even hung their heads. Isaac was made of sterner stuff, he winked at this feisty lady.

"And don't you wink at me, Detective Howard," she said, but without any heat. "A bit of respect, please, you stand in the room holding your future." She stopped talking and looked at the group triumphantly.

They remained silent. A puzzled silence from Isaac and Mokti.

"Oh, for heaven's sake. Have you men no souls? This is the main storage facility for this continent. The main LifeCorps vault."

More silence until Isaac spoke, "Still not with you, Michelle. What is it that LifeCorp needs to keep this secure.... oh, I get it, the cells." He felt like a complete fool. "Our cells."

"At last," said Michelle. "Yes, detective," she put a slight emphasis on this word, Isaac had the grace to wince a little, "this room holds the two cells taken from every child born on the continent. You'll all be in here somewhere, everyone is."

"Ahem," coughed Jim "Nearly everyone, Michelle. Not everyone believes in regeneration."

"You mean those idiots from OneLife! Good grief, Jim, we're better off without them. Let 'em die, I say."

Even Isaac was mildly shocked by this statement. Manners indicated you didn't overtly wish for the death of an entire sector of the populace. Not aloud, at least.

"Steady on, Michelle, visitors present," said Jim, obviously used to her outspoken ways. Needing to bridge this social gaffe he asked the detective, "So, what did you want to know, Isaac?"

"Since we're all so upfront and honest, tell me how someone could break in and steal some of these cells," asked the big man.

"Don't be ridiculous," snapped Michelle, "No one gets in here easily. And certainly no one can just waltz in and open up one of these drawers and pinch a cell or two. This is more secure than any bank you have ever seen," she concluded with finality.

"Prove it," challenged the detective.

And so, she did. After an hour of being lectured and shown the security protocols, Isaac had to admit the place was impervious to anything but a sustained military attack. Certainly not vulnerable to someone like Leonardo, a psychotic mad dog killer.

"Satisfied?" she asked him. He grunted and walked back out of the vault, Jim at his side talking softly to the big man.

Michelle looped a hand through Mokti's arm and guided him after the other two men; she crooked a finger at Edward who fell in behind with an easy smile. He loved his job, so much entertainment, better than a daytime soap.

"Tell me, my dusky friend," asked Michelle to Mokti "Why is that particularly lumpy man ahead of us so upset that none of our cells are missing?"

"He wants to find a man, a man who has been through multiple regenerations. A bad, bad man."

"Oh, dear. And he thought that if we were leaking cells, it would explain how this miscreant got himself reborn?"

They exited the room, Michelle locked the door, nodded to the seated guard and then walked over to where the men were waiting at the elevator.

"What will you do now, Isaac?" she asked.

The detective raised his arms over his head and stretched out hard, he rotated his neck listening to the litany of pops from a tired, tired body. "Dunno," he said, "I was hoping this place would...show me something..." The men stepped into the elevator, Michelle stayed in the room.

As the doors began to shut Isaac saw her again in the arms folded stance, feet evenly balanced, a blood-red fingernail keeping time on her arm. A very assured and competent human being.

"Sorry, Isaac," she said, "no help here."

Chapter 28

"Who's doing black market regenerations?" asked Isaac as the elevator rose.

"No one. Can't be done" replied Jim.

"In that case, someone in your LifeCorp is doing it. Which might mean that your company is corrupt." Isaac was in no mood for niceties.

"I am sure no one at LifeCorp is involved, Isaac."

"Bloody hell, Jim!" exploded Isaac, "You can't have it both ways! IF Leonardo is a bad regeneration, then he had to be cloned by someone. The options are someone inside your company or someone outside it. Not a lot of choices."

"But you'd need so much gear and expertise," said Jim, "Not to mention the basic cells to start the clone."

"The cells from the donor when they were still a baby?" put in Mokti. "Why?'

Edward felt he could contribute, "Any cell can be grown into a clone, but only the baby cells will produce a viable body capable of living out a normal life span. Clones from any other cell will degenerate rapidly." He'd been reading manuals.

The word triggered something in Mokti, "Degenerate? What do you mean by that, Ted?"

"I mean the clone would have some serious abnormalities and a short life span."

Isaac and Mokti looked at each other, each sharing the same thought.

"Leonardo isn't a clone from the original cells!" declared the big man. But from where neither would guess.

The elevator arrived and the group exited, Isaac and Mokti moved towards the front door, Jim and Edward had a brief consultation before Jim ran over to catch the detective as he reached the exit.

"Edward's had another thought," said Jim, "must be his day for it." Isaac didn't say anything, just waited for Jim to keep talking.

"Go and see Michelle's grandfather."

Isaac snorted and turned to leave, "Not looking for a relationship, Jim."

Jim grabbed the big man's arm, "No, hold on, Isaac. Her father is Thomas Glanville, he pioneered the research that led us to the ability to regenerate. Remember those notes I read out to you, the ones explaining the defects a clone picks up? They were his notes, Isaac. He knows more about how a body is cloned than any person alive. Go and see him."

"How old would he be?"

"I don't know, well over a hundred. He was a brilliant mind, won a Nobel prize by the age of twenty-two for his research. Child prodigy. Edward's gone to find his address and call ahead. We can text you the details." He paused and looked at Isaac with sincerity and trust "We'll help on this, Isaac. I'll make sure LifeCorp gives you whatever you need."

I am so out of my depth in these gatherings, thought Mokti. If these two big guys want to have a pissing contest, then I don't want to be here.

"Come on, Mokti, let's go see Michelle's revered ancestor," said Isaac. "If he's anything like his granddaughter he should be a real sweetheart." As he pushed through the doors he spoke over his shoulder to Jim Brodie, "Thanks, mate."

THE DOOR WAS OPENED by an elderly man wrapped in a loose dressing gown over comfortable clothes. In one hand were some pages of a folded newspaper, he bit off a mouthful of toast and chewed. He wore scruffy slippers and the expression of a man who did not relish his peace being disturbed.

Stiff, thought, Isaac, I'm a copper. It's my job to piss people off.

"Thomas Glanville?" asked the policeman.

"I'm Professor Glanville and this is my day off," replied the man, he hadn't shaved yet. Mokti surreptitiously checked his phone for the time, it was almost mid-afternoon." Stop looking at your phone, boy, if you've got somewhere better to be then please go." He squinted back to Isaac, "Are you the irritating policeman Jim Brodie called me about?"

"May we come in, please?" asked Isaac.

Glanville swallowed, blinked testily and turned back into the house. "Oh, God, give me strength. One of those idiots who answer a question with a question," he muttered.

Mokti made sure Isaac went first, he tried to calm himself by thinking invisible thoughts. He followed the big detective's broad shoulders, a man whose entire life was one of confrontation - and confrontation was something he normally avoided, numbers didn't snarl at you.

Isaac was a good man to stand behind, he decided. A long way behind.

They entered a small hallway and followed their unwilling host back into the depths of the house, finally emerging into a kitchen area. On an old table stood the remains of a late meal, toast, jams, coffee. Other pieces of newspaper were scattered over the table and any nearby chair.

Glanville saw them surveying the room, "No comments about my housekeeping. This is my day of rest, I send the servants away and get to lounge around in my pyjamas all day, drip egg yolk onto the carpet and read any damn paper I please. Any that are still being published, that is. Until today, when my perfect solitude, my brief respite from the cares of the world is interrupted by two goons from security."

Mokti felt a bit chuffed about being called a goon, he hunched his shoulders and slit his eyes in a vain attempt to live up to the sobriquet.

"Stand up straight, boy, don't slouch!" snapped Glanville. "Your mother would be so disappointed, I'm sure." He sat in a tatty chair and resumed eating, "Now, what can I do for you, constable?" he asked.

"I'm a detective, sir, a constable is a uniformed police officer," said Isaac. He sat on another chair, crushing the sports pages. "You said this was your day off. Would you mind telling us what it is that you do? I was led to believe you had retired."

"You're like, really old!" blurted Mokti, instantly regretting his lack of control.

Glanville dipped a piece of soggy toast into a runny egg and theatrically slurped it into a wide wide-open mouth. "Indeed. And you are, what, twelve? Be quiet, boy, let the grown-ups talk." He turned back to Isaac, wiped his mouth with a napkin and said "Now that I've had my fun.... I have indeed retired from paid employment, detective. But I am just as occupied as ever; I firmly believe that the onset of decrepitude and senility can be offset by keeping oneself busy. Both mentally and physically. I walk for an hour each day and combine a vigorous Pilates routine into my schedule." He gazed meaningfully at Isaac's girth before continuing, "I shall outlive you by several decades, you are a cholesterol train wreck about to happen."

Isaac ignored the tone and message of Glanville's words. While he did not appreciate cruelty or meanness, he suspected that Thomas Glanville was neither. People invent personas for themselves, he knew, and he believed Glanville had invented this image of an irascible, cantankerous old coot to entertain himself. Fair enough, he thought, I guess I play the role of crusty detective a bit much, too. He decided to wait for a response to his question, so he stood gazing expectantly at Dr Glanville's face.

The old man returned the look and realised he had run out of play time, especially with this big detective. He sighed, smiled and said, "I do charity work, my earlier research led me into, well, an unpleasant place." He paused, the nightmares flooding through his mind again; broken babies, dying children, tearful parents and fellow researchers; all looking at him. It was his responsibility, for some time he had barely been able to cope with living each day knowing the harm he had done. "When I retired from LifeCorps – in fact, even before then – I realised I had to do something positive. Something to make up for the dreadful errors of judgement that I and others made in the early days."

His eyes glazed over for a moment, but he dismissed the shallowness of inherited guilt. If you made a mistake then you tried to fix it, you apologise and move on; he knew he couldn't undo his past mistakes, no one can. And a constant revisiting of past errors was both useless and selfish, fraught with self-defeating breast beating. The Glanvilles had never been breast beaters.

"I set up a clinic, a clinic for those who had some form of deformity or handicap due to the regeneration process. I support it financially as well as practically with my work as a medical doctor; surprisingly, I have found many other high-profile people willing to give of their time to work in the kitchens, as cleaners or simple workers."

Isaac tried a tentative ploy, "A lot of guilt out there, Doctor."

"Don't be patronizing, detective, I'm too wise and you're too old to think it will work," snapped the old man. "Yes, I do use all sorts of emotional blackmail to fund and staff my clinic, but I have the privilege of being the pain in the arse who runs it."

"My apologies, doctor," said Isaac. "Now, I wonder if we could ask you a few questions?"

"You've got until I go to work in about half an hour."

"I thought you said this was your day off?"

"I lied. Get on with it." Glanville began clearing the table, placing dishes in the sink, untying his pyjama robe. Underneath he was dressed in comfortable but well-made clothes, a pale blue shirt, no tie, high quality slacks and shoes for the man who spends a lot of time on his feet.

Isaac was impressed, the old man still had a lot of kick in him. "You are very healthy for a man your age, sir," he said.

"My research showed me a thing or two about longevity, detective....., what is your name again?"

"Howard. Isaac Howard."

"Yes, well," said the doctor, "You also have benefited, or would benefit if you took any sort of care of your body. Our current health system now has a rash of drugs and procedures to lengthen life. Naturally, I mean, not just with a regeneration."

Mokti had to ask, "Does it make you angry that you can't regenerate? The process can only be performed on babies, you miss out. Yet you were the one who, sort of, invented it?"

Glanville moved to a coat rack and took down a white lab coat, putting it on he addressed the young man, "No. Some things we can control and some we can't. Even though I devised the procedures I was unable to benefit from my work personally - do I feel cheated? No. I wasn't born handsome, athletic or charismatic. I can't play any sort of musical instrument, can't paint, sculpt or perform any of the many artistic tasks some people do so effortlessly. But do I hang my head and berate my Creator because he 'cheated' me? Such whining is selfish and pointless. You play the cards you're dealt." He moved towards the kitchen door, "Besides, I got my share of aces. Now, are you two coming?"

Isaac was caught off guard, "Where to?"

"My clinic, of course."

Mokti and Isaac followed the doctor out of the kitchen, both men expected a turn to the left and so on back to the front door. Instead, Glanville picked up a small bag from a narrow hallway table and moved off to the right, deeper into the house. He beckoned for the two men to follow him and led them through several rooms before ending up at a door towards the back of the house. He fished a small key out of his pocket and unlocked the door, stepping back he gestured for the others to join him, "Gentlemen," he said, "my clinic."

Mokti blurted "It's in your house?"

"Don't be ridiculous, boy. I bought the property behind me and built the bloody thing there. I don't mind paying for its upkeep, but I'll be damned if I have to drive to work each day. Come on, in we go." The three entered the clinic, walking down a long corridor with several doors on each wall before they finally entered a reception area. Behind a functional but plain desk sat a functional but plain man. When he saw the doctor, he smiled and it transformed his face, a joy and life leapt from his visage as he regarded the approaching Professor Glanville.

"Professor!" he exclaimed happily, "How are you, sir?"

"I'm well, Frank. Who do we have today?" The young man gave the doctor a clipboard.

"The dinner volunteers are in the kitchen. We have one walk-in waiting in room 2 plus the regular group in meeting room 3. I have had a phone call from a chap who wants to see you to discuss his regen. He thought he was fine but now it's all going bad."

"Any details?"

"Nothing over the phone, I asked him to stop by in an hour; that'll give you time to do your routine visits."

"Well done, Frank, I'll just pop into the kitchen to say hello to the volunteers. Is it the usual Tuesday night bunch?" Frank nodded.

Isaac felt the interview had well and truly slipped out of his control, "Professor Glanville!" he exclaimed, "May we please finish our discussion?" Glanville stopped his walk towards another, larger corridor, the walls held signs indicating the kitchen, some wards and the meeting rooms. Mokti noticed the sign back over the corridor leading to Professor Glanville's house, it read "Private".

"What is it, Detective Howard? Come on, man, I'm not getting any younger."

Isaac took a breath and gambled it all, "Doctor, is it possible for someone you know to be carrying out illegal cloning? And would these clones exhibit the symptoms of fused fingers and ear, plus milky eyes?"

"Illegal cloning?" responded the doctor. "Someone I know?" he thought a moment and said "Yes." He opened the door to the kitchen a spoke again, "The symptoms you describe would be presented by someone after multiple incorrect cloning. By 'incorrect', I mean the cells for the clone would be from the original body, but continued regenerations would lead to more and more catastrophic clones. Of course, multiple defects such as you describe would have one other symptom ..."

Isaac pushed after the professor as he entered the kitchen "Which is?"

"He'd be mad," said Glanville as he walked through the door. "Barking".

Mokti followed Isaac and the doctor into the kitchen where the volunteers worked at stainless steel benches, cutting, stirring and carrying out an array of domestic chores.

"Evening, all," greeted the doctor. He indicated the two men following him, "Liz, I believe you might know these characters." Isaac stopped, Mokti collided with his back.

Behind the nearest bench, Black Betty was dishing out the soup.

Chapter 29

Isaac's mouth opened and closed a few times before the inspector spoke, "Get on the end of that spoon, Detective Howard," she instructed.

Mokti followed Isaac to the serving area where they were both given jobs to do; it seemed to be assumed that they had turned up to do volunteer work. Isaac found himself next to Black Betty, each dishing out a different food, serving as people moved past the benches.

"What are you doing here, Detective Howard?" asked the inspector. A middle-aged man stood before her, all the fingers of both hands were fused together with only the thumbs distinct, holding the tray was a challenge; his clothes indicated he had been sleeping rough. She ladled a scoop of soup into his bowl, Isaac passed him some bread.

Isaac watched the man as he moved passed them, the regenerated man kept his head down; his body had that posture of defeat, of acquiescence to the world's harsh treatment. "I'm following a line of enquiry over the Leonardo killings," he replied. "I have reason to believe that Leonardo is a regeneration gone wrong, a clone with multiple defects."

The man with the fused fingers shuffled to Mokti who placed a salad onto the tray, the young mathematician felt guilty of his limbs, his purity of form. He knew from various generalized discussions with friends at university that he was experiencing 'survivor's guilt', but the knowledge didn't diminish the feeling. He wanted to help these people, mostly he wanted to run away and pretend they didn't exist, go back to his world where he didn't have to confront deformities and human carnage.

Looking up he saw Doctor Glanville moving from patient to patient, stopping to chat occasionally. The doctor moved to a door and left the meal room, he nodded to Mokti before closing the door, mouthing, "I'll be back".

Black Betty and Isaac had been talking in low tones as they served, finally, Betty turned to him and said, "I can't believe what I'm hearing, Detective Howard. You think this Leonardo fellow is some clone gone mad? Let's hope the press doesn't get wind of your theory, they'd have a field day, especially with Professor Glanville."

"How do you know him?"

"I've been doing volunteer work of one sort or another all my life. When I moved here, I was contacted by a very charismatic member of his staff who enlisted my services. I'm happy to help and having some big names working here has spin-off benefits for the clinic. We not only serve the food, but he gets to throw our names around when he goes into fund-raising mode."

"You don't feel he's taking advantage of the situation?"

"Of course, he is! And good luck to him, poor man's spent his life giving the rest of us slobs a second chance at life with no possibility of one for himself. He's almost the last of his generation, the last of the enforced 'onelifers'."

"As opposed to the intentional ones," said Isaac, "the ones who demonstrate outside of maternity wards."

"He gets them here, too. Hate mail, burning in effigy, the whole box and dice. Poor man."

"So, you met him here at the clinic?"

"Don't be such a detective, detective; you're allowed to turn yourself off sometimes. But yes, I met him here. And his granddaughter, of course."

"She's a bit of a live wire," commented Isaac.

"You've met the vibrant Michelle? Yes, she doesn't suffer fools gladly. I like her."

I just bet you do, thought Isaac. They had been chatting quietly for some time, the last of the diners had been fed and they began to clean up. Mokti had signalled he needed a bathroom break and left the room.

As Isaac carried more dishes over to the national news anchor busily stacking the dishwasher, he noticed a young staff member enter the kitchen area and look around as if searching for someone. No matter what Black Betty said, old habits die hard, and Isaac stepped back a little to watch the young man in his search, he was curious for no particular reason.

The staff member saw his quarry and walked over to Black Betty, handing her a note. Isaac watched her unfold the slip of paper, read it and then become thoughtful. She gave the plates she was holding to the young staff member, tossed the note onto the pile of food refuse on the top plate and left the room. Before leaving she retrieved her uniform jacket from a coat hook and put it on.

The young man carried the dishes over to where Isaac was standing and prepared to empty the food scraps into a recycling bin. Before he could carry out his action Isaac moved forward and said, "I'll do that, mate. You shoot off back to wherever you're supposed to be." The young man smiled his thanks and handed Isaac the dishes. The detective carried out the required tasks, but first, he took the folded note from the top plate and put it in his pocket.

He had no reason to know what was on the note, none at all. But he wanted to read whatever was written there. Unfolding the pieces of paper, he read, "Your son is here to see you, he's in the library nook."

It wasn't the stuff of conspiracies or the missing clue. Just a note about a boy meeting his mum. Isaac sighed, pocketed the paper and went back to doing the dishes. He was stopped by a voice over his shoulder, "She's gone and left you to it, has she?" The doctor had reappeared.

Glanville smiled at the detective, "Liz is a good old stick, been a great pal to my girl. They both love shoes. Shoes and handbags, don't see much in it myself. So, where is she?"

Isaac shook off the mental picture of Black Betty being as frivolous as to try on shoes and handbags. Especially the sorts of shoes beloved by the feisty Michelle Glanville.

"Her son's dropped by for a visit," he replied absently.

Glanville paused in his perusal of the kitchen to stare at Isaac, "Her what?"

"Her son," said Isaac, knowing as he spoke that something was wrong, Glanville's face showed a mystery, a worry.

Mokti re-entered the kitchen, saw Isaac and quickly walked up to the detective, "Isaac, saw something, saw him!"

Isaac found himself confronted by two sets of questions, one for each of his interlocutors, he decided to go with Mokti's obvious agitation rather than Glanville's puzzle. "Who did you see?" he asked.

"Leonardo! When I came out of the bathroom, I could see into the reception area through the little window in the door. He was at the desk." The young man gulped "What'll we do?"

"Liz doesn't have a son," said Glanville, "Not anymore, died years ago."

Isaac's body was moving before his brain caught up, he grabbed Glanville and pulled him towards the door. Over his shoulder he yelled at Mokti, "Call the precinct and ask for Patricia Lee or Harris; tell them to get here quickly!"

He barged through the doors into the hallway, still dragging the doctor with him, once outside the kitchen he spun Glanville around to see his face, "Where's your library nook?" he demanded.

"Off our Common Room, through there," said the professor, pointing to another door off the corridor. "What's going on?"

"Shut up," commanded Isaac, he weighed up his options and concluded he didn't have a lot. "I have to go in there and find Liz, Black Betty. The man posing as her son is a mass murderer and I think he intends to kill her." It made sense, he realised, Betty had the right birth date and she was certainly in uniform, he saw again her putting on her uniform coat before leaving the kitchen.

Glanville stared at this new man before him; gone was the dishevelled, prying bureaucrat. Gone was the shambling caricature of a time-serving government worker. He was looking at the real Isaac, the man who went into dangerous places to make people safe. The man who looked society in the eye and didn't blink.

He shut up.

Isaac drew his weapon, squashed his fear back into its old familiar box and went through the door. Betty's only chance was quick action, Leonardo seemed like a gloater so he might have a few moments before he killed Betty. He knew he did not have enough time to wait for reinforcements, negotiators or a SWAT team. They might be in time for Leonardo but not for Betty. It was up to him, he shrugged off the thought that Leonardo might end up with two bodies for the price of one.

The Common Room was an austere, plain room. The floor was tiled, tables and chairs scattered randomly around the large space, decks of cards and chess sets sat waiting to be used. A side bench carried hot water facilities, mugs hung off hooks, and a small fridge nestled in a corner. The sink area was covered in used mugs and plates, tea bag refuse, spilt coffee and sugar granules; above the sink was a hand lettered sign "Please wash and put away your dishes."

The far wall had two closed doors, above each was a small sign. The first said "Storeroom"; the second announced "Library", Isaac was across the room before he realised it, his eyes registered the action of his hand pushing against the closed door and then he was in the Library Nook; a passenger in his own body.

THE ROOM NOW HELD THREE people, Isaac, Black Betty and Leonardo. They formed the points of a triangle, separated by distance but joined by events; Betty had her back to the door and did not see Isaac enter.

Leonardo did, he was facing the door and on the far side of the small room. His eyes widened in recognition at the sight of the big detective as he burst into the room, Isaac's face was set in a fierce, grim visage, a face bent on action. Violent, violent action.

A flood of almost ecstasy burst through Leonardo, this was even better than the public slaying of the police constable! What fun! What joy!

Isaac heard the end of Black Betty's question, "What do you want?"

"Say hello to the nice detective, Inspector," said Leonardo. From behind his back, he produced a pistol which he pointed at Black Betty. "Careful now, Isaac. Wouldn't want any misunderstandings to break out, would we?"

Betty turned and saw Isaac, saw the weapons each of the men held. She was unarmed. The moment held a brief pause.

"Inspector," said Isaac, "I have reason to believe this man to be Leonardo."

"I have reason to believe this man to be Leonardo," mimicked the other man. "Oh really, Isaac, such formality between us. Surely, we can have a civilized chat considering how much we mean to each other. By the way, how's the wife?"

Oh, God, thought Leonardo, he's going to shoot me! How delicious! He watched the big detective grapple with the surge of anger caused by the taunt, watched as it fought with the big man's self-control. For a few ecstatic moments, Leonardo wondered if he was about to be shot. This feeling, he decided, is just too good, it's even worth money.

"Inspector," said Isaac through clenched teeth, "Please move towards me." His pistol was already pointed at Leonardo, but he emphasized his intent by taking deliberate aim at the other man's face. "Leonardo," he instructed, "put the gun down. It's over."

"I must disagree, Zaccy-poo. One more to go in this sequence and then I can start again with the delightful Sally. How good's this, eh?" he asked.

The Inspector, Black Betty, had not moved, she saw the resolve pass across Isaac's face and knew he was moments from shooting Leonardo. She deliberately stepped in front of the killer. Putting her back to the smaller man, she faced Isaac.

"Inspector!" cried Isaac "What are you doing? Move away!"

Betty smiled softly, "I can't Isaac." A softness entered her voice, calm crossed her face, "I can't."

Leonardo grinned at Isaac over the woman's shoulder, "Bit of a surprise this, eh, Isaac? Go on, have a go, say it, 'What's going on here'? Oh, I know, can you say in your best Policeman Plod voice 'What's all this then?' Go on, do."

Isaac was flummoxed, what was going on here? Betty should know better. As this thought left his brain another entered, a realization which blossomed. "He is your son, isn't he?"

Black Betty stared into her detective's face, saw the confusion, saw her world crash. Again. She nodded sadly, "Sorry, Isaac. This is my boy, Joshua," in a whisper.

"Where are my manners?" said Joshua. "Isaac, I'm very please to meet you. Let us drop my *nom de guerre*, my alias, my AKA, as it were, and let the name 'Leonardo' drift from your mind. Please call me 'Joshua.' It means 'God is my deliverance' but I daresay a Jewish scholar such as yourself is well aware of that meaning. Lovely to drop the mask and see you in the flesh, as it were."

Joshua pushed the barrel of his pistol into Betty's side, "Hello, mum," he said. "I have to say, mother dear, I just wish you would let me go. But no, you keep bringing me back, again and again. I'm a bit over it, dear heart, and so I've come up with a way to stop the whole 'bring me back to life' thing. You'll get a kick out of the idea."

The tableau held for a heartbeat before Joshua placed an arm around Betty's waist. With the gun pressed into her side he began to edge towards the door, "Just stay there a bit, please, Zaccy," he commanded. "Mum'll see me out."

The two moved closer to the door, Black Betty's face sagged with anguish and torment, her eyes pleaded with Isaac for something. What was it, he wondered, forgiveness? Understanding?

"I didn't know what he was doing with the women's names, Isaac," she was pleading her case now, seeking forgiveness.

"Told mother I was seeking Miss Right," said Joshua. "Wanted to settle down with just the right gel. Oh, what a hoot!!" He stopped at the door, keeping his mother as a shield between himself and the detective. He placed the pistol barrel against the policewoman's neck and said, "Now just stay still for a moment while I check that the coast is clear." He used his free hand to open the door a crack and peered outside.

"All clear," he announced. "Now, what do we do here? How do I extricate myself from this seemingly impossible dilemma? Oh, Isaac, I must thank you, this is just the best fun!" He moved the pistol to press into the policewoman's back.

Betty spoke up, "Let him go, Isaac. Let him go, I can explain what happened. He won't hurt me." Over her shoulder Isaac could see Joshua's face watching his mother speak, eyes agleam with interest, fascinated by what she was saying.

"He's a killer, Inspector," stated Isaac.

"No," she said, "I don't believe it. You've made a mistake, you've got something wrong. He's not a killer. He's not!"

Isaac saw Joshua's face break into a wide, beatific smile, his eyes wide as he watched his mother.

"Actually, Mum," he said, "I am."

And he pulled the trigger.

Chapter 30

Black Betty stiffened as the bullet entered her back, and a look of astonishment crossed her face. Her red-lipped mouth opened in a little 'O' of surprise.

She was still erect as Joshua darted out the door, he pushed the falling body towards Isaac. The detective reached and caught her as she fell, the weight of both their bodies causing him to stumble backwards into the now closed door leading to the rest of the facility.

"He...," she stuttered, "he shot me." Isaac lowered her to the floor, blood streaming between the fingers of his hand as he pressed against the entry wound. Black Betty settled against the door, her head slumped onto her chest and final betrayal in her eyes. "My boy ... my boy...."

Isaac moved her onto the floor, allowing him to crack the door a little. "Help!" he called into the corridor "Help!" He moved Betty to her side and examined the wound, the entry site was ragged but small, the bullet still inside the body. She coughed a little, specks of blood foaming at her lips, Isaac knew her lung had been punctured; he placed her on her side, the wound down so any blood might drain out of her body and not fill her lungs. He swapped hands to get better pressure on the wound, blood pooling as they slumped on the floor.

Using a blood-smeared hand he fumbled for his phone and called for an ambulance. He could run after Joshua, follow him through the other door and perhaps catch him. Or he could stay here and try to save Betty.

He stayed.

MOKTI PUSHED AGAINST the door, behind him was Professor Glanville followed by other staff members.

"Push hard!" he heard Isaac yell, "I'll try to move. We need medical help here!"

After a heave, Mokti was able to push Isaac and his limp charge away enough to allow others to enter. Glanville immediately went down on one knee to examine the wounded police officer, Isaac quickly told him of the bullet and its entry point. Glanville snapped some instructions to his people while he opened Betty's uniform jacket and blouse.

Isaac stood up beside Mokti, both men looking at the doctor as he worked on the patient. Betty's eyes had rolled back, she was unresponsive to any of the tugs and prods; her whole body quivered whenever it was moved, a wave of motion rippling through her inert form. Isaac was worried, Mokti thought she was dead.

Harris and Lee arrived before the ambulance, running in with guns drawn. A host of uniformed officers followed shortly after. They found the sad little scene in the library, Glanville still toiling over the inert policewoman, Isaac sitting slumped on a chair with blood dripping from the fingers of each hand. Mokti hadn't moved, he stood transfixed by the unfolding battle before him, watching Glanville rummage through a small bag brought in by an assistant.

"This is a clinic, for God's sake!" he was saying. "Not an emergency department! I don't have any tools for a bullet wound!!" He muttered and cursed, continuing to pack the wound with a series of bandages that came to hand, blood trickling between splayed fingers.

Betty remained unresponsive.

The paramedics arrived and moved the professor out of the way. Within moments they had a drip inserted and a more secure dressing applied; they quickly moved Betty onto a gurney and efficiently transported her out to the waiting van. Patricia Lee followed her out, she and Harris had already discussed roles and both agreed that Isaac was out of the running for a while. So, Harris would do the follow-up here while Patricia sent uniforms to stand guard over the Inspector in case of another attempt on her life. If she survived this one.

Isaac placed a smeary hand on the white sleeve of the last departing paramedic; the man stopped and looked down at the seated detective.

"How is .... I mean, will she?" asked the big man.

The paramedic shook his head, "Don't know, mate. She's still alive but we have to move. That bullet could be anywhere inside her, tearing up God knows what. We have to go." He gently prised the bloody fingers from his sleeve, patted the detective on the shoulder and left the room.

Harris sat down beside Isaac, gestured to another chair for Mokti. Patrica rejoined them after finishing up with the paramedics.

"What happened?" he asked them.

Isaac rolled his shoulders, stretched his back, leaned his hands on the table and began to speak, filling in his fellow detective on all that had happened.

At the end of the recital, Harris leaned back and said, "Shit."

JOSHUA WALKED TOWARDS his parked car, unable to believe the feelings surging through his emotional account. The blood pounded in his ears, the air was fresher, the sky a sharper blue than he had ever seen before.

Surely, those other idle pedestrians could see the same majesty to the day? Why were they walking so hang dog? He felt he had to make an effort to keep his feet on the ground, at any moment he might begin to walk on the very air!

He opened the door to his latest vehicle and experienced a fleeting concern that it was too small for him. Would he fit within that small space, surely he had grown in stature; he possessed an immensity, not a mere human form.

The drive back to Sally and Evie was one of barely contained euphoria. He must do that again, he must talk to the police, taunt them with his power, dangle a hostage in front of their myopic and pale lives.

And then take that life away, kill in public. Let others, many others, see him, feel his presence.

This was just too good. Forget the Fibonacci Sequence, its usefulness had finished, he had found a better game now. No more tricks, little mysteries and games for silly little policemen like Isaac to follow. Now he would merely walk into any public building and kill at random.

Perhaps kill many? Oh, yes. He writhed with anticipation.

But first, he would tidy up his garage, his little room where Sally waited for his will and the van containing the still sleeping Evie. Perhaps a scenario involving the lissom young girl and her previous employer, the doctor? Perhaps both found naked in bed together, arms entwined in death. Yes, a fittingly embarrassing tableau, the doctor was of no further use and the scene would make a wonderful statement for the media.

He considered Sally's death. A simple slaying as she lay captive would do, but perhaps something else? He drove the rest of the journey blissfully debating the many ways he could kill Sally, the manner, the place and the time.

Life can be so much fun, he thought.

ISAAC, HARRIS, MOKTI and Patricia continued to talk, trying to make sense of the killing.

"Leonardo's real name is Joshua? He's Black Betty's son?" said Patricia.

"That's what he told me," said Isaac. "But Professor Glanville said that Betty doesn't have son. I don't understand."

"She hasn't got a son, mate" replied Harris. "The family split up early on in the piece, husband was a drunk, shot through and took the boy with him. The story goes that the son grew up bad. Not surprising, with an abusive, addictive father and an absent mother. One night, years later, he was tanked up pretty well when he drove their car off a bridge and into the drink. The son was in the passenger seat. Betty was told about it when she was at work and went on to finish her shift before going to identify the bodies. She only claimed the son's body, left the husband for the state to deal with."

"What about cloning them? Did they each get a second life?" asked Mokti.

"No life insurance, he'd cashed in their policies and drank all the money away," said Harris. "The husband was buried and his LifeChip extracted for storage. It'll be in the LifeCorps facility somewhere, with all the other personalities who couldn't afford a clone. His cells would still be in the main LifeCorps vault, don't know what happens to them."

"What about the son? asked Patricia.

"No one knows," said Harris. "The rumour mill said she took her son and had him buried privately. Came back to work two days later."

"When was that?" asked Isaac.

"Four or five years ago," said Harris.

The coldness of Betty's persona crept back into the room, a mother who would see her job done before viewing her dead family. A mother who would bury her son, choosing the solitude of her grief over the comfort of others.

"Betty said he was her son. Joshua confirmed the relationship when he spoke to me," said Isaac.

"Did she have other children? Any adopted?" asked Patricia.

"No," said Harris, "or if she did, she kept it very quiet. Her police bio doesn't mention any family and the checks are very rigorous before someone is promoted to Inspector level. I think we can say there were no other children."

"Which makes Joshua the son who was killed and buried," said Patricia.

"But Joshua is a clone, right?" asked Isaac to the room, the others looked at him. "Where did he come from? He was cloned because he died! Where did he die?"

"But we checked all the deaths, all the hospitals and morgues," said Harris.

"He didn't go to a hospital or a morgue," stated Isaac. "His mother took him. Took him somewhere."

"There's no death certificate on file, no record of the burial. I checked," muttered Harris.

"Hang on," said Mokti, stepping forward, "If he died and we can't find a record then it isn't about where he was **buried**. Because he wasn't buried! The question isn't about his body, it's about the accident, it's about where he **died**!"

Patricia Lee returned an encouraging look and squeezed Mokti's arm, so he went on. "After Mary's death, did you check all the local accidents which led to a fatality?" he asked. Patricia nodded. "What about accidents that **didn't** have a fatality reported? But an accident where **maybe** there was a fatality!"

"Shit," repeated Harris, "there was one, I remember it. That's what I meant when I said I wanted to check on a few things – I wanted to look at all the serious accidents near the scene that day, the same afternoon as Mary's murder. I was just looking, no real reason, just, you know, that feeling." He stood up, pacing as he remembered, "A motorist reported a hit and run with a motorbike, said the guy came out of nowhere, cut directly in front of his car. The driver was sure he hit him and said his car had a hell of a dent. I remember reading the report and thinking we had a possibility, that the biker could be Leonardo/Joshua - but there was no linked ambulance callout, no hospital visit. The police on the scene found a motorbike but no rider, they figured he had run off. Nothing was recorded and there would have been if someone was hit by a car that hard. The report was filed as a 'Fled the Scene." He stopped and ran fingers through his hair, "Maybe he didn't flee, maybe he was dead or dying. Mybe his mum took him again. Damn. It still doesn't help us – where did they go?"

After a moment Mokti spoke, "No address, then." He sat down; the others went back into themselves, defeated.

"Yes, there bloody well is!" shouted Isaac, leaping to his feet. "The motorbike! The bloody bike, Harris. Didn't the stupid sods check out the address for someone fleeing the scene of an accident!"

Harris gawped at the big detective for a moment, then plunged his hand into his coat and extracted a mobile phone.

SALLY HEFTED THE CROWBAR, she had found it on the bottom shelf of a locked metal cabinet, the door of which hung broken and unhinged. She looked at the damage she had done, her rage had blossomed and she had kicked and kicked the cabinet door. The old Tae Kown Do lessons finally earning their keep on the thin metal. The cabinet was useful for keeping things away from children and casual busybodies, but not a feral, trapped woman.

"Anytime now is good for me, Joshua," she whispered and swung the crowbar at the deadlock on the main door.

The lock held but the door around it broke, pieces of the wood splintering under the repeated blows. Finally, the door groaned open, the last sag of wood joining the lock snapping away in disgust; a small gap appeared. She was almost free.

Sally dropped the crowbar and ran back to pick up the bag containing the laptop. She snagged the strap on her shoulder and returned to the door, stepping back on one foot she released a yell as she snapped her right foot into a full-blooded front kick. The door lost the argument, swinging open to reveal her path to freedom; the next room was some sort of garage, a roller door shutting off the rest of the world.

In the large garage space was a Medical Transport van, there was plenty of room for another vehicle. As Sally moved past the van towards her freedom she heard a noise. A little sob. It was coming from the van.

Was someone else in there, she wondered, had Joshua taken another prisoner?

She opened the rear doors and saw a prone figure trussed to one of the gurneys, a woman with fear in her eyes, a fear Sally recognized. She quickly entered the vehicle and, remembering her own discomfort and terror, she untied the gag.

Before either woman could speak, they heard a rattle, a clanking noise.

The roller door was rising.

JOSHUA SWUNG THE NOSE of his car into his garage and saw Sally in the back of the medical van. He could see that Evie was still inside the vehicle and a quick glance showed him Sally had found a way out of his secure room. His supposedly secure room with the now broken door.

So much for DIY, he thought. Next time I get a professional.

He stopped the car with just the nose poking into the garage and the rest of the vehicle blocking the entrance. Sally stood framed in the rear doors of the van, bag over her shoulder.

Their eyes met.

Joshua smiled. Sally snarled.

Evie whispered, "It's Joshua! Run!" She swallowed, "Untie one of my hands and get out of here, get help!"

Evie knew she wasn't being noble, she wanted Joshua to chase her rescuer. She had been a silent witness to Sally's capture. Joshua had not explained his fixation on the girl and Evie had not sought an explanation. Evie would do anything to keep his gaze off her and on Sally, this strange woman who had just appeared. This strange woman who moved with deliberation and something else – assuredness? An implacability? In any event, Evie did not want anything to do with her. While Joshua chased her rescuer, she reasoned, she would be able to free herself and get away.

"Get away!" Evie urged, as Sally freed one of the bound girl's hands, "GO!"

ISAAC DROVE, HARRIS sat beside him, visually confirming their route with the dash-mounted GPS. In the back seat, Mokti sat beside Patricia, both rocking around corners as the big man drove with passion, determination and a disregard for road rules. Some of the corners seemed particularly fierce, pressing the two together with a warmth the young Muslim found fascinating yet unsettling; he looked a question at Patricia, but she just smiled a particular smile into his rabbit-like face.

Now I know what 'inscrutable' means, he thought.

Harris had found an address. The owner of the motorbike in the accident listed a workplace as the point of contact. A workplace located in a row of industrial sheds in one of the seedier parts of town. The car containing Isaac, Harris, Mokti and Patricia sped towards these sheds.

"Nearly there, mate," said Harris to Isaac, not a little worried over their ability to survive the journey. "Steady down a bit, drive to survive, and all that."

Isaac wasn't hearing anything. All he could see was the need to find Sally, find her before Joshua did something dreadful to her. Find her safe and whole. He relived the finding of Mary, the moment of realization when his world went away, the flash in time when he pushed the bushes to one side and saw her lying on the cold, leaf strewn earth. Chest cut open, eyes open, face surprised.

That was what he saw, he never heard Harris, not a word.

The car erupted into a row of light industrial sheds, Harris saw the glow representing their car on the GPS come closer and closer to a similar glow which showed their destination.

They were nearly there.

SALLY SAW THE SMILING face of her tormentor, he waved at her as he opened the car door.

His car effectively blocked the roller door exit, but to her right was a stairway leading up. A smaller door was next to the big roller bay, but Joshua was very close to it. To reach that door she would have to approach the vile man, an action she briefly considered before she saw him reach a hand into his jacket and withdraw a gun.

She turned and bolted up the stairs.

JOSHUA SNAPPED A SHOT off at Sally and missed. He was not too interested – if he had hit the girl he would have been amazed at his marksmanship. A miss was to be expected, a hit would have just been too good for words.

He saw that Evie was still on the gurney in the back of the van, her struggles indicated she seemed to be still tied down securely. Anyway, he thought, onwards and upwards. Things to do, places to go.

People to kill.

He shut the van's rear doors as he passed the vehicle; Evie stared wide-eyed back at him. She struggled against her bonds, twisting her body so that her freed hand was hidden. Her survival depended upon Joshua walking by and he would only do that if she was still secure. As the door shut, she squeezed out some tears and managed a dry sob. She hoped she was projecting helpless fear.

Josua got off on helpless fear.

He had considered just shooting her on the spot but decided to keep her for his later plans. She was still secure in the van, Sally was the main game. Just so much to do.

How good's this? he thought as he walked towards the stairs, I get to have a quick game before moving on. Little game of hide and seek with Sally and then back for Evie.

What fun.

Chapter 31

The stairs led onto a narrow walkway which opened out onto a wide, flat storage area. Some boxes were scattered around the floor and an old motorbike lay tiredly on one side. The rest of the space was taken up by discarded tools, piles of paper and dry refuse.

Nowhere to hide.

Sally ran to the centre of the walkway and looked back at the stairs, Joshua was slowly walking upwards, examining his gun as he lightly ascended. Her movement had caused the walkway to rock and a slight vibration was transmitted back to the stairs and to the feet of her tormentor. He looked up and saw Sally, smiled and gave her a little wave. He pointed the finger of his right hand at her and mouthed the word 'bang' before continuing up the stairs, smiling every step of the way.

She turned and ran to the storage area, casting around for a weapon, a solution. She was out of options.

Nowhere to run.

"HERE! HERE!" YELLED Harris. He grabbed the dashboard to steady himself against the sliding stop the car executed, bits of dust and some discarded paper blossomed around the skidding tyres.

Isaac was out of the car before it stopped, he drew his heavy pistol while casting around for spoor.

The sheds were all closed except for one, in the open roller doorway of the facility immediately in front of his vehicle there stood another car. Isaac ran to it and squeezed past the vehicle, the interior of the shed was dark after the outside glare and he could not see anything.

He stood stock still, waiting for his vision to adjust. When it cleared, he saw the broken door in the far internal wall but no people.

No Sally.

"Yoo-hoo!" called a familiar voice, "Up here, Zaccy-poo."

Isaac looked up to see Joshua leaning on the safety rail of an upper walkway; the little man had both hands extended as they rested on the railing, he was smiling. In his hands was a gun, pointing steadily at the big detective.

Joshua squeezed the trigger.

SALLY SAW A DOOR.

A little door sat at the far end of the storage area, it was set into the sloping metal ceiling next to a window. Anywhere was better than here, she decided, and ran past the boxes and the motorbike. When she arrived at the door, she was not surprised to find it locked. Yet another obstacle.

"Bugger this," she said and kicked the metal. With a loud crash, the door flew backwards on its hinges revealing a small patch of blue sky. She stepped up to the opening and saw that it opened onto a narrow service walkway running alongside the sloping roof. From behind her came the sound of a shot.

JOSHUA MISSED.

Isaac stood watching the man as the trigger was squeezed, he held the other man's gaze during the entire episode, not flinching. He stood as an indestructible pillar in the face of evil.

Joshua stood up, wondering where his shot had gone. The loud bang behind him must have put him off, he realised. Sally was such a nuisance, time to finish this.

"Be down in a minny, petal," he called to Isaac, "Just want to see Sally off." He waved down at the big detective, subtly impressed by the other's imperturbability. The big clown didn't even flinch when I shot at him, he thought, just proves he has no brains, no imagination. Policeman Plod.

Other people pushed passed Isaac and carried him with them into the body of the shed.

More audience, thought Joshua delightedly. Be still my beating heart, another public slaying.

Oh, please, Sally, he silently begged, find somewhere wonderful for your final moments. Somewhere with space for others to see.

He turned and ran down the storage area towards the open door onto the roof.

THE WALKWAY RAN AROUND the edge of the sloping roof, each side rising to a tall peak jutting bravely into the sky; a low wall separated the walkway from a descent into nothingness. Sally looked over the side into the long drop to the ground.

Not so bad, she thought, only one flight and a bit, I could probably survive a fall. Broken leg maybe, if I'm lucky. Could be worse.

Then her brain tapped her on the shoulder with a replay of the words from Joshua: "Zaccy-poo"?

Was Isaac here?

She ran around the walkway, slowing at the first corner to take the sharp right-angled turn. Before she disappeared, she looked back and saw Joshua poke his head out of the small door.

"Honey!" he called, "I'm home."

"UP THE STAIRS!" COMMANDED Isaac, pressing forward. He ran up the stairs to the storage area and stopped, waiting for another shot from Joshua. When none came, he scanned the space around him, searching for signs of his quarry. Slowly edging forward, he kept his pistol out, the barrel following his eyes around the room; behind him, the others clattered up the stairs.

"There!" exclaimed Patricia. "The little doorway! I saw his leg as he went through!" Pushing aside her bulkier companions she ran to the doorway, running past some old boxes she reached down and grabbed an empty carton.

"Pat!" called Harris, afraid of an ambush. Joshua could be just standing on the other side of the door, waiting to shoot whoever showed their head.

But Mrs. Lee did not raise her daughter to be a fool. Patricia stopped before she reached the door and placed her back against the wall; with a gun held high in her right hand, she used her left hand to throw the empty box through the doorway.

Harris, Isaac and Mokti arrived in time to hear it clatter onto the roof; no gun sounded. The three detectives exchanged knowing glances and readied themselves. Mokti knew they had passed some arcane communication to each other, the way they stood, the way they shuffled their feet, the way they took up different positions around the door. It all said they knew what they were doing, and what they were doing was very, very dangerous. Mokti took a few backward steps, whatever they had planned was way out of his skill set.

Isaac nodded and leapt through the door, closely followed by Patricia and Harris. Mokti took a deep breath and followed.

The three detectives were in single file on the walkway, it wasn't wide enough for more than one at a time to pass along. Patricia was facing off to the left, and Isaac crouched with a gun raised towards the right. Harris was peering over the edge when Mokti emerged from the doorway and bumped into him. The black detective lurched forward, close to tumbling off the roof and threw out a hand, Mokti caught it and pulled him back. Harris glared at the young man.

"Yeah, er, sorry, mate," Mokti said.

Harris shook himself back to normalcy, then turned to Isaac. "See him?"

"I think he went around that far corner," said the big man, moving forward rapidly. "Pat, stay here in case he doubles back." Looking back over his shoulder, he caught sight of his young friend, "And you stay inside, Mokti. Too much bloody paperwork if you get hurt."

"I love you too, man," muttered Mokti.

"Take that pretty head indoors, sweetheart," murmured Patricia in his ear. "You wouldn't want to distract a girl, would you?"

The young man stammered, felt his ears grow hot and found himself stepping back into the safety of the storage area.

Joshua was not the only scary one out there, he decided.

THE ROOF WAS NOT HIGH, certainly not high enough to bother a man such as he, decided Joshua.

Now, where had Sally gotten to?

He knew the detectives were close behind, knew it and savoured the delicate taste of pursuit. Exquisite.

The walkway turned another corner, and when he reached it, he looked back for a moment and saw Isaac doggedly following but still some distance behind. He gave him a little wave, he was such fun to taunt, and the big man responded so wonderfully to teasing. Joshua was going to miss him.

Still, life goes on, as mother would say. Used to say.

Looking ahead, he finally saw Sally, she had stopped about halfway down the walkway and was looking over the edge. Just in front of her a plank led across to another higher building. A much higher building.

"Don't jump!" he called. She mustn't jump, no, no, no. "Sally," he pleaded, "have a heart!" Where was the fun in that?

He put his gun away and ran towards her, arms outstretched. Her saviour cometh.

SALLY SAW ISAAC'S CAR down below, he was here! Then she heard Joshua pleading with her not to jump. She realised he was very close. Planning went from her mind, replaced by the need to flee, the need to escape the predator.

She stepped up onto the plank and ran up it to the higher building where it led to the very apex of the adjacent roof. This building ran lengthways to the one she had just left, the entire building was side on to Isaac and Harris. Stepping off, she felt the plank vibrate and realised Joshua was close behind.

She had stepped onto the centre of the peak of a very high building. Her feet were at the start of a narrow walkway, probably an inspection ledge for maintenance men; it ran to both ends of the roof, a distance of about sixty feet. On each side, the roof sloped away, and there was no matching walkway down below around its circumference. If she fell from this height she would die. A misstep would send her sliding down the rusted metal of the roof until she disappeared over the edge into certain death.

Knowing Joshua was behind her, she moved forward, a little way ahead she saw another of the small doors in the roof. If it was unlocked, she might have enough time to get through it and escape!

As she reached the door she heard a crash, looking back she saw Joshua dusting his hands. He had pushed the plank off the roof, there was no way Isaac could reach her in time.

Her fingers scrabbled on the door, finally finding the recessed latch. She heaved up with all her might.

The door remained shut. Locked or jammed, it didn't matter.

"Couldn't you just spit?" asked a voice behind her.

MOKTI DESCENDED THE stairs while thinking about the best way to make himself useful; he decided the best place for him was outside in the street – he could meet the reinforcements and fill them in on developments.

As he passed the van he saw it rock. Puzzled, he opened the rear doors and saw Evie. He grinned tentatively at the prisoner. Evie hit him with her megawatt smile, Mokti's brain lurched as his primal response skipped past the thinking centres.

"Uh," he dribbled.

"Please," whispered Evie. "Untie me. Help me, Joshua forced me to drive the van and then put me back here." She swallowed and paused, wetting her lips with a moist tongue she gave it her final pitch, looking pleadingly into the young man's face she husked, "Rescue me?"

Mokti leaped into the van and untied the young woman, she sat up and flung her arms around his neck. "Thank you," she nuzzled into his ear.

He dissolved, all decision making given over to his hormones.

Evie released her newest conquest and took stock of her situation. It would not take a lot of work to discover her involvement with Joshua, the clones and all her illegal activities. She had a few moments until someone with a brain came by and started asking unwelcome questions.

"I need to get out of this van," she whimpered, "I feel so trapped in here."

Mokti jerked into action, he hustled himself out of the van and raised a hand to assist his fair damsel. Evie bent low to exit the vehicle but stopped before stepping down to the floor, looking back into the van she saw the small briefcase containing the illegal tech. The very valuable tech obtained from Jimmy that afternoon.

She was conscious of being in a moment, one of those rare moments of opportunity; that brief pause before the jackpot pays off, that breath before the lover acknowledges his obeisance. She could take the tech and set herself up, get away from the doctor and whatever fallout came down over the events of the last day. A brief montage ran through her mind, the doctor hitting her with the ashtray, Joshua's eyes, his pleasure in killing, the handing over of the two clones, but most of all she remembered poor little Charlie Knox.

She didn't want to be a Knox.

"Just a moment, sweetie," she said and ducked back into the van, quickly retrieving the case.

Mokti's mind kept reliving the experience of Evie's arms around his neck. the feel of her soft breath on his neck and now the clamouring trumpet call of her voice calling him, 'sweetie'. He smiled inanely at her as she finally exited the van holding a small briefcase.

"Would you like to sit down?" he asked.

Evie looked around, so far she was alone with this drone but she knew moments were precious. She moved towards the driver's side doorway of the car blocking the garage doorway, a quick glance revealed the keys were still in the ignition. Time for Evie to shine, she thought, time for me to give this kid a memory he'll have wet dreams over.

"Where is everyone?" she purred, placing one hand gently on Mokti's chest.

"Up on the roof. Chasing Joshua." His brain debated staying or handing over controls to baser thoughts while Evie's hand performed a slow, sensual rub against his chest.

"Isn't there anyone else around? Any police?" A thought struck Evie, "You're not a policeman, are you, sweetie?" He didn't look the type but she wasn't about to take any chances; her hand moved and played with the hairs on the back of his neck.

The young man gurgled, "Me? No, I'm a uni student." He maintained his vaguely imbecilic gaze at this young goddess; Evie recognized the puppy look and sighed with relief.

"I need a drink. Could you please find me some water?" Evie touched Mokti's cheek as she spoke, giving it a gentle stroke to communicate at a baser level; her lips parted and a tongue darted out to moisten their glistening surface. "There might be some in that room." Evie indicated the room which had recently held Sally as a captive; she let her body brush Mokti with the gesture.

He shuddered and jerked, his entire world now revolved around this holy quest. Find some water! His brain conceded defeat and went to sit in a corner to watch how things played out.

The young man scanned the garage, saw the doorway and disappeared into the room. Inside he ran from cupboard to shelf before wrenching open a refrigerator. On the door were several bottles of water and juice – he stood and thought a moment. What if his queen would have preferred juice? She said water but maybe he could take a bottle of fruit juice out as well, she would be impressed with his thoughtfulness, amazed at his ability to see to her every need. She would fall into his arms and he would gaze proudly over her head, the master of the situation. A man among men.

Grabbing two bottles of water and two of juice – just to be sure – he moved back out into the garage.

Evie was now where to be seen.

After a moment Mokti realised that Joshua's car was also missing. His brain asked if it could come back into the control room and take charge.

SALLY STOOD AND FACED the milky gaze of Joshua, a soft smile on his face, a gentle, quizzical expression on his face. He was too far away for one of her kicks, but if he got in close then she would try.

Joshua waited for Sally to do or say something. Surely, she had some witty remark? Remembering the kicked in door, he drew his gun and waved it at her, "Since I can't do the cutting business with you, Sal, I may just have to shoot you and get on." He gestured over his shoulder to where Isaac and Harris stood helplessly on the other side of the chasm.

From that far distance, Isaac watched, impotent and angry. The two figures were silhouetted against the blue sky, two tiny bodies perched on a thin strip of safety.

"What about a shot?" asked Harris. "Reckon we could get him?"

"Not me, a handgun's hopeless at a distance, we try only if Sally's dead. At this range, we could hit anything. You get back downstairs and across the road to that building, we have to catch that bastard." Harris moved off back the way he had come.

Across on the other roof, Joshua saw Harris move off and knew he only had moments to make good his escape. If he shot Sally now, he could break open the door in the roof and get away. But he had to do it now.

He raised his gun, he would not miss.

"Detective Harris!" called Sally. "Please stop!" To Joshua, she whispered urgently, "You don't want to shoot me." She unbuttoned her blouse, tugging the material from her waistband.

Joshua was perplexed and amused, he could see that Harris had stopped and wondered what Sally had in mind. Surely not a bit of sex, a bit windy up here and besides, did she think she was so good he would spare her life?

This game just kept getting better and better.

"What's on your mind, Sal?" he asked.

"Look," she said, "you could just shoot me. No problem, you get away. All done. But what about this?" She opened her blouse to reveal soft white skin and two small breasts.

Joshua was puzzled, "Not sure if I'm quite with you, old girl. Lovely body and all that but my dear child, there is a time and a place. Where do you think you are, for goodness' sake?"

"I don't mean sex," she said, "I mean what's under here." She tapped her chest "Do you have a knife?"

Harris had returned to Isaac, both men watching the scene unfold before them, both transfixed. They could not hear what was being said but they could see Sally's actions.

Joshua stepped forward, an idea blossoming in his mind, "Do you mean your LifeChip?"

"That's right. I know you're going to kill me, I know there's nothing I can do about it. But I'll set you a challenge, a game."

Joy exploded into Joshua's soul, a game! "What game would that be, Sal?"

"You come here and shoot the lock off that door and open it, I'll step well back. You'll be between me and the door, nothing I can do to escape."

He teased the idea around, "Don't see any gain in it for you, Sal. And I can't see why you'd give me a free chance to escape. What's on your tiny mind, lassie?"

"Here's the game. You can still get my LifeChip, but to do it you have to spend a few moments cutting me open. And once I'm dead those men over there," she nodded to Isaac and Harris, "will rush to capture you. So, can you get my LifeChip and be quick enough to get away? That's the game. How good are you?"

He squirmed with delight, what a rush! Those two wallopers across the way would see it all, would see him cut open Sally! Oh, the deliciousness of it all. And getting away? Piffle. He'd had a bit of experience extracting LifeChips, in a special pocket of his jacket was a small device that would perform the whole manoeuvre in the blink of an eye. He would not need a knife, speed would allow him to win this game.

Sally backed up a few steps, away from the trapdoor to freedom.

"You're on, Sal. Now just stand still, this won't hurt a bit." He began to walk forward, gun outstretched, alert for any sudden trick. As he reached the locked door into the roof he bent down and fired a shot, the lock was destroyed and he easily opened the door. Freedom beckoned, but first for Sally; she just stood still, serene and erect.

Joshua took out a small device, a hand-held LifeChip Extractor. He held it up towards his prey's chest and smiled.

She was far from serene. She had expected to see a knife, something to slow Joshua down. The LifeChip Extractor would give him an edge and

Sally knew she was going to die. Her tormentor approached with his gun outstretched, ready to shoot her at the slightest provocation.

She summoned all her willpower and remained still. The nervous young girl from a few days ago had gone, replaced by someone with steel inside. She had a solution.

As Joshua placed the device on her chest, she looked into his eyes, his milky, crazy eyes.

She smiled and said, "Time to go, Leo," and threw her arms around him.

He struggled, and writhed in her grip, "What are you doing, woman? This wasn't part of the game!"

"It's a part of my game," she responded. Then she jumped off the roof, dragging Joshua with her onto the sloping tin.

As they slid painfully down the metal he shrieked, "You'll die too, you stupid, stupid woman!!"

"But I'm coming back, you sick bastard!" she spat.

They both tumbled over the lip and plummeted to the ground. To their deaths.

Isaac was running back along the walkway the moment Sally grabbed Joshua, he heard the sickening splat as their bodies hit the pavement. Mokti and Patricia were just flashes as he sped past them and down the stairs, "Get the paramedics in! Now!!"

He reached the ground floor and rushed passed his car towards the two bodies, both in that awful repose of brokenness that can only be finished by death. "Sally!" he cried, cradling the young woman in his arms.

She opened her eyes to see the big man over her, his face a mask of anguish and rage, the pain was far away, and she felt her life trickling out. "See ...," she coughed, "see you in a few months."

Then Sally died.

Chapter 32

The paramedics bent over Sally's body, one of them took Isaac off to one side and made sure he could not see the chip extraction procedure. The man performing the task positioned his machine and depressed the switch. A slight click sounded followed by a meatier noise. After a few moments, a small screen lit up and a series of messages were displayed. He looked at his partner and gave him the thumbs up.

"All good, mate," said the paramedic, "we'll get her LifeChip back to base. She'll be up and about before you know it."

Isaac felt both relieved and sad. The new Sally would be fine, but even so, he couldn't help but feel a sense of loss for the poor sad body at his feet. This Sally was gone.

Patricia held a laptop bag in one hand, "Sally was pretty keen on this, reckon it might be worth looking into, Isaac."

He sighed and turned to find Harris standing over the body of Joshua. "What's the situation with him?" asked the big man.

"He's gone. Gone and not coming back; I doubt we'll be cloning him again." The two men moved away and joined Patricia and Mokti at the car.

"Funny thing, though. He was still alive when I got to him" said Harris, "So I asked him."

"Asked him what?" queried Mokti. The others knew the question.

"I asked him why he did it. Why he killed so many people? Damndest thing"

The silence lengthened.

Mokti gave up trying to be cool, "What'd he say?" he blurted.

Harris looked at the three of them, "Joshua said he was tired of his mother always bringing him back. No matter how hard he tried, she would not let him go. He said he needed to have a purpose in life, something to do. His final words - 'A man's got to have a hobby.'"

SOME MONTHS LATER, Sally opened her eyes in the hospital bed. People stood around her, some medical, others her new friends.

"Hiya, Sally," said Mokti. "Good to see you again."

"Joshua?" she croaked.

"All gone," replied Patricia. "The courts decided it wasn't worth the expense of bringing him back, especially after the expert testimony of Professor Glanville, his words carried a lot of weight. He didn't recommend cloning Joshua, but he will be bringing Black Betty back. She's now facing criminal charges herself. We've uncovered some interesting things in her back story, she was involved with Michelle Glanville, the doctor from LifeCorps. Betty came across her some years ago, discovered her little secret and has been blackmailing her to clone Joshua each time the sad bastard died. Lord knows, he tried often enough, but she just kept on cloning him again and again. He was so damaged, poor bugger."

"The professor's daughter, the lovely Michelle, she's broken his heart," joined in Isaac. "She had a lucrative side hustle selling clones. Betty had a firm hold on her. Unfortunately, she made her escape but Jim Brodie and LifeCorps are opening their files and being cooperative, Harris is leading a team over there now."

Sally gazed with strong affection at the big detective, "We did it, Isaac, didn't we? We caught him."

"You caught him, Sally," said Isaac. "We put it all together, Mokti and the team did the thinking but it was you, Sal, you and your courage that stopped him."

Sally blushed. Her heart went out to the big man, "What about Mary's cells and her chip? Are they ... ss she ... viable?" She sank back into the pillow, hearing cold words coming from her mouth, cold words describing the fate of a woman she had never met but who loomed so large in Isaac's life.

"We think so," said Isaac. "LifeCorps are making her cloning and second life a priority. Even Professor Glanville is having a look. I find out next week." He paused, "I'd like you with me when we go to the hospital to ... to meet her again. I could do with a friend."

She felt warm, squeezed his hand and nodded, moisture starting from her eyes. Isaac grunted, stood up and continued, talking about anything to change the subject.

"LifeCorps have put you on their payroll; Jim Brodie wants you and Mokti on call as security consultants. The company's picking up all the medical bills for your treatment, they've also been paying you a salary for the last few months. You might be able to afford a car now."

"It's all over, then?" asked Sally. In the corner of the room, she could see the lumpy form of Sergeant Flannery beaming at her.

Mokti shuffled his feet, "Well, some girl called Evie got away with a briefcase containing useful tech," he said.

Patricia ruffled his hair, "You let her off, sweet cheeks. Sigh," she said, emulating the last word. "My new boyfriend is just catnip to the ladies."

They chatted a while longer before a nurse came to move them on, citing the need for Sally to rest. Mokti squeezed her shoulder while Patricia leaned in for a hug. The nurse chivvied them out and returned to gather up Isaac and Flannery.

"Good to see you again, Sally," said the big man. "I'll see you next week at the hospital, but if you ever need me, reach out." He chuckled, "You know where I live." He gave her a final, caring look and departed.

Flannery growled, moved up to beside Sally's bed and placed a box on her nightstand, "We chipped in and bought you a little something, Sally. Now that you're a top-notch private detective you need something better than that little child's taser."

Sally raised her eyebrows, "That better not be a gun, Flannery."

Flannery laughed, "Perish the thought, little one. What you've got here," he tapped the hard plastic case, "Is a top-of-the-line security Taser, it'll stop anyone."

Sally was touched and also a little mystified, why had these hard-bitten cops pooled their money to buy her such a thing? "Why?" she asked.

"Why?" he repeated. "Because you stood by Isaac, because you brought him back to us, Sally." He leaned in and patted her shoulder.

She spoke in a soft voice, "I'm not sure I need a Taser anymore."

"You surely do not, Sally girl," he said before turning to leave. He grinned, "You are one tough chick."

Sally snuggled down into the bed and closed her eyes, ready for some sleep.

"Damn right," she thought, a smile settling on her lips.

THE END

Bonus story
Jim Brodie Regrets...

JIM BRODIE DEEPLY REGRETTED his death. The rock ledge had looked firm but simply crumbled when his weight came on. He remembered watching his hand as the piece of shale came away from the cliff face; he remembered thinking, "That's not good."

The fall had hurt, his body bouncing down several outcrops of jagged rock, each one breaking more bones and flesh. At some point he lost consciousness; he could not remember finally contacting the ground and lying very, very still.

Marge saw the fall. Her heart stopped, she watched the man she loved tumble like a rag doll bouncing down the cliff face. The ground crew reached him within minutes of his final landing, he appeared conscious for a few moments before his eyes closed, his frame shuddered, and he died. Died in her arms. Marge was devastated.

The medics arrived, their white van slewing to a stop in a cloud of dust and noise. Marge knew one of them murmured a few words to her, a white noise of consolation but nothing to stop the drowning in a sea of grief.

Grief and rage. Rage and hope. Such a maelstrom of emotions. One of the medics took her away from the corpse, she heard one of them say, "He's implanted."

"I need some details, Mrs. Brodie." The medic spoke carefully, smoothly professional while still warmly human, ensuring Marge kept her back to the body, loved ones should not see the small box placed over the corpse. Should not hear the soft plop as it worked its way into the deceased's chest and extracted the memory chip. Sitting in the front seat of the ambulance she recited the details - name, address, insurance company.

She knew they had insurance, knew there would come a day in the hospital when she would hold his hand again, look into his face and see that loving smile spring from his eyes. She loved his eyes. For two months she held onto that memory. Starting in the car on the way back from the accident, she decided to hold on to the memory of his eyes. It helped, it pushed away the strange mixture of grief and anger an hope. Grief over the accident, anger at Jim for letting it happen, and at herself for being so heartless. How dare she be angry with someone who had just died? Fortunately, the hope was also there, strengthened by the interviews that followed, discussions with the technicians, visits to the clinic to view the progress.

And now, here he was, tucked up between the crisp white sheets. She looked at him, saw the eyes, saw the face, saw the smile. The hard knot of grief, tension and anger dissolved and went away. She had no regrets over the expense. The sun came out and her life began again.

Jim loved Marge. She sat beside him now, holding his hand and occasionally turning it over to check its fresh perfection. No scars, no nicks or bumps, none of those little bits of physical memory that a body picks up over thirty years of roaming the world. Jim's hand, like the rest of his body, was unblemished and would remain that way until he christened it by stubbing his toe, cutting his finger or just living life. All this would start today when he got out of bed.

"Daddy says you are to take as much time as you need to get back on your feet," said Marge, "He misses you a great deal and sends his love. Your father wants to see you this evening for drinks, sort of a coming out party, I guess." She looked at him for a moment before continuing, "And no more rock climbing or other dangerous sports. That was our deal, Jim, you promised me that you would stop doing these things if you died."

She looked nervous, thought Jim, probably wondering if I'll keep my word. "I promise, honey, no more foolishness, I've had a good run. Don't worry, I don't plan on dying any more." He surprised himself to find he meant it. Ah well, time to settle down and be responsible. "After all, "he said, "I want to be around when our kids and grandkids grow up."

Marge stood up and leaned over the bed, stroking his forehead with one hand. They gazed at each other for a few moments before she whispered, "I love you, Jim Brodie."

His hand held a piece of her skirt, clutching it to never let go. "I love you, Margaret Brodie."

Margaret smiled down at her husband. She hadn't liked watching his death. She knew it would come one day, earlier than most given his desire to push himself to extremes. While not wealthy, they had decided to keep up the insurance policy for all the family, the policy which allowed for a mistake

– the car crash, the accident, the sudden sickness or long term illness - any horrible piece of life's unfairness. Today she was glad of that decision.

She was even more glad of Jim's decision to honour his promise to stop extreme sports.

"Dad!" The door burst open as two small boys hurtled towards the bed. "Here's your clothes!" Each boy held some article of clothing, generally crunched up so tight that all semblance of tidiness had long since walked off in disgust. One blue sock was still being fought over as each boy attempted to wrest total control of the garment while also trying to be the first to their father.

Both boys crashed into the bed which gave a small shudder. Clothes were thrust at Jim while two faces looked adoringly up at him, big eyes, smooth cheeks and life abundant.

"Well done, boys," said Jim as he surveyed the intertwined jumble of shirt and slacks. "Just give me a moment." He swung his legs over the side revealing a hospital gown neatly slit up the back, offering no protection to the naked buttocks as both boys exploded into gales of laughter. Apparently seeing dad's bottom is the highest point in the comic life of a four year old.

MR. CHARLES JONES SAT on the wooden bench outside Interview Room Number 1, his hands resting on his company issued briefcase. The hospital corridors gleamed with polish and disinfectant, cold and clean and shiny. Occasionally a door would open as a competent-looking nurse trod this channel of sterility; swishing, clean uniforms thickening the austerity. His wandering eyes ran over the door opposite his seat, 'Patient Discharge' said the black letters. Patient, indeed, he thought. I certainly am.

He spent a lot of his working life waiting, sitting in hospitals just like this one, waiting to close one chapter on a person's life and open another. I suppose death could be called that, he thought, the end of a chapter. Charles Jones sometimes thought of himself as one of God's editors, doing the paperwork on a death and a resurrection.

The door opened and a well-dressed man emerged. Charles knew it was his client, the newly resurrected had a certain smoothness to their skin, a lustre known only to newborn babies and bodies fresh from the clone vats. They were bathed in the arrogance of new life. Jones stood, introducing himself.

"You're from the insurance company?" repeated Jim, he shook the agent's hand with real warmth, "Well, I certainly owe you a lot. Not sure how to say it but thank you. Thank you very much." Jim beamed at Mr Jones, still mildly surprised to find himself in a hospital corridor, whole and healthy. A bit unreal, actually.

Mr Jones opened another door leading into a small interview room. His dark suit chafed across the shoulders where his years on inactivity had begun to express themselves with a thickening torso. A nurse turned a corner and caught his eye, silently questioning his presence in her territory. He glared back, clutching his briefcase tightly, and ready to wave it in her face if challenged. His clenched jaw and stiff posture were enough for the nurse to identify an officious clerk, she turned and left.

The two men entered the room and sat on opposite sides of the small desk. Mr. Jones placed his briefcase on the floor, sat stiffly erect on the uncomfortable chair and folded his hands in his lap. Silence entered the room. Jim Brodie grinned the amiable smile of someone waiting to see what happens next. Charles Jones pursed his lips, needing a conscious effort to speak.

"Mr. Brodie," he said, they both sat, eyes meeting across the table. Jim Brodie smiled harmlessly, Charles Jones seethed.

I dislike you, Jones thought, my faith tells me to be charitable yet I find it such a struggle. Your money has given you another chance, but for what? Aren't you still the same selfish, spoilt brat who could so blithely flaunt your will and ego? How dare you decide that your will should supplant God's, he thought.

The pause stretched on, Jones closed the door on his opinions and retreated into emotionless efficiency. "I am here to complete the formalities concerning your death. I must necessarily seek your response to some questions and then ask for further instructions. May I begin?" He spoke in a low, quiet voice, leached of all feeling.

A pause developed.

LOOKING ACROSS THE table at his visitor, Jim felt detached from his surroundings. He sensed the absurdity of discussing his recent death with a life insurance salesman, surely one of the strangest interviews which could be envisioned, After all, he was dead, what right did he have to be walking around and talking about policy claims?

All he could manage was a mumbled response; Jones took this to be assent. He continued, "Mr. Brodie, you had a life insurance policy with my parent company, Mercantile & Legal, into which an annual premium had been paid by, first of all by your parents, and then by you. This policy contained the standard 'Second Life' Clause and upon your recent death this clause was activated. I must ask if you are satisfied with the service with which you have been provided."

Jim's mind was empty, what was he talking about? A Service? "I'm sorry," he asked, "I'm not sure I quite follow what you mean?"

Mr. Jones paused and looked at Jim with a totally blank face, he could have been discussing fabric patterns. "I will require you to attest that my company has fulfilled its part of the contract. This document before you asks for a signature to confirm that you have been delivered of your body and that your memories and personality have now been inserted. This is a standard form, Mr. Brodie. I must advise you that you may have it examined by your own solicitors before signing, but until you do sign, we will require that your current body and all its appurtenances such as memory inserts and personality upgrades remain in this ward which is under the direct control of Mercantile and Legal."

I could well be mad, Jim thought. "You mean I have to stay here until I sign this form?" he asked. "Um, how can you ... I mean, what .... Er ..." He ground to a halt.

"This is all very straightforward, Mr. Brodie", said Mr. Jones. "I understand it is the first time that you have died but I have been dealing with clients for some ten years and there is certainly nothing to fear. Your current body represents a considerable financial outlay and, as such, the transfer of ownership must follow certain procedures. You will have one week to sign this document and then the agreement becomes null and void and Mercantile & Legal will repossess the items in question."

Mr. Jones folded his long fingered hands together and looked across at Jim. "What are you wishes, Mr. Brodie?"

"Uh...," Brodie's mind came to a complete halt, gave up and lurched off into the unknown, "so if I don't sign this document you will take back ... er ... me?"

"Your body, Mr. Brodie, just your body. Your personality, the "you" to which you refer remains in the original piece of hardware we retrieved from your corpse." Mr. Jones gave the ghost of a smile before continuing. "That, of course, remains your property."

A stillness descended upon the room as Brodie tried to assimilate his situation. He was aware of the chair on which he sat, the table with its neat pile of papers, the surreal presence of Mr. Jones. They all seemed to sit in a huge cavern; the walls growing, the roof stretching off into some unimaginable height. In the stillness of his mind, he considered the absurdity of the negotiation.

JONES FELT HIS BIG toe rubbing against the inside leather of his shoe. His socks always had holes and as the day had drawn on his toe slowly enlarged the tear. Another painful reminder of his financial status. Somewhere, he thought, somewhere there is a small tube containing my DNA, taken from my body when I was a baby. It waits for the summons to grow into a new me, a new Charles Jones. I am a truly faceless man. It waits for the chip to be taken from my chest when I die. It waits for all my memories, my knowledge, my very self to be uploaded into the new and undamaged brain.

Too late, he thought, I'm already damaged. I have no money for that task, I did not plan ahead, I have but one life. And one eventual death.

What did my pastor say, "Who are we to take life or to give life? We are not God!" Amen to that, thought Jones, I will follow His plan for death and not seek to negate Divine will.

Not like this shallow, weak one before me, he thought, only now does he understand what he has done. Does he have any regrets at all, Jones wondered.

I HAVE TO SIGN THIS paper to take delivery of me, Jim thought. If I don't then I have to hand me back. He stifled a giggle.

He reached across the table and picked up the document. Try as he might he could not focus on the words, he read the first paragraph several times before finally giving up and placing the paper neatly back on the pile. Looking up at Mr. Jones he spoke, "I have no idea what to do. I suppose I should ... but then I ... um ..." He finally realised his brain was not doing any thinking.

Mr. Jones sat in his own personal stillness for a few more heartbeats and then slowly reached across and gathered up most of the documents. A single sheet remained on the table.

He began to place the others into his briefcase, moving with a degree of sureness that sent waves of messages across the table. Brodie sat and watched, aware that there was a level of communication occurring, Mr. Jones wanted to say something, he had an opinion about all this.

A person acquires many skills in life, Brodie could sense a person's moods, he could read a person by their body language. Sitting back, he folded his arms and watched Mr. Jones radiate a message and decided to make a guess "You don't approve of this, do you?" he asked.

A moment of inspiration flashed, "You hate the idea of multiple lives?"

There was a brief hesitation in Mr. Jones, then he slowly pushed his chair back and stood up. Reaching down, he picked up his briefcase with great deliberation, paused, and looked down on Brodie like a great, still, black bird. "You are a dead man, Mr. Brodie, your time on this earth ended when you fell. You made choices, no one forced you to live your life the way you did. And now, you use your power and influence, your wealth and advantages to ... to ..." He visibly gained control of himself, stopped speaking and moved towards the door.

"What power? What advantages?" asked Jim, "I just had insurance. Just ...life insurance," he finished.

Mr. Jones stood with one hand on the door handle, he waited a moment and then spoke once more without turning back, "Regretfully, you are a cheat, Mr. Brodie." And then he left.

Brodie sat quietly watching the tall man exit the room. Silence lay in waves, washing up the walls and filling all the spaces, the shadows lay in the corners, watching the man at the table.

"All I did was have insurance," he repeated to himself. Looking at the closed door he reviewed the interview, seeing in his mind's eye the angry man who had just left. Again, he saw the fire in the eyes of the agent, felt the waves of distaste and disapproval. Was I wrong, he questioned, am I a cheat?

He heard Marge's voice in his ears, "I love you, Jim Brodie."

Picking up the pen he signed the paper. No regrets.

Don't miss out!

Visit the website below and you can sign up to receive emails whenever Terry Hornby publishes a new book. There's no charge and no obligation.

https://books2read.com/r/B-A-ZYBAB-JEOHD

Connecting independent readers to independent writers.

Also by Terry Hornby

Valentine and the Devil
Valentine and the Undead
Valentine and the Mobsters
Sally's Got A Taser

www.ingramcontent.com/pod-product-compliance
Lightning Source LLC
Chambersburg PA
CBHW031942010726
47493CB00007B/2047